Death of A Well-Travelled Man

Faukon Abbey Mystery 3

A. K. Lakelett

Faukon Abbey Publishing

Authors note:

Please note, this book follows British English spelling, grammar, and punctuation.

EBook ISBN: 1-945479-08-6

EBook ISBN-13: 978-1-945479-08-3

Paperback ISBN: 978-1-945479-09-0

Praise for A.K. Lakelett

Remember Me?

"As with the best of crime novels, Remember Me proves a tense and compelling debut as A K Lakelett takes a tried and tested formula and adds her own impressive twist. Creating something innovative in such a popular genre is no mean feat..." BookViral *"Bravo to the author for taking a chance by using a combination of a very untraditional format for a novel — a play — and yet combining it with a standard novel storyline that's suspenseful, skillfully paced, and intriguing."* Amazon Reviewer

Missing Alibi

"A timely and classic blend of suspense laced with one twist after another it's one of those rare offerings that actually encourages the reader to solve the crime. Dense with plot intricacies, thick with atmosphere, and packed with a well-nuanced ensemble of characters..." BookViral *"Ms. Lakelett's plotting is devious and there is more than one candidate for villain in the running, which always makes the story more interesting, albeit more complicated. I thoroughly enjoyed this book and heartily recommend it to mystery lovers everywhere."* Amazon Reviewer

Death of a Well-Travelled Man

"A thoroughly enjoyable read. Layering one crime over another, Lakelett remains in command of multiple threads in true Agatha Christie fashion as the puzzled investigators move from one theory to another, exposing motives and laying bare doubts and insecurities as they negotiate human nature in their search for the truth." BookViral

Also By

Remember Me? – Faukon Abbey Mystery 1
Missing Alibi – Faukon Abbey Mystery 2
Faukon Abbey Mysteries Companion

The Good Riddance Project – Occupational Hazards Novella

DEATH OF A WELL-TRAVELLED MAN

A.K. LAKELETT

Even when you travel,

you are still you.

Sunday, 1 February

The intense rays of the midday sun filter through haphazardly closed curtains illuminating the pale face of a man sprawled out on a sofa. He lies there, with his right arm dangling off the side and his mouth open. His clothes are all rumpled, buttons partially undone, exposing pale skin. His face bears the imprints of the sofa cushions, and his dull brown hair stands on end.

One muddy shoe peeks out from under the sofa, its mate hidden under the table. On the table, a nearly empty bottle of single malt lies on its side, and a large yellowish stain is visible under the table where a small glass has toppled over.

The man, in his 50s, winces as the sun's rays touch his bleary eyes. He slowly raises his arm to shield them. Moving deliberately, a moan escapes his parched lips as he gingerly pushes himself upright trying to avoid the sun's intense glare. Drawing a deep breath, he cringes at the smell of the room. Peter Greene, Detective Inspector with the Faukon Abbey police, with a serious hangover, finally opens his eyes and tries to remember.

Monday, 2 February

DI Peter Greene and DC Terrence Ford

Detective Constable Terrence 'Terry' Ford, also known as Beanpole behind his back due to being tall and on the skinny side, is intolerably happy and smiling broadly on Monday morning. Detective Inspector Peter Greene, on the other hand, sitting on the opposite site of their shared office in the Faukon Abbey police station, had grunted a barely audible good morning upon arriving at work and hasn't said a word for the past two hours while shuffling papers on his desk and occasionally signing them. Terry tries to concentrate on his own work, filing reports on his computer, but he's having a tough time of it.

A knock on the door saves Terry's sanity.

"Morning Terry, how was your weekend? I'm collecting some dues for the next week's birthday cakes." Constable Bertie Lawson shakes an envelope and looks around the small office. "What did she say?"

"Weekend was fantastic," says Terry, smiling broadly, "she said yes!"

"I knew it, whee! Good on you mate! Congratulations! And her parents?"

"They gave their blessings, looked happy too." Terry can't stop grinning.

"They'd better, she's marrying a proper copper! So, when's it gonna be?"

"No date yet. Going to be in the summer though. Christine said her parents want a church wedding, of course." Bertie nods towards Peter, who hasn't indicated he's heard anything at all. Terry shakes his head, lifts his shoulders, and rolls his eyes. He digs in his wallet to find a five-pound note to give to Bertie.

"By the way, have you seen anything about a bad bicycle accident on Eastern Green junction in Penzance on Saturday evening? Someone knocked a cyclist off the road there. Christine and I were on our way to pictures and dinner when she noticed a bicycle upside down with a leg attached to it in the shrubbery by the road. I pulled over. We found a guy bleeding and unconscious, collapsed on the ground. Big gash on his forehead. Called an ambulance. They showed up in less than five minutes, so that was good. A rookie uniform came a minute later. Told him we hadn't seen the accident happen and didn't know anything else. Ambulance drove off with the guy. The rookie took our names and drove off, but not before he walked around my car to see if there was any damage on it! I've tried to find some info in the system today, but no luck."

"Really? Did you tell him you were a copper? Can't say I've seen anything, but I'll take a look. If they don't know who the guy is, it may take time for the rookie to register it, and it was the weekend too. One of my old pals works there so I can call him. "

"Yeah, Christine actually told him that I was a cop. He just looked, didn't say a thing. I guess he figured he'd better do a proper job, which of course he should've. Anyway, thanks, it would be good to know if the poor guy is okay. Christine was rather shocked, so she'll want to know if he made it. He was bleeding pretty badly."

Peter's temples are throbbing and he has a tough time trying to focus, to think.

What did Terry just say about an accident? Pretend that you're concentrating on the report, he tells himself, *keep looking down. And where did they find that guy? Think man,* he tells himself again, *think! Did something happen after I hit the gas and raced to get out? Or when I fishtailed in my haste to get home?*

Peter closes his eyes and does a mental check on his beloved BMW. *Any damages?* He can't remember off-hand. *Wasn't anything in the front, was there?* Cold sweat now runs down his spine. *Could I've hit a cyclist on my way home and not even remember it? Granted, I'd had a few more than I should've, and I'd been driving too fast too. But surely I'd remember something like that, wouldn't*

I? His hands feel shaky. *It wasn't me, was it? Oh God, I should've called in sick today. Why didn't I,* he asks himself.

Clearing his throat, Peter coughs loudly, scrambling to his feet. Terry and Bertie freeze.

"Congratulations Terry. I'm not feeling well. I'm going home. Call me if there's anything urgent."

He rushes out of the door.

"What's with him?" Bertie asks.

"No idea. He hasn't said anything at all since he came in this morning."

"Odd. Thanks for the money Terry, and congratulations again. I'll let you know if I find anything."

With every step he takes, a jackhammer clobbers Peter's head. The glare of the lights in the corridor pierces his eyes. He squints, but tries hard to look normal, waving to the desk clerk as he walks towards the door. Walking gingerly, he gets soaked, his umbrella forgotten. *Damn, damn, shit!* He keeps swearing, gets in his car trying to blink drops away from his eyes. Raindrops pummel the car roof, hard. Peter sits there for a moment, feeling the rain, wiping water from his face with his hand, trying to focus before starting the car, but his brain feels as foggy as the steam clouding the windows.

Peter drives home slowly and carefully, grabs a bottle of aspirin and downs a few pills with two glasses of water and crawls into bed. *Please, let the pills help. Never going to drink anything ever again!*

***

A young woman, with short thin blonde hair and thick-rimmed glasses, comes to the station wanting to report a missing person. She says her name is Ingela Marsh and she hasn't heard from her boyfriend for nearly a week. Front desk staff call in a response officer, who on this day is PC Bertie Lawson.

"Please sit down. Tell me who you want to report missing."

"His name is Ryan Bolan. He's 25 and he's my boyfriend. I haven't heard from him since Thursday!" she says, her voice rasping with tension. "Please help, something must've happened to him! Please!" She keeps twisting and grinding a paper handkerchief in her hands.

"Why are you reporting him missing? What about his parents, siblings?"

"He's the only kid. His mum died a few years back. He never knew his father."

"How long have you been together?"

"Since Easter last year."

"Do you live together?"

"No, not yet. We each have our own place. What's that got to do with anything?"

"As he's 25, he's an adult. He could've just decided to leave and not tell you."

"Oh no! You don't understand. Ryan loves me! He wouldn't just leave. He's a very responsible person." Ingela fishes another paper handkerchief out of her pocket and blows her nose.

"I'm sure he is." Bertie tries to project calm. "But, you know, sometimes people do change their minds. Why'd you think he's gone missing? Doesn't he answer his phone? Maybe he lost his phone or has no signal, or his battery is dead? Have you tried his house? Doesn't he answer his door?"

"It's a quiet time at the hotel." Ingela sighs. "Ryan works as a night porter at Levington. He took a week off from work to train for that big cycling event later in April. I forget what it's called. I saw him off last Monday morning on his bike."

"Where was he heading?"

"He was supposed to ride from Faukon Abbey to Minehead, then to Barnstaple, to Tintagel, to Penzance, to Bodmin and then to return to Faukon Abbey on late Saturday afternoon or early evening. But he hasn't come back! I've been to his place several times, he's not there! I have his keys. Please, please find him! Something must've happened to him!"

"Penzance you said? Now, don't get your hopes up. There was an accident involving a cyclist in Penzance recently. The person was knocked off his bike on Saturday and taken to hospital. He was unconscious on arrival..."

"Tell me which hospital! I'll drive there now!" Ingela jumps up. "Tell me!"

"Calm down, please, calm down. It may not be him. We could check…"

"No! It's faster if I drive there myself. Which hospital?"

"He was taken to West Cornwall Hospital. Now let me make a call and confirm. They may have moved him…."

"No, I'll drive there! That must be him. Thank you!"

Terry comes downstairs as Ingela runs out of the police station and hops into her Smart car, zooming out from the parking space.

"Your latest girlfriend running out on you?"

"Ha ha, we can't all be steady eddies like you," Bertie says. "She was reporting her boyfriend who's gone missing while on a cycling tour."

"Cycling tour this time of the year, huh? It's been pretty cold and rainy too. Why'd anybody want to go pedalling in this kind of weather?"

"Dunno, I wouldn't! She said he took a week off from work to cycle around as prep for a race or something later this year. He's supposed to have been riding through Penzance, so I mentioned you finding a cyclist in a ditch and she just took off!"

"Let's hope it's him then. Do they actually know who he is yet?"

"No idea. I saw the accident was reported, but that was all. No details."

"Maybe it's her boyfriend. We haven't had any other bicycle accidents reported, have we?"

"Nope, no reports of any accidents that I've seen. Anyway, wanna go to *The Daily Cuppa* for bacon sarnies?"

James Carter, *The Abbey Chronicle*

It's Monday, again. And it's raining, again. And it's too early. A gloomy James Carter, known as Jimmy, is on his way to work. Jimmy is a lanky 27-year-old with keen brown eyes and short, brown, flat hair. He stops to get coffee for himself and his boss from *The Daily Cuppa* near *The Abbey Chronicle* office where he works as a reporter.

"It's raining, as in pouring," Jimmy calls out when he gets to the office.

These days *The Abbey Chronicle* office consists of just four people: Mike Kings, who is the editor, publisher, and owner of *The Abbey Chronicle,* Eddie, who does sports part-time, Molly who does advertising and admin work, and Jimmy, of course. The small office now only takes up half of the upper level of a 1960s built concrete two-storey building. The only modern equipment consists of the computers and monitors on everybody's desks.

Jimmy shakes his parka and sends water flying onto his trousers.

"Great, just great! Just what I needed," he mutters to himself.

Helen, his girlfriend, had actually ironed his chinos and shirt for the first time ever. Something he himself never does. Permanent press, he claims, was made for journalists. Jimmy has a genial personality once you get to know him, and he has a very sharp mind - doggedly pursues the facts. He dreams about getting a big scoop so he can be a star reporter at *The Guardian*.

Jimmy and Mike start their usual Monday morning meeting after Jimmy arrives with the coffee. Mike shows Jimmy an email he's received from a source in Gwedrow Glassworks. The sender is anxious and claims that the new head of IT, who was brought in a few months ago to 'bring the company into the 21st century', is now apparently making plans to give the heave-ho to a lot of folks.

"He doesn't mention what kind of plans, but Gwedrow has been going through some tough times recently, with their sales dropping. And, of course, when changes are needed, those usually come with lay-offs and redundancies," Mike says. "Gwedrow management may claim it's just modernisation, but I'm not buying that. There are other rumours too, including a possible sale of the company, so we need to find out what they're actually planning. Set up interviews with the union rep, the GM and the new IT guy."

"You sure it's not just rumours?" Jimmy asks. "I didn't know they even had an IT department; the place seems so ancient somehow."

"They do. How'd you think they design and make those glass panels according to tight specifications?"

"Hmm, right, didn't think of that. So, if they brought in a new head of IT, who was taking care of their IT before him?"

"I think it's the stepson of the founder or maybe he's a nephew or something, not sure. Mark, I think his name is. Got the job right after uni, back in what 2004 or 5. Supposed to be a sharp guy, although he didn't actually graduate, if I remember correctly." Mike crunches his brow. "As I recall, hmm, I think he won some hacking or IT competition at Exeter uni. Should be on file."

"Okay, if this Mark guy is so sharp, why did they need to bring in an outsider?"

"That's the question for you to find the answer to."

They finish their meeting after talking about other daily news items. Jimmy returns to his own desk and looks out of the window. It's still Monday, and it's still raining. Contrary to his usual aptitude for sniffing out a story and going for it, his head is filled with personal plans. He and Helen have been talking about taking a week off, or rather Helen's been doing the talking, to fly to the Canaries to meet Helen's parents who retired there a year ago, leaving their bookshop, now named *Cliffhanger Books*, to Helen. Jimmy keeps ruminating about it all. This whole thing with Helen is suddenly getting a bit more serious. *While he likes her, does he really actually love her? And does he really want to spend the rest of his life with her?* She wants to get serious, but Jimmy's not so sure, he keeps hesitating. *She's great company but...* Jimmy sits and watches the raindrops making their way down, carving their path through the grime. *Helen's clever, looks great, and has the nicest smile, and she's good fun to be with, but ...* They've been going on, sometimes off and back on, for more than a year now. *But is she really the one? Do I really want to go and meet the parents?* Jimmy keeps asking himself. *It's not like I haven't met them before, but this time it would be the real 'meeting the parents' thing.* Jimmy keeps pounding his mouse on the mouse pad and sighing, loudly.

Mike comes by.

"What's going on? Aren't you getting anywhere with Gwedrow?"

"No, it's not that."

"So, what is it? Out with it, I'm not sure that mouse can take any more beating."

"Not sure what to do."

"About what? Have you and Helen broken it off again?"

"No." Jimmy sighs.

"So, what is it then?"

"She wants me to meet her parents."

Mike is silent for a moment.

"Oh, I see. She wants to get serious, and you don't, is that it?"

"I don't know. That's the problem! I mean, how do you know if you actually want to spend the rest of your life with someone?"

"Sorry mate, you're asking the wrong person. I've never had much luck with the ladies. They usually want kids or money or both. And since I'm not rich and can't make kids, they soon give up. Dogs are much more loyal."

"But you were married once, weren't you?"

"Ah, you found that out, didn't you? Of course you did!" Mike sighs. "Yes, well, right after I got back from the Falklands, I got married, because my girlfriend at the time claimed she was pregnant. I got invalided out of the Navy and got a job at the *Leeds Evening Post*. Thought it would be a 'new start', you know, job, family, and all that. Except it wasn't. The kid was born with red hair. None of my family or her family had red hair. She tried to explain that the hair didn't matter, it would change as he got older. Yeah, hair does change, but after two years it was clear the kid's hair didn't. It was red and it stayed red." Mike keeps staring at the window. The pounding rain makes it nearly impossible to see out.

"One evening, when she was supposedly going to visit her sister, I followed her. She'd started seeing her sister a lot. I saw her getting into a car, a green Volvo. I wrote down the number. Next day I went to see a mate, a copper. He gave me a name and an address. The following day, I went there. I saw him." Mike stops again. "His hair was dark curly red, just like the kid's. We divorced."

"I didn't know. I'm sorry."

"Never mind that. It's ancient history. Told you I wasn't any good with women." Mike turns around and walks back to his desk. "Now get back on to Gwedrow."

Jimmy bangs his mouse one more time and logs onto the internet to check Gwedrow's site to find out who to call.

Tuesday, 3 February

DI Peter Greene and DC Terry Ford

Peter is finally feeling better, or at least his head isn't killing him any longer. His thoughts are still on the gloomy side though. Before driving to work, he walks around his car and carefully inspects it from all angles. He loves his old BMW and takes great care of it; spending time washing and polishing it several times a month. But as it is a few years old, it has some dents and minor scratches here and there. But, as far as he can see in the early morning light, no dents or anything indicating he has recently hit something, or, heaven forbid, someone. *At least that's good*, he thinks, and drives to work.

Terry is in the office when he gets there.

"Congratulations Terry! I'm thrilled to hear that you've found the right one and are prepared to tie the proverbial knot. When's the wedding? Sorry about yesterday, I had a terrible headache, couldn't think straight. Anything happen?"

"Thank you, sir. Nothing much going on. You're feeling better now, sir?"

"Yes, thank you, very much so. Nothing urgent going on, is there? If not, let's get to work. Do you have anything more about those cases Exeter wanted to know about?"

Jimmy Carter, *The Abbey Chronicle*

It's misty in the morning when Jimmy drives to Gwedrow Glassworks. He's so busy thinking about Helen, he passes the plant's entrance and has to turn around. He finds a spot to park his car in front of a tired-looking, two-storey dirty yellow office building. Flagstone steps lead to the entrance with a glass door. A rather dark and gloomy entry hall contains a few display cases propped with Gwedrow products, a receptionist's desk in the middle, and a few closed, dark wooden doors on both sides. Four brown leather chairs and a low table are positioned near the receptionist's desk. A winding staircase with a metal railing leads to the next level. The floor is covered with dark green, wall-to-wall carpeting. An efficient looking middle-aged woman in a grey twinset sits behind the desk, typing on a computer keyboard. She looks up when Jimmy enters.

"Good morning, I'm Jimmy Carter from *The Abbey Chronicle* and I'm here to meet with Jon Geldenhuis and Tom Linkled."

"Good morning. They're waiting for you in the meeting room, if you'd care to follow me."

Jimmy checks his watch. It's 9 a.m., he's right on time. The receptionist walks to a door near the staircase and knocks, opening the door.

"Jimmy Carter from *The Chronicle* is here."

She motions Jimmy to go in. Inside, Jimmy looks at the same dark green, wall-to-wall carpeting, dark wooden table and half a dozen chairs. A whiteboard hangs opposite the window with drawn curtains. Two men sit at the table, and both stand as Jimmy comes in.

They all shake hands. The younger of the two is Tom Linkled, who is the General Manager of Gwedrow Glassworks. He's in his 40s, slightly built, with short, dark hair and brown eyes. He's smartly dressed in a blue suit and light blue shirt with a dark red tie. Jon Geldenhuis is older, about 50, Jimmy thinks, with salt and pepper curly hair, wearing dark blue chinos and a grey shirt, both with sharp creases, and a dark blue tie.

"Please sit," Linkled says.

They all sit and both Linkled and Geldenhuis look expectantly at Jimmy.

Jimmy clears his throat and digs out his notebook.

"We've received some information that there are major changes planned at Gwedrow, with possible redundancies and lay-offs. And, as Gwedrow is a major employer in our area, our readers are obviously interested in what happens here. Many livelihoods can be impacted."

"I wonder where you got that information?" Linkled says. While he sounds polite, there is also a hint of annoyance in his voice.

"It was sent to us anonymously. Is it true?"

Linkled sighs audibly. "There are always rumours. Someone hears something and then it just spreads. But yes, in this case, there's some truth in it. We're planning some changes. I'm not sure how familiar you are with our business, but Gwedrow Glassworks currently makes about 120 varieties of laminated, tempered, and other kinds of glass for different purposes. We sell most of our glass to museums, banks, modern buildings, and even as artworks. Our glass can be bent to shape and can even stop bullets. But currently, our product portfolio doesn't match the demand, thus changes are necessary. We need to orient our production to the market and make it more efficient."

"I see. What kind of changes are you planning?"

"I'm sure you're aware of computer-aided design," Geldenhuis says, "it's been around for quite a while." He has a slightly nasal voice and speaks with a clipped accent.

"Yes," Jimmy says.

"To ensure improved production, we need to get our computer systems up to speed," says Geldenhuis.

"Oh, okay. So, are you also going to computerise more of the production?"

"Yes," Linkled says. "It's already computer aided in many sectors, has been for years now, but if we're going to get our costs to the level of the competition, we have to increase our use of computers and even add robots. But before we can do any of that, we obviously need to plan carefully and obviously also negotiate with our unions and workforce."

"Right, I see," Jimmy says. Before he has a chance to ask more questions, both Geldenhuis and Linkled stand up and walk to the door.

"Thank you for coming. We'll send out a press release with more information as soon as our board has approved the plan."

Jimmy is guided out of the room. Geldenhuis and Linkled walk upstairs and Jimmy is left standing with his notebook in his hand.

He walks to the receptionist and asks where he can find Jeff Ruddy, who is the union rep.

"You'll have to ask his union about his whereabouts."

"So he doesn't work here?"

"I'm not allowed to give you information about our workforce. Have a good day," she says, returning to her typing.

Jimmy heads back to his car.

A minute or so after Jimmy returns to his desk, Ingela Marsh, who is Helen's friend, rushes in.

"Hi Jimmy, do you have a minute, please. Can I talk to you, please?"

"Sure, what's going on? Sit, sit."

Jimmy pulls out a chair for Ingela who plops down and drops her handbag on the floor.

"Ryan's missing!" Ingela sniffles.

"What do you mean, missing? I thought he'd gone on that cycling tour. Isn't he back yet?"

"No! He was supposed to come back on Saturday. He called me on Thursday about noon and I've heard nothing since."

"Where was he? Was he okay?"

"Yes, he was fine, a bit sore, he said. The weather'd been chilly, but pedalling had kept him warm. He was heading to Penzance. Said he was going to stay overnight there in a hostel, get a hot shower and then head to Bodmin early in the morning. But I haven't heard from him since then."

"Maybe he lost his phone, or the battery died?"

"No, not you too!" Ingela's voice rises shrilly. "I reported him missing to the police yesterday, but all they said is that he's an adult, and maybe he just didn't want to call me; that he's just gone because he wanted to! Ryan would never do that! You know that. He's a responsible person." Ingela's eyes start to well with tears.

"Indeed. Deffo doesn't sound like Ryan not to call you. Did the police say they were going to do anything at all?"

"No. All they said was that there'd been an accident in Penzance on Saturday involving a cyclist. As they had no more information about who it was, I drove there yesterday and went to the hospital. The hospital didn't know who the cyclist was either. The poor guy was badly concussed and couldn't tell them. They let me see him, but it wasn't Ryan." Ingela sniffs and wipes her nose. "Can you help, please?"

"Sure, of course, but what can I do?"

Mike comes around. "What's going on?"

"This is Ingela. She's an assistant librarian and Helen's friend. Her boyfriend went off on a cycling tour, from here to Penzance or so. He was supposed to come home on Saturday, but he hasn't shown up so Ingela reported him to the police as a missing person, but they aren't doing much about it."

"Not much we can do either, is there? A bit of a vast area to do a search. I suppose we could post a misper note on *The Chronicle* online page. Would that help, do you think?" Mike says.

"That we can do, right? I'll post the missing person info right away. Do you know the editor in Bodmin online? Maybe they could pick it up too and share it?" Jimmy says.

"Send them an email and ask or call. I'm sure they'd know about any accidents there."

"Thank you. At least that's something." Ingela smiles weakly. "Hopefully someone will see it!"

"Don't worry. He's probably just lost his phone somewhere," Jimmy says.

"I hope so! Thank you."

"So how did it go at Gwedrow?" Mike asks Jimmy after Ingela has left.

"A lot of business-speak and very little substance. They talked to me for like five minutes and then promptly escorted me out."

"You met the new guy?"

"I met with what's-his-name, Tom, Tom Linkled who's the General Manager, and Jon Geldenhuis, he's apparently the IT guy."

"Ah yes, that Linkled guy. He arrived there about three, or maybe four years ago. He's a business guy, no engineering background at all. There was quite a bit of rumbling when he came. But he's apparently managed to bring in a lot of new business."

"If that's the case, why was he complaining that the business wasn't good?"

"Who knows. There's always more money to be made, I suppose. Anything interesting?"

"No, not really. All they said was that they're going to get new computers and maybe robots."

"Aha, now that's interesting; robots."

"How do you mean?"

"Robots come in, humans go out, so lay-offs."

"Oh, okay, I didn't think that's what they meant. I'd better go back to talk with the IT guy again and find that union rep, Ruddy."

"Oh, don't bother with Ruddy, he's not going to tell you anything. I'll talk to him. There's a black guy there, Kirwan something. He's been there forever and a day. Talk to him and you'll find out more."

"How do you know all this?"

"I've lived and worked here longer than you. This place isn't big, so you talk to someone, who knows someone else, who knows everything about someone else. Small towns."

The Abbey Chronicle - online

Missing Person - Have you seen Ryan Bolan?

We are appealing for your help in locating Ryan Bolan, aged 25, who left his home and girlfriend on the morning of Monday, 26 January for a cycling tour from Faukon Abbey to Minehead, Barnstaple, Tintagel, Penzance, Bodmin, and back to Faukon Abbey.

He was due to return home to Faukon Abbey on Saturday, 31 January, in the late afternoon/early evening. The last known contact with him was on Thursday, when he was near Tintagel, making his way to a hostel in Penzance, before continuing to Bodmin the following morning. We are greatly concerned for his welfare.

Ryan is 6ft (1.80m) tall, slim, with brown hair and eyes. It is unknown what he was last wearing. If you have seen him or have any information on his where-abouts, please contact *The Abbey Chronicle* or the nearest police station imme-diately.

Wednesday, 4 February

The Abbey Chronicle, Page 1

Major changes planned at Gwedrow

The Gwedrow Glassworks has announced the commencement of a 45-day consultation period to discuss plans for a comprehensive company restructure following a reduction in volume over the past year, necessitating some changes. General Manager, Tom Linkled, emphasised that changes are vital if the company is to remain competitive. But the level of interest in Gwedrow Glassworks products has been strong, he said. He hopes to be in a position in the near future to give further details about the progress which has been made. Jon Geldenhuis, the newly appointed head of IT, said, in an interview, that most changes would be concentrated on restructuring the IT, implementing cutting-edge computer systems to enhance workflow and integration with automation technology.

Currently Gwedrow employs 203 people on a full-time basis in Faukon Abbey and the company said redundancies are obviously the last and most regrettable option. A spokesman said alternative approaches will be explored to avoid redundancies and that the company intends to reach the goal through voluntary means. Gwedrow Glassworks plans to offer affected employees a comprehensive package of support, including services aimed at their transition to new employment. Jeff Ruddy, Chair of the trade unions' committee, expressed his deep concern at the news and pledged to do all he and the trade union can to support those affected by the announcement.

DI Peter Greene and DC Terry Ford

At 4.20 p.m. Ben Rivers calls 999, saying that he has found his mother in the bathtub, not breathing. Looks like she has slipped. He can't get her out on his own. Please come fast.

Emergency Services sends a call to both ambulance and the police. Peter hears about the call and feels he needs to do something to stop thinking about Maggie and bicycles and all that jazz and goes with Terry to the site to check it out.

Terry drives them to Glowburn Terrace where they see the Emergency Response team. Police constable Jones is already standing outside a well-maintained, red brick, mid-terrace house. Peter and Terry walk over to get more details. Jones explains that the person who made the call, Ben Rivers, is the son of the victim, Marion Rivers. It's her house. When asked, Ben Rivers said he'd arrived there only to find his mother unresponsive in the bathtub. The ER team is still upstairs, but apparently nothing could be done.

"That's him there, Rivers." Jones points out a man in his mid-40s, standing in the doorway greedily smoking a cigarette. Both his rumpled red T-shirt and dark wrinkled trousers are wet in the front.

Peter and Terry introduce themselves and Peter asks what happened. Ben's not entirely coherent; just keeps repeating how he'd got into the house, and how he'd tried to lift his mother up, but couldn't get a proper hold, all that soap and water, and how she was so slippery and heavy that she just kept slipping under.

"I had to pull the plug, didn't I, she was so heavy!" he says. "Couldn't get her up, just couldn't; she just slipped under. I had to call for help."

Ben lights another cigarette.

"Can we call anybody for you? Is there a neighbour who could come?"

"I'm okay, I just need some fresh air."

Terry and Peter head upstairs.

The ER team is packing up when Terry and Peter arrive upstairs. The doctor has already left. The naked body of an elderly woman is on the floor, partially covered with a towel and her body is being readied to be removed by the ER team. They explain to Peter that they tried to revive her for a while, but despite all their efforts, Marion Rivers was unresponsive and was pronounced dead at the scene at 4.55 p.m. The ER tech says that she has an injury on the back of her head; an indication that she had likely fallen and hit her head, and then presumably drowned.

More information will be available after a post-mortem. Another ER tech takes pictures of the tub and the scene to document it, while the other two deal with their own equipment, as well as moving the body. Peter and Terry step out of the bathroom to allow the body, covered with a white sheet, to be removed. Terry takes a few pictures with his mobile as well. The ER team then heads out with the body, leaving one wet towel on the bathroom floor.

"Seems pretty straight forward. An accident, right?" Terry says.

"I don't know," Peter says, "something about this bothers me. Let's go back downstairs and talk to the son." They check that the water and lights are off and go downstairs.

Ben Rivers is still standing by the door, smoking. There's now a considerable pile of half-smoked cigarettes and butts on the ground. He's pressing his lips together tightly, watching his mother being transported away. The ambulance drives away and Ben lights yet another cigarette.

"I'm very sorry for your loss, Mr Rivers," Peter says. Ben grunts and nods. "Unfortunately, when someone dies alone we have to follow procedure, ask questions and investigate. Are you up for that?"

"Sure."

"Did your mother live alone?"

"Yeah, she lived alone."

"So, you don't live here?"

"No, I've got me own place."

"What time did you get here today?"

"I came about... about 4 p.m. Didn't really look at the time."

"You have your own place. Why did you come here today?"

"She called me, wanted some help with something. I couldn't really talk to her as I had a customer in me car. So, I told her I'd come when I could."

"Do you have keys to your mother's house?"

"Yeah, she's me mum, isn't she?"

"Again, I'm sorry, but I have to ask you for the keys."

Ben digs the keys out of his pocket and hands them to Terry.

"Is there another door?"

"Yeah, the back door."

"Same key?"

"Nah, that one hangs on a hook by the kitchen door."

Terry goes back inside, checks that the door to the back garden is locked, and takes the key with him. He then locks the entry door, bags, and tags all the keys and hands the bag to PC Jones still standing by the door.

Terry asks if Ben needs help getting home. Ben says no and points to his car.

"We won't bother you anymore. Could you leave your address and contact information with PC Jones, in case we have any more questions, please?"

When Peter and Terry walk back to their car, they notice that Ben's car has a small dent in the front. There is a hint of orange residue on it.

"Ben must have bumped into those new orange parking barriers at Asda," Peter says. "I've done that too; those are way too low to be properly visible, shouldn't be allowed."

"You don't think this was an accident, sir?" Terry asks, when they're on their way back to the station.

"But it looks like one, doesn't it? Accidents often happen, and old people are prone to falls. Obviously, it could be an accident, but I don't know. Something didn't seem right." Peter furrows his brow. "Let's try to find out a bit more about Marion Rivers, and also about the son, Ben Rivers."

Jimmy Carter, *The Abbey Chronicle*

As usual Jimmy's ears perk up when he hears a request for Emergency Services for a person who has fallen and is in distress at home on his police radio. He's just about to leave to get a story but decides to call his contact with the police first. Jimmy's contact says it looks like an elderly lady has had an accident. Apparently she'd slipped and fallen in the tub, knocking herself unconscious. Nothing much to write about there, so Jimmy decides to stay in and continue digging for more information about Gwedrow instead.

The Abbey Chronicle, Page 10

How to avoid falls at home

Falls are uncommonly common. We all fall, we trip, we stumble, mostly without sustaining serious injury. However, for some, and older people especially, falls can cause broken bones and other injuries. Keeping fit and doing regular balance exercises, like dancing or *tai chi* can help. To prevent falls, you can also make simple changes to reduce your risk at home.

Here's our list:
- Spills—Mop them up immediately.

- Wires and cables—Keep them tucked away, fasten them along walls.

- Non-slip—Only use non-slip mats and rugs, especially in bathrooms and kitchens. Remove loose mats and secure carpets, especially on stairs and near staircases.

- Stairs—Make sure the stairs are not slippery and always hold on to the handrail.

- Don't walk about with socks on—Use shoes with non-slippery soles.

- Lights—Make sure all parts of your home are well lit, especially staircases.

- And most importantly—get help if you feel unsteady.

Thursday, 5 February

The Abbey Chronicle, Page 2

Marion Rivers dies

We are sad to report that former Faukon Abbey Library assistant librarian, Marion Rivers, 66, who retired only last year, was found dead yesterday at her home in Glowburn Terrace by her son, Ben Rivers. He called Emergency Services at 4.20 p.m. after finding her unresponsive in the bathtub. The Emergency Services arrived at the scene within minutes, but despite all their efforts to revive her, she was declared deceased at 4.55 p.m.

Dr Percy Slater, Home Office Pathologist

It's a slow day for dead bodies, and Percy Slater, who is the Home Office Pathologist, is able to perform a *post-mortem* on Marion Rivers in the morning. Dr Slater is in his mid-40s, with short, blondish thinning hair and says that he's just well-rounded, not over-weight as his wife claims. A real introvert, he enjoys giving long speeches using short sentences and assumes nobody knows anything about anatomy. He's always very meticulous.

Peter calls him in the morning to find out about the post-mortem, only to hear it is just about done. Slater asks them to come over.

Instead of Terry driving them, Peter decides to drive them to the Brookside hospital morgue. When they get there, Slater is finishing with the body.

"Good of you to come."

"What's up, Doc?" Peter says. Slater raises his eyebrows and peers over his glasses.

"Based on the statements made to the ER team, it was assumed that Mrs Rivers had slipped in the bathtub, hit her head, knocked herself out, and drowned, correct? She has a contusion on the back of her head and the drowning part is correct. She did drown."

"So, she slipped and fell, hitting her head?"

"Yes, except the fall didn't appear to have rendered her unconscious. It seems she was still alive when she drowned since she had water in her lungs."

"What you mean she was alive when she drowned? If she was alive, why didn't she get up?"

"That's a question for you, gentlemen. See these," he continues, and points out multiple red contusions on her arms and some red contusions on her ankles, "they could've been due to having worn too tight socks before taking her bath or...."

"Yes?"

"The contusions on her arms indicate she was probably banging her arms against something, likely the sides of the tub."

"Could those have been caused when someone was trying to help her get up?"

"Possibly... but that would still mean she would've had to have fallen back down and drowned."

"It's awfully hard to get hold of a body to get it out of water. They tend to be slippery, especially if soapy. I remember that when Andrew was small he loved being in the tub, but getting him out of it was a battle." Peter smiles remembering, then becomes serious again. "Ben Rivers said that he tried to get her up, but she kept slipping back as he couldn't hold her. And when he couldn't get her out while she was in the water, he tried to find the plug to drain the water. In the meantime, she drowned?"

"Again, possible. But you're the detectives. I can only tell you what I've found."

"What you're saying is that her death wasn't an accident?"

"I'm calling it undetermined for now, likely suspicious."

"She wasn't drunk or under the influence of anything, was she?" Terry asks.

"No, nothing in her system shows that she had had anything which could have caused her to faint or lose balance."

"Her son claimed she liked to take hot baths and used to fall asleep."

"Apart from some arthritis impacting mostly her hands, and a few extra kilos, she was in fairly good shape for a 66-year-old woman. Her muscle tone was good. Brain appears normal, no clogged arteries, no sign of stroke, pneumonia, or epilepsy either. She'd had eggs with ham for lunch about an hour before she drowned. A bit of an odd time to take a bath, I would think, in the middle of the day, but maybe she was feeling a bit frozen? It's been quite chilly recently. The warm bath likely helped with the arthritis too. Drowning due to falling asleep in the tub, however, is not common."

"Thanks Doc, undetermined it is."

Peter drives them back to the station.

DI Peter Greene and DC Terry Ford

"Falling and not being able to get up and then drowning? That must've been terrifying," Terry says.

"Indeed, a horrible way to go if that's what happened. Drownings are difficult to determine. For all we know it's possible that she had decided to top herself, changed her mind and couldn't get up again. Let's go and check the rest of her house a bit further, see if we can find anything. The Emergency team only dealt with her and the bathroom. We need to find out more."

Peter drives back to the police station. He waits in the car, checking his phone, but there are no messages from Maggie. *Damn*! Terry collects the keys to Marion Rivers' house from the evidence room before driving to Glowburn Terrace.

Terry unlocks the door and they enter. On the ground floor there's a small WC to the left of the entrance, further down, on the right, a door to the kitchen, and, at the end of the hall after the staircase, an opening leading to the lounge at the back of the house. A small kitchen with light blue cabinets with snap closures, curtains with bright yellow roses, and a dark blue linoleum floor make the kitchen look nice and bright, if somewhat dated. Every surface is clean and polished. Peter finds the dishwasher, and in it, just two plates, one with a bit of dried egg residue. A teapot and a mug stand on the counter. Terry checks the lounge where there's a round mahogany dining table covered with a lacy tablecloth and four chairs. A burgundy sofa, two easy chairs, a light oak coffee table, TV, and an oak bookshelf with shelves with books interspersed with porcelain cats. The books, all organised alphabetically by author, mostly about gardening, and a few cookbooks thrown in, are in excellent shape. A grey wall-to-wall carpet covers the floor, and an old-fashioned yellow wallpaper with raised medallions adorns the walls. No clutter, no dust, no photographs either. Large windows and a door to the patio, with a round table and two chairs and a few bags of chicken manure piled up next to two empty pots looks out on a small, well-tended back garden with a couple of trees.

"She must have read all those gardening books. Look at that garden, sir. Even now, in the middle of the winter, there are a lot of flowers. What are those small purple ones?"

"Don't know, crocuses maybe? Let's check the upstairs. There's no basement, right?"

"No basement."

The stairs lead to a hallway with doors to three bedrooms, one with a small *ensuite* with shower and the main bathroom with a bathtub where Marion Rivers was found. The smallest bedroom has a little table with a sewing machine and shelves with clear labelled plastic boxes containing fabrics and other sewing materials. Not a speck of dust anywhere.

"This one must have been Ben's old room which she'd made into her sewing room by the looks of it. And the other bedroom looks like a guestroom."

"What happened to the husband? Is he dead, or did they divorce?" Peter asks.

Terry checks his notes. "The husband died about ten years ago."

"And Marion Rivers worked in the library? What did the husband do?"

"I think he was a foreman at the Gwedrow Glassworks."

"What did he die of?"

"Don't know, sir, I haven't checked that out yet."

"Let's find any relatives and talk to them as well. We also need to talk to the son again."

They walk into the main bedroom. A big bed, with a bedspread covered in purple roses occupies pride of place, accompanied by two side tables and a dresser with a few small, framed photographs. The bedroom has dark maroon, wall-to-wall carpeting, and the same yellow wallpaper as in the lounge downstairs covers the walls.

"All clean here too. She must have cleaned the house the day she died."

"Maybe she just kept things clean? Living alone things don't get dirty. Let's see the bathroom."

They open the door and look inside. The bathroom has a big, old-fashioned, clawfoot tub with a hand shower. The lower half of a small window over the tub is covered with contact plastic. White-tiled walls, beige vinyl floor and a toilet with a black seat complete the bathroom. Terry stays in the hall while Peter walks to a small mirror cabinet over the pedestal sink. It only contains a few cosmetics, a toothbrush, and a tube of toothpaste. On the top is a basket with brushes and combs and, beside this, another basket, with a small shampoo bottle, a bottle of purple bubble bath and a sponge. The tub has some foamy residue covering the bottom.

"What happened to the towels? And I assume there would have been a bathmat as well?"

"I think they took the towels when they took her away. Don't remember any bathmat."

"Okay, let's get out of here. I want you to come back here with a forensics kit and cover both bathrooms and the kitchen for fingerprints. Don't forget the plates in the dishwasher and the mugs. I want to know who was here yesterday, and what they were doing."

"Very well, sir. I can call Bertie Lawson and ask him to come over with a kit, and we can get to it right away."

"Good, you do that, and I'll go and talk to the neighbours."

Peter walks out and rings the bell next door. A woman in her mid-60s, standing outside on the other side of Marion's house, yells that he's not at home.

Peter walks over to her and presents his warrant card.

"DI Peter Greene. Do you live here?

"Yes, I do. What's this about?"

"And you are?"

"I'm Maureen Crowley."

"Do you have a moment? I'd like to ask you some questions about your neighbour?"

"Sure, come on in. I expect you want a cuppa?"

"That would be very nice, thank you."

They walk to the kitchen which looks like a mirror image of the Rivers' kitchen, except all in green, and Maureen sets about making tea.

"Sit, sit," she says, pointing to a small table and chairs by the window.

"Thank you. Have you lived here long?"

"Yeah, my family and the Rivers are the original owners, the only ones left." Then she sighs deeply and pulls a paper handkerchief out of her pocket and blows her nose. "We're the only originals left now. Or rather, I am. My husband, just like Marion's, died ten years ago in that horrible accident at Gwedrow. You may remember that one?"

"No, sorry. What happened?"

"The chains holding two enormous sheets of laminated glass meant for the Exeter Museum failed. The glass tipped over on my husband, Arthur, and Scott Rivers. It flattened them on the concrete floor. That glass was so heavy they were killed instantly! They were directing the placement of it on the glass transporter, and for some reason the glass just keeled over." She sniffs again and blows her nose. "They classified it as a workplace accident, of course, and Marion and I got apologies and insurance pay-outs."

"Were you and your husband close to Marion and her husband?"

"Oddly, not really. We were neighbours. The men worked in the same place, they got along, went to the pub and so on, but Marion and I, well, you know, we were friendly, but not friends, if you get my meaning. We just never really hit it off."

"How come?"

"She could be nice, and helpful too, but she was such a nosy parker. I don't want to speak ill of the dead, and it sounds terrible, but she was always poking her nose into other people's business, always eyeing what everybody was doing. Working in a library, she thought she knew it all. And, of course, she knew what everybody read too." Maureen shakes her head and blows her nose again. "But, after that Golden guy moved in, what eight or ten months ago, she started behaving like an infatuated teenager! Can you believe it, at her age?" She rolls her eyes.

"By the 'Golden guy' you mean the neighbour on the other side?"

"Yes, he works at Gwedrow."

"Do you know him?"

"No, not really, but, as I said, he and Marion were thick as thieves! Or at least that's what she claimed."

"Really?"

"Yeah, she took to him like he was the second coming! It was unbelievable." She rolls her eyes again. "More tea? She's old, retired, 66 she is... was, I mean. Her next birthday is in two months and he's at least 15 years younger, if not more. Although it's hard to tell how old someone is with that salt and pepper hair, so I guess he could be older? Mind you, he's a pretty good-looking guy for his age; lean, tanned, in decent shape. Although his nose is more like a beak and he limps a bit. But Marion went totally gaga over him, always asking him to come in for this and that. Embarrassing, to say the least!"

"And his name is?"

"Jon Geldenhuis. Jon, no ' h'. A bit fancy leaving it out, but then he's a foreigner."

"And Mr Geldenhuis is single? Living alone?"

"Well, I haven't seen any women going in or out, but that doesn't mean anything these days, does it? Or maybe, who knows? Perhaps he just likes older women. The way he keeps running in and out of Marion's place just about every day. She cooks him meals too. I've even seen her buying wine! A woman who goes to church every Sunday and doesn't even drink! She tilts her head and asks if he could come over and fix this, or help her with that, and complains about how Ben is never around to help with anything. Like she was some damsel in distress, at her age!" Mrs Crowley shakes her head. "Incredible. It's pathetic to run after a guy like she does. And he's some hot-shot manager at Gwedrow. Surely he could afford to do his own cooking and buy his own wines?"

"And yet he willingly helps her?"

"Seems so."

"When did Ben move out?"

"As soon as he could. Joined the military when he was barely 18. He was first a driver, and then a car mechanic. He left the military and worked in a garage for a while. But he was never really into it, drifting between different jobs until he finally got the job as a minicab driver a few years ago."

"He hasn't married?"

"Oh no, I don't think he's ever even had a girlfriend, or a boyfriend either, for that matter. Come to think of it, if Ben had come home with a boyfriend Marion would've just died!" She chuckles. "For all her bookish knowledge she was a very small-minded person."

"Did you see or hear anything yesterday?"

"No, I wasn't home yesterday. I had to go to see my sister in the hospital in Exeter. She's got cancer. I took the 10.15 bus and came back what, going on 6? I heard about Marion when I came home. Old Grubbins who lives opposite told me."

"Thank you for the tea, Mrs Crowley."

"So, I thought she just fell in the tub and drowned? Marion? Why are you asking questions?"

"When a person dies alone we always have to investigate. You have been most helpful, thank you. If you can think of anything else, here's my card. Please don't hesitate to call."

Peter walks back to Marion Rivers' house.

"Terry," he calls as he opens the door, "is Lawson here yet?"

"Yes, he is," Terry comes out of the kitchen. "Bertie's checking upstairs."

"Good, then you can drive back with him. Check and double-check everything. I'll go and talk to the other neighbour.

Geldenhuis is not at home, so Peter continues to the other side of the street, further down the row of terraced houses to talk to anybody he finds there. Nobody seems to be at home. He walks back on the other side, nobody there either. Peter walks back to the Rivers' house again.

"Terry," he calls out.

"We're done, sir."

"Good, get everything expedited. Bertie can take things back to the station, you and I can go to meet Ben Rivers."

Terry and Bertie pack things up and lock the door, this time adding crime-scene tape to it. Bertie drives off while Terry directs Peter to Ben's small flat, a bed-sit really, near the golf course. They walk upstairs but get no response when they ring the bell. A neighbour, a short elderly woman with curly grey hair opens her door and peeks out, leaving her security chain on. She inquires what they want with Ben. Peter and Terry show her their warrant cards and ask if she knows anything about Ben or where they might find him.

"He's likely at work, driving somewhere. He's a cab driver, you know. He usually drives Thursdays; those are his long days."

"Thank you. Do you know where he's stationed?"

"No. Hold on a second, I have his card somewhere." She pulls the door closed and returns a moment later with a business card. "Here it is, you can call him there. He's not in any trouble, is he?"

"No, we just want to ask him a few questions."

They thank her and drive back to the station.

***

When the officers get back they see Ingela, who has returned to the station. She is very distressed and tells them that the guy in the hospital in Penzance isn't her missing boyfriend. Peter is concerned about the poor girl. Maybe something actually has happened to the guy. He asks Terry to talk to her and get all the details. Terry interviews her at length, asks for a picture and all other information, how he'd left last Saturday morning, cycled to Bodmin, etc., and whether he has any friends he might have visited along the route. And if she knew which hostel he'd stayed in Penzance.

"That's the thing, I don't know where he stayed in Penzance. Yesterday I called just about every hostel in Penzance myself and asked if he'd stayed there, and they all said they couldn't tell me! Can you call them? Maybe something happened to him in Penzance?" Ingela asks, her voice breaking.

"Could it be possible he'd been camping?" Terry asks.

"No, he didn't have a tent with him. His plan was to stay in hostels."

"But you're sure he was heading to Bodmin from Penzance?"

"Yes, that's what he said."

"Do you know if he had any friends or family there he could've stayed with?"

"No, I don't," Ingela's eyes behind the thick lenses start to fill with tears, "something must have happened to him."

"We'll do our best to find him," Terry says, "try not to worry."

***

Peter calls it a day and drives home. It's dark and it's as gloomy outside as he feels. Judging by what he heard from Terry, Ingela's boyfriend must have been pedalling back to Faukon Abbey around the time he, himself, was speeding home on Saturday. He tries to remember how he drove home and keeps wishing that he could be certain that he hadn't hit anybody while trying to convince himself that, if he had, he'd remember it. Despite his promise to himself never to touch a drop of alcohol again, he pours himself two fingers of scotch when he gets home. He checks his answering machine, no calls. No word from Maggie; no texts, no calls. He's even kept an eye on his private email account which he never really uses. But nothing.

"Damn woman!" he says out loud and downs his drink.

After heating and eating a microwave pizza and going over and over in his mind his drive home, Peter feels the need to hit something, anything, just hit something, do something. To find something to do he goes upstairs to his son, Andrew's, old room. Andrew had been home over the last Christmas holiday from the University of East Anglia where he's studying Environmental Sciences. His girlfriend Gina came for New Year's. And obviously a single bed had been too narrow for the two of them. They were no longer kids, as Andrew was 23 and Gina something similar, so Peter had no issues with them sleeping together. He was simply happy that Andrew wanted to come home every now and then. Peter and Andrew had gone after Christmas to *Ikea* to get a new, wider bed. When Gina came, the two of them promised to put it all together, instead they'd headed to London. The bed was still in flat-packs, leaning against the wall. *Maybe it was time to get it all done? Andrew might come home in a week or two with the girlfriend.* At least it would give him something to do, a chance to bang something. And it would help him not to think about Maggie or driving too fast in the dark, or anything else.

Jimmy Carter, *The Abbey Chronicle*

Jimmy has managed to dig up information about Ben Rivers and drives to the minicab station to talk to him. To call it a station is an exaggeration. It's an old construction shed which has a small room with a desk and a phone, a sofa that has seen better days, a small table with overflowing ashtrays and a couple of chairs. A door with a big sign, WC, looms at the other end. Two drivers are watching a football game on TV. They indicate Ben's car which is just leaving. Jimmy hops in front of the car, and Ben stops with an inch to spare.

"Watch it, you pillock! What the bloody hell do you think you're doing, fucking idiot?" Ben yells.

Jimmy apologises and explains that he wants to talk about Ben's mother. "It's customary for prominent citizens to have an obituary in *The Abbey Chronicle*. So, if you could spare a few minutes?" Jimmy asks.

"All right, all right. Hop in, I'm on my way to a customer. We can talk on the way."

Jimmy gets into the front passenger seat. He barely manages to pull the door closed before Ben speeds out of the yard.

"It's a bit tricky to try to write in a moving car, you mind if I record this?" Jimmy asks. Ben glares at him. "What for?"

"I'd like to make sure I get my facts correct."

"All right, I've got nothing to hide."

"Let me start by offering my condolences," Jimmy says. "I only met your mother a few times in the library, but she was always very helpful when I visited the library for research."

"Thanks. Well, you already know her and where she worked, what more do you want?"

"She retired about a year ago. Did she have any plans to do anything particular?"

"She had her garden. I helped her with it. She was happy."

"Many retirees want to travel, pick up new hobbies. Did she want to do anything new?"

"Nah, she was happy pottering about in her garden. She usually went to see her sister in Spain once or twice a year, but auntie died a few years ago."

"And your father?"

"He's been dead for around what, 10 years now. Don't you do research?"

"Sorry, I didn't know. I haven't been here that long. Any other relatives?"

"Nah, just me."

"When's the funeral?"

"The cops haven't told me yet. She died alone so they have to investigate, they said. What's there to investigate? She slipped in the bathtub, hit her head, and drowned! I found her; I should know. But did they ask me, no."

"I see."

They arrive at the far side of Mulberry Hill.

"Your ride's up. I've nothing more to say. You can find your own way back. Now get out."

After work, Jimmy ambles to *The Whistle & Tin*, his and Helen's favourite pub. He gets his pint and finds that their usual table in the corner is taken. He finds another table and sits down, taking a deep swig of his beer.

"Hi sweetie, how are you?" Helen asks, kissing Jimmy on the cheek. "You're looking right down in the dumps. What's the matter?"

"Terrible day, let me get you your drink. Want your usual white wine or a G & T?"

"White wine, please."

Jimmy comes back with the wine and a second pint for himself.

"Thanks. So, what was so terrible about your day? Have you heard something about Ryan?"

"No, nothing about Ryan. Nobody seems to have seen him. Maybe he's just staying with friends somewhere. I think he mentioned having some friends in Bodmin?"

"Very odd for Ryan to go missing like that. He loves Ingela, I'm sure of that. She's worried sick. I hope he's with friends or something. If he is, it's still strange he hasn't called."

"Yes, it is."

"So, if it's not about Ryan, why are you so miserable? You're not getting laid off too, are you? I heard about the 'rightsizing' at Gwedrow."

"No, nothing like that. Did you know Marion Rivers?"

"Yes, sort of. She worked at the library. I met her a few times."

"What was she like?"

"I don't know, she shushed a lot at the library if people were too loud. And she was very inquisitive, to put it politely. Ingela told me that Marion was always keen to chat with people when they came with books, always asking questions, and after they left, she'd tell Ingela who they were and what kind of people they were. Ingela thought Marion was nosy because she may have been lonely and didn't meet many people elsewhere. She said that maybe by asking questions, Marion tried to show she was interested in people but didn't quite know how else to show it. Ingela always thinks best of people. Why'd you ask?"

"She died the other day."

"Yes, I saw that. Bathtubs can be dangerous, especially if you're old."

"So, you don't think there's anything else?"

"Oh, you're being Sherlock again. If you are, maybe we should get something to eat before we dig into it all?"

They order their food. While they're waiting for it to arrive, Jimmy complains about having to walk all the way from Mulberry Hill to the other side of the cricket field where the minicab drivers have their station.

"Oh, poor baby!" Helen pats Jimmy's arm. "Such an arduous trek!" She grins.

"Well, it was." Jimmy smiles. "Anyway, that Ben's a bit of an odd one. I mean, if you've just fished your own mum out of the bathtub and she's actually dead, wouldn't you show some signs of, I don't know, grief or sorrow or something?"

"I certainly would, but others might keep it bottled inside and not let it show."

Their food arrives and Jimmy fetches wine for them both.

"I don't think he was keeping it all bottled inside. It felt like he didn't give a toss."

"That's a bit harsh. So, what did he say?"

"He didn't say much of anything, nothing I didn't already know. Basically, talking to him was a waste of time. I was lucky that it didn't rain when I had to walk all that way back. And he drives like a damn maniac too! Drove too close to some cars and nearly hit a couple. I was hanging on for dear life!"

"But you survived!" Helen smiles. "Have you asked Mike for time off yet? I can't close the shop for more than a week. But if we leave on a Saturday, come back the following Sunday, we'll get a few more days in the sun. I got a call earlier from my mum. She'd like to know when we're coming. Their neighbours are going to go to Italy, I think she said, so we could stay in their place instead of on a couch with my parents."

Jimmy masks a sigh behind a napkin. *Do I want to go? And if I say no, guaranteed she won't see me again! How bad can it be if I go?* He takes another sip of his wine and promises to ask Mike for a week off.

Friday, 6 February

Jimmy Carter, *The Abbey Chronicle*

Jimmy arrives at Gwedrow again promptly at 9a.m. The receptionist calls for Geldenhuis who asks for Jimmy to be sent upstairs.

"Third office on the right," she says.

Jimmy walks upstairs. The place looks run-down. The harsh glare from industrial strip lights shows every scratch and dent in the worn-out grey linoleum floor. On the right side of the long corridor, the office walls, which seem to have originally been painted to imitate dark wood, have now depressingly faded to the colour of dried mud. Each office has partially opaque windows to the corridor. To the left, big, dusty windows open to the front of the building with a view of the yard and the manufacturing building.

Jimmy finds Geldenhuis's office. The door is open. He knocks on the frame. Geldenhuis stands up to meet him. They shake hands and Geldenhuis limps back behind his desk. The office isn't big, a large mahogany desk takes up most of the space. There's shelving on the wall. The only light comes from the corridor and two industrial strip lights in the ceiling. One wall is taken up by a small fireplace with a stone surround. Just as before, Geldenhuis looks like someone has put him between the pages of a heavy book and slammed the pages shut. Both his pale blue shirt and his dark blue trousers have creases so sharp they could cause injury. Jimmy, in his chinos and his never-ironed shirt, feels rather shabby by comparison.

"Hello Mr Geldenhuis, thank you for meeting me again."

"Please sit," Geldenhuis says, and points to a visitor's chair. "And, here you are again. What do you want to know this time?"

Jimmy digs out his notebook from his bag.

"Can we start with a little bit of background about yourself? You came to Gwedrow about eight to nine months ago?"

"Yes."

"How come you wanted to come here? Faukon Abbey isn't exactly a well-known place?"

"I was working in Exeter for a consulting company. We had done a few jobs for Gwedrow before and they offered me the job. So I moved over here."

"You're from Sweden?"

"No, I'm from South Africa. I was in the SA military and the Swedes wanted to know who killed their Prime Minister, so I moved there."

"Really?"

"No, of course not! After graduation, a pal and I were running a windsurfing school in Eilat, Israel. I met a Swedish girl there, we married, and I moved to Sweden."

"That must have been a major change. The climate is a bit cooler."

"I like snow. I like skiing."

"Do they do much windsurfing there?"

"No. Well, they do, in the south, in the summer. But no, I got a job in a computer company there. I had done quite a bit of programming when I was in the military in SA, so it wasn't a problem getting a job there. My wife went to work at the university. She's an anthropologist."

"Sounds like you enjoyed living in Sweden. By the way, did you know that there's a Swedish chef who runs the kitchen in *The Whistle & Tin* pub? They make amazing Swedish meatballs."

"Didn't know that. Not a great fan of meatballs, Swedish or otherwise."

"And then you came to the UK?"

"Yes, after the divorce I needed a change. The consulting company I worked for in Sweden had an office in Exeter, so I just transferred here." Geldenhuis checks the time on his phone. "I take it you didn't come here to talk about me. What do you actually want to know?"

"Ah, yes, you mentioned when we met that you were planning to introduce robotics and change the IT here in

Gwedrow. Can you tell me a bit more about what kind of robotics and changes you're planning?"

"We are basically changing the entire manufacturing set-up. Currently, we have incredibly old software used for both planning and manufacturing. It has all been in use for over 15 years. Now, the plan is to update that software, as well as put in place a proper server support. And, once we have our own servers and network set up in our own data centre, we can increase the robotic support in the factory as well. Then we can offer much more cost-efficient production, minimise the errors, and improve quality. And we can also offer more custom-made products to our clients.

"Sounds like a major overhaul?"

"Indeed, it is. We have to drag this company into the 21st century if it's going to survive."

"Does this mean reductions in the workforce?"

"In the IT no, not really, maybe some changes, but IT isn't over-staffed."

"What about the manufacturing and other parts?"

"Changes will happen, but of course, nothing has been determined yet. You'll have to speak with Linkled about the changes, but what I can say is that we must have our systems in place before anything else can really happen."

"Then the workers shouldn't be worried?"

"You know I can't give you any specifics. Linkled is the one you'll have to ask about that. I only deal with IT. I hope that is all. I must get to a meeting."

"Yes, thank you. I may come back if I have more questions?"

"Of course."

"I'm very interested in robots."

"Then you must ask the manager of the factory for a tour, they have a few robots there for testing."

Geldenhuis stands up and walks to the door.

"Thank you for your time," Jimmy says. They shake hands and Jimmy saunters out. Geldenhuis goes back to his desk.

Just as Jimmy is leaving the building, Terry and Peter walk in. Jimmy walks over to Terry, but Peter waves dismissively as they walk in.

Jimmy returns to his office.

"Did you get anything useful?" Mike asks.

"Geldenhuis said he was only talking about changes in IT. They're adding robots."

"Nothing about the workforce or planned reductions?"

"No, he said no reductions were planned in IT."

"*Ergo*, nothing useful. Did you speak with Linkled?"

"No, he wasn't around. And I didn't get to speak with that union guy there either, Kirwana. He was in a meeting. I'll go there again and try to talk to him. But there was one odd thing, Terry Ford and Greene walked in just when I was leaving. And I overheard that they wanted to speak with Geldenhuis too."

"Now why'd they want to speak with him? What's he done?"

"Dunno. They looked very officious."

"Didn't say anything to you?"

"Nope."

"Odd. So did Geldenhuis say anything of interest?"

"Not really. He said he's divorced and moved here from Sweden. He made an odd joke about South Africa, though, saying that he moved to Sweden because the Swedes wanted to know about Olof Palme."

"A joke? Hmm. Well, there was a long-running story way back about how the Swedish Prime Minister Olof Palme was supposedly murdered by the South African military in 1986. Palme had been rather vocal voicing his opinions about apartheid and the war in Angola, as I recall. South African leadership back then didn't care for his views. Maybe he thought you were going to ask him about that?"

"Could be. I didn't know enough to ask. Although he did say that he'd been in the South African military."

"I think they had conscription back then. Nothing else?"

"No, not really."

"So, a wasted visit then and nothing to print. Guess you'd better find out a bit more about Marion Rivers or that Bolan guy. Heard anything more about either, have you?"

"I talked to Ben Rivers yesterday; nothing about Ryan."

"Well get on digging and find out! We have a paper to publish."

Instead of checking on Ben or Ryan, Jimmy sets off dig up anything he can find on Geldenhuis. He's convinced there's more to the man than meets the eye. The first thing he finds out about Geldenhuis is his address. He was Marion Rivers' neighbour. *That explains why the cops went to talk with him*, he mutters to himself.

"Mike, Geldenhuis lived next door to Marion Rivers."

"So," says Mike, "why does that matter?"

"If the cops went to Gwedrow, they went there to talk to Geldenhuis, which means there's something fishy about her death."

"They have to investigate when someone dies at home alone," Mike says. "You know that."

"True but..."

"No buts, dig up something we can use instead!"

But for once, Jimmy decides not to dig. Instead, he heads back to his car to drive to Glowburn Terrace where Marion Rivers had lived. Maybe the neighbours there can tell him more about her and about Geldenhuis too. He gets lucky, a few hours spent, and he manages to speak with three of her neighbours who all have a lot to say about Marion Rivers and about Geldenhuis too.

What a neighbourhood though, Jimmy thinks. *Retirees or folk who don't work, so they're all at home. And they all seem to know a lot about each other, what everybody is or was doing. For better or worse, you couldn't get out of your door or come home without at least one of your neighbours seeing you, not matter what time of the day or night. Always someone watching. A bit scary that.*

Jimmy whistles as he gets back to the office to write the obit for Marion.

DI Peter Greene and DC Terry Ford

In the morning, Terry drives with Peter to Glowburn Terrace again. This time they want to talk to the other neighbour who hadn't been at home the day before. Peter knocks on the door. A man in his late 40s, with a sizeable beer belly hanging over his belt, looking like he has just woken up after having slept with his clothes on for the past week, opens the door. His greasy, unwashed hair stands upright, his eyes are puffy and he stinks of yesterday's beer.

"Whaddya want?" he asks. He has a voice that has suffered far too many cigarettes.

"You're Ken Preswick?"

"Yeah, so?"

"I'm DI Peter Greene and this is DC Terry Ford. We'd like to ask you some questions about what happened around here on Wednesday?"

"Yeah okay, whatever. What'd you wanna know?"

"Can we come in?"

"No."

"Were you at home on Wednesday?"

"Yeah."

"Did you see anybody coming in or going out from number 8, Marion Rivers' house?"

"You mean before the ambulance and you lot?"

"Yes."

"Ben came by."

"You mean Ben Rivers?"

"Yeah."

"What time was that?"

"Musta been about 1 p.m."

"You sure about the time?"

"Yeah, I was upstairs and I saw him."

"So, you saw him coming in the front?"

"Nah, he came through the back, carrying some compost bags he was, chicken shit bags too. Phooey! Smelly! Had to close me windows."

"He came from the alley through the back gate. Did he go inside?"

"Dunno, can't see that from me window."

"Did you hear him or Marion?"

"Nah."

"What time did he leave?

"Dunno, I took a nap. But he must've left, as he came back again later."

"Later, you mean before the ambulance and all?"

"Yeah."

"How long was it before the ambulance came?"

"Dunno."

"Thank you. If you remember anything else, please give us a call. Here's my card."

Terry and Peter walk back to the car.

"He wasn't very forthcoming," Terry says.

"No. What do we know about him?" Peter says.

"Nothing much." Terry pulls out his notebook. "He inherited the house from his parents who died several years ago. Only child. Owns an old Nissan. Found out nothing about where he works or if he does. Previously married for only a few years it seems, divorced 2002, no kids."

"Check him out a bit more. I'm sure he's done something, not sure what, though," Peter says. "Let's go and talk to that Geldenhuis and find out what he knows."

While they're on their way, Terry gets a call from the police officer in Penzance telling him that an observant dog walker had found a wallet in the ditch and handed it in to the police. It turned out to belong to the cyclist Terry and Christine had rescued. They now know who he is, a 25-year-old named Lucas Hart who is recovering nicely and wants to send his thanks to Terry for his help and for calling an ambulance so quickly. The Penzance officer continues, saying that, based on the traffic cams in the area, they were able to find out that Hart was hit by a dark sedan, driving fast, and turning left. Lucas Hart didn't have a chance while crossing the road. He was hit on the rear wheel and was sent flying. He didn't see who hit him. Lucky for him he landed in the shrubs, and not on the road. Unfortunately, a few of the streetlights in the area were out as Terry had observed. The Penzance team hadn't been able to see the registration number or the make of the car on the traffic cams. The car had continued towards the main road, one camera not working, again. There was too much traffic at the time to pinpoint the car, so they're still without intel.

As Terry had accepted the call on loudspeaker, Peter had heard the full discussion as well and tried to think. *A dark sedan they said. My BMW is a dark blue sedan. Where was this again?* He hasn't time to dwell on it as they arrive at Gwedrow.

As they're approaching the door, Jimmy Carter comes out and starts to head towards them, but Peter shakes his head and waves his hand dismissively. They walk briskly inside.

At the reception they ask for Geldenhuis. The receptionist calls him, stating that two police officers want to talk to him. Geldenhuis comes downstairs and extends his hand.

"Gentlemen, what can I do for you?"

Peter and Terry introduce themselves.

"Is there somewhere we can talk? We'd like to ask you a few questions about your neighbour, Marion Rivers." Peter says.

"Sure." Geldenhuis checks his mobile. "I have about 20 minutes before a meeting. Follow me."

He walks ahead of them to a small meeting room near the entrance, with dark, fake-wood-panelled walls, dark green wall-to-wall carpeting, and a table with a pale, laminated top and half a dozen fake leather chairs. A dusty-looking green curtain covers the window.

Geldenhuis sits down and offers Peter and Terry chairs.

"Mr Geldenhuis, you've heard, I take it, that Marion Rivers was found dead on Wednesday at her home?"

"Yes, I have."

"When someone dies alone at their home we are required to investigate, so it would be helpful if you could tell us where you were on Wednesday between 1 and 4 p.m?"

"That's easy. I was here at work."

"You were here all that time?

"Yes."

"How well did you know Mrs Rivers?"

Geldenhuis sighs audibly. "I didn't really. She was my neighbour."

"Did you get along with her?"

"I suppose so."

"How do you mean?"

"She was a rather nosy old biddy."

"Sounds like you didn't like her."

"I didn't say that. Look, of course I'm sorry that she's dead. She cooked a mean chicken à la king, but she was nosy, and constantly asking questions."

"What kind of questions?"

"How did I like living in Devon? What was it like living in Sweden? How does it compare to living here? Wasn't it cold there? Why am I here? Etc. etc. etc. Non-stop! She was nice when I moved in. She knew people: who to hire for help, where to buy this and that. She was a good neighbour. So, when she asked for my help to fix her ancient laptop, or a terrace door that didn't close properly, or a kitchen tile that had fallen off, I helped her. But it was wearing me out."

"Sounds like you're happy that she's dead?"

"No, of course I'm not! Don't be stupid. I'm sorry that she's dead. But it has nothing to do with me."

"You're from Sweden?"

"No, I'm originally from South Africa. I moved to Sweden in 1989. I moved to the UK after my divorce in 2012."

He looks at the clock on the wall.

"And now you must excuse me, unless you have something else to ask, I have a meeting to attend. If you feel you need to talk to me again, please call and I'll be happy to help in any way I can. This way, please."

Geldenhuis walks them back to the reception and leaves them there, while he heads further towards the back of the building.

Peter approaches the receptionist and asks her if she can provide them with Mr Geldenhuis's schedule for Monday, as he'd like to set up an appointment with him.

She checks and says he should be available around 3 p.m.

"Thanks, I'll call you and set up the appointment once I've had a chance to check my own calendar," Peter says. "Oh, could you let me know what Mr Geldenhuis's calendar looked like on Wednesday?"

She clicks on the keyboard again.

"Oh, on Wednesday he can see you earlier."

"No, I meant what did his calendar look like on Wednesday, 4 February? Did he have a lot of meetings? Was he here all day?"

"Oh okay... let me check." The receptionist points the mouse and clicks buttons. "Yes, he was here, he had meetings just about all day long."

"Thank you," Peter says, and walks out with Terry.

***

Terry and Jimmy meet at the pub later and Terry pumps Jimmy for what he's heard from Geldenhuis, which wasn't much.

What Jimmy doesn't tell Terry is the background info about Geldenhuis, the part where he was saying he'd been a spy, etc. When Helen comes to the pub, Terry leaves.

"Hi Terry, bye Terry!" Helen calls out. "He didn't have to leave on my account."

"No, he had to go and call Christine, his girlfriend in Penzance. You know they're getting married?"

"Oh, good for him and her. He's actually a pretty nice guy. He should bring her here, and we'd have a bit of an engagement party for him."

"I'm having another pint. You want your regular white wine? What about eating, should we get some meatballs too, I think today's special is Greek ones?"

"Yes please, to both. I'm starving."

Jimmy comes back with two glasses and a carafe of white wine. "I thought white would go nicely with the Greek meatballs."

"Any news about Ryan? Ingela is falling apart, poor thing."

"I wish I could tell you girls something, but no, no news. I called the Penzance local news site and Bodmin too, but they haven't heard about any accidents. Terry just told me that a wallet belonging to the guy they found in Penzance has been found. The guy was thrilled about it. But nothing about Ryan. It's like he's vanished into thin air. You don't think he's just hopped on a ferry to France or a train and gone somewhere else?"

"No, he would've told Ingela. He loves her, I'm sure of it. Poor Ingela she's going out of her mind worrying."

Their food arrives.

"Yum! These are so good. Anything more about Gwedrow? Are they going to close the factory?"

"Where'd you hear that? Yeah, these are really nice. More wine?"

"Yes please. Two women came to the store earlier to-day and were talking about it. They claimed they had an inside source and that there'd be big lay-offs; half the factory closing!"

"Wow, I haven't heard anything like that! I was there today. Talked to that IT chief, the new guy. It seems he moved here from Sweden."

"Another Swede? Next thing you know we'll get a Swedish coffee shop too. They like coffee there, I'm told."

"Actually, he's from South Africa."

"But you said he came from Sweden?"

"Yes, he met his wife in Israel. She's Swedish, he moved there, they split up, and he moved here."

"Well, at least he kept to the same time zone, or near-ly."

"Eh?"

"I've been reading these travel books and how it's better for your health if you travel within the same time zone, meaning you travel from north to south as much as you can, instead of going around the world."

"Really?"

"Yup. What else did this Geldenhuis tell you?"

"Nothing much really, which is a bit odd. He said he's planning to fix the entire manufacturing; robots, and all, and yet he claimed to know nothing about any lay-offs."

"I don't think I've ever met anybody from South Africa. How was he?"

"Don't know if it's typical for South Africans, but he looked like someone who's been dunked in a bucket of starch and ironed flat."

"Funny!"

"No really! His trousers and shirt have such sharp creases it's amazing he can put those on without cutting himself."

"Do I detect a bit of an inferiority complex here?" Helen smiles and wipes a bit of sauce from Jimmy's cheek.

"Nah, suppose he learned that in the military. They get that way there."

"Wasn't Ryan in the military too? Although, he looks nicely put together, he doesn't look that starched and ironed."

"I think he mentioned something about that. He had to get out because he was too close to some explosives which affected his hearing."

The pub is getting crowded, and rowdier.

"Want to get something more to drink? Or just go home?"

"Let's go home."

Jimmy gets to spend the night with her at her place.

Saturday, 7 February

The Abbey Chronicle, Page 6, Obituaries

Marion Rivers

Marion Rivers, aged 66, born in Taunton, has passed away. After she married Scott Rivers, who had been offered a job at Gwedrow Glassworks, they moved to Faukon Abbey. They had a son, Ben Rivers, and Mrs Rivers stayed at home taking care of her son and husband. She was also active in the church and was an appreciated member of many committees. After her husband died in 2005, and Ben had moved out, Mrs Rivers became an assistant librarian.

While there she met many residents of Faukon Abbey and was always keen to offer help and guidance.

DI Peter Greene and DC Terry Ford

Faukon Abbey police receive a call at 11 a.m. from a cyclist who reports seeing what looks like a bicycle and a body in a ditch about five miles from Faukon Abbey. The Emergency Response team is dispatched together with the uniforms to go to the site and cordon off the area. Once the emergency team arrive, they realise there's nothing they can do. They leave and one of the officers on site calls Slater and his team who arrive at the scene. Terry also heads out there.

The cyclist who found the body, is still there. Terry talks to him, but he has nothing more to tell. He'd seen an article online about a missing cyclist, so, when he saw a rear wheel sticking up from the mud, he stopped and went to look. That's when he saw the body. He touched nothing, calling the cops right away.

"Poor sod," he says, "must've been hit by someone passing too close." He leaves his contact information with the police.

Terry and Slater's tech take a lot of pictures of the location, road, and the dead cyclist. Terry walks with the uniforms along the cordoned area and the side of the road to see if there are any marks on the road or anything which could reveal what had happened. Further away from the body they find one pannier, one strap broken, similar to the one still attached to the bicycle. Terry finds the dead man's wallet in the pannier and in it, his driver's licence, a few pound notes, and two bank cards. Slater and his team collect and tag and bag everything to take with them, including the bicycle and parts of it found scattered about. The uniforms extend the cordon to cover a longer section of that side of the road.

***

Jimmy hears about the dead body on his police radio scanner when driving home from Asda with his weekly shopping. He speeds up to get to the site. He spots Terry and asks if they know yet who the cyclist is, what's going on, etc. Terry is not telling him much except that a cyclist has been found in a ditch, and that they are not releasing any additional information until the next of kin has been informed. He asks Jimmy not to report anything, not to tell anybody, not even to mention that a body has been found. The post-mortem is on Monday and then they'll know for sure. Terry promises to call him. Jimmy drives home hoping that the dead guy isn't Ryan and dreading that it is.

***

As usual, on Saturdays, Ingela is at work in the Faukon Abbey library. Terry finds her sitting at the desk. He greets her. Her eyes light up.

"You found him? Is he okay?"

Terry doesn't reply immediately.

"Is there somewhere we can talk privately?"

"Yes, there's a small office. Come with me."

Terry follows her into a small room in the back, furnished with a laminated covered table which has seen better days, with a few chairs around it. Behind the table is a narrow counter with a small fridge on top, a sink with a few mugs, a kettle, and a drip coffee maker. Stacks of books in various stages of disrepair are piled on a side table and, next to the table, a row of grey steel lockers is bolted to the wall.

Terry goes to the counter, pours some water in the kettle. He finds a mug, tea bags, and sugar.

"You'd better sit down," Terry says, pulling out a chair.

"Is he going to be okay?" Ingela sits down somewhat unsteadily, her eyes wide open, tears beginning to well up as she looks at Terry.

"I'm afraid not. I'm so deeply sorry to have to tell you this."

"He's dead, you mean?"

"I'm afraid so."

Ingela draws a deep breath, big tears slowly running down her cheeks. She tries to blink, gives up, takes off her glasses and searches for a handkerchief. Terry pulls one out of a packet and hands it to her. He gets milk from the fridge, pours it into the mug, adds a tea bag and water with several spoons of sugar then hands the mug to Ingela.

"You'd better have some tea. Careful, it's hot."

"He can't be dead! He just went for a cycle. I talked to him! I talked to him last week, I told you!" Ingela cries out. "He was just a bit cold, that was all. He was going to Penzance to stay in a hostel and..." She blows her nose. "I told you all this on Monday! And again on Wednesday! Why couldn't you find him? Why didn't you believe me? What happened? Where was he? Why's he dead? An accident?" Ingela cradles the mug. Her big blue eyes are filling with tears again. She wipes her nose with the back of her hand.

"I am so sorry. We're not yet really sure what happened to him. He was found about five miles from Faukon Abbey. It looks like an accident. But we don't know yet for sure. We have a team investigating."

"Can I see him?"

"Not yet. I'm sorry, but I have to ask you some questions. Are you up to answering now?"

"Yes."

"When you reported him missing you said his parents are dead, correct?"

Ingela nods.

"As you can understand we'd like to find his next of kin. Do you know any of his relatives, siblings, aunts, uncles, grandparents?"

"No, I don't. He was an only child and he never talked about his family."

"Do you know where he lived before he came to Faukon Abbey? He's only lived here for the past four years it seems."

"No."

"One more question, you said you didn't live together, correct?"

"We each had our own places."

"When you reported him missing you said you had keys to his apartment?"

"Yes, I do."

"Do you have them with you? With your permission, we'd like to go to his apartment and see if we can find any information about his relatives."

"Don't you use computers?"

"Yes, of course we do, but when people die and live alone, we have to investigate a bit more, as I'm sure you understand."

"I'll get the keys."

Ingela gets up, steadies herself a bit and trudges to the locker. She fishes a key out of her jeans pocket. Her hands shake and it takes a few tries before she manages to open the locker door. She pulls out her big handbag, rummages around and finds a key ring with an orange unicorn on it. Terry gets up and helps her to lock the locker again.

"Here's the key."

"Thank you." Terry helps Ingela back to her chair.

Ingela leans her head on her hands with her elbows on the table.

"I can't believe he's dead. You're sure it's him?"

"We found his wallet, in it his driver's licence and bank cards. So, we're fairly sure it's him. We'd like you to come in to identify him formally, if you're up to it, on Monday?"

"Of course!"

"Would you like me to take you home? Is there any-body I can call for you? You shouldn't be alone at a time like this."

"I can't close the library. I'll go to my mum's."

"You sure you don't want me to take you to her? Can't the girl at the counter close here?"

"She doesn't have the keys."

"Can you give me the keys, please?"

Ingela sits by the table cradling the warm mug in her hands and just stares at it. She hands him a big key ring and Terry goes out to the library. There are no patrons at present.

"Can you put a sign on the door saying the library is temporarily closed, please?"

"Sure, what's going on? Is Ingela okay?"

"Not really, she's had a terrible shock."

Terry helps to tape the sign to the library door and locks it. The girl goes to the back office, gives Ingela a hug and leaves.

"Now, let me take you to your mum," Terry says. "Where does she live?"

After delivering Ingela to her mother's place, Terry calls Peter.

Peter is flipping the instructions for the SO-VASASOTT bed, down on his knees on the floor, twisting and turning among plastic wrappers, cardboard, scattered screws, and assorted tools trying to find an elusive wooden peg. One side of the bedframe is propped up with three books, the other one has screws missing. When his phone rings, it takes a while before he finds it under a pillow in the corner. He manages to stretch his hand to it and pushes the button.

"What?" he barks.

"Sorry to bother you sir, but we've found the missing cyclist."

"Ah yes, Terry, I'm sorry." Peter gets the phone to his ear. "I've been trying to put together this bloody bed for hours now and I'm still missing screws and other bits, I think. I had to take the damn thing apart again for the third time! But you didn't call me to hear about that. So, what about the dead cyclist? Do we know who it is? What happened?"

"It seems it is Ryan Bolan. At least the driver's licence says so. He's gravely injured and covered in mud. And dead."

"Ryan Bolan? That's the guy who that girl wanted to report missing?"

"Yes sir."

"What happened to him?" Peter manages to move and push himself upright, leaning his aching back against the wall.

"Not sure about that yet, but, by the look of it, it seems he was hit from behind and sent flying into a ditch. Landed headfirst on the sharp rocks there."

"And when did this happen?"

"Slater wasn't sure. But it was a few days ago."

"Did he have any family here?"

"No, she said his parents were dead."

"Check anyway. Did you tell her?"

Terry swallows audibly, breathing in a few times. "Yeah, I did. She was working at the library. I went there," Terry says quietly.

"She was devastated, I'm sure. Poor kid, how terrible! So young too."

"Yes, she is." Terry draws a deep breath. "Have to ask, how do you manage it, sir? I never get used to telling people news like that!"

"You never do. It's hard, I know," Peter says, "but you have to remember, it's much harder to hear it. Poor kid. Did you get her any support?"

"I took her to her mum's place."

"Probably the best for her now. Go home, Terry, call your wife-to-be and tell her you miss her. See you on Monday."

"Yes, I will. Hope you get the bed put together."

They end the call.

Peter throws a spanner on the wall, it bounces, and buries itself in the cardboard packing. *Oh shit, it wasn't me. I'm sure it wasn't me. Please, please God, it wasn't me!*

Sunday, 8 February

Jimmy Carter, *The Abbey Chronicle*

After a leisurely breakfast, Jimmy and Helen descend to the bookshop from her flat above. Helen received a load of new stock on Friday, and she wants to get it all properly stacked on the shelves before her bookshop opens. She climbs busily up and down the ladder, while Jimmy opens the boxes and hands books to her to place.

"We're nearly done, Jimmy. How about coffee and maybe even one of those lemony cupcakes? Can you go and get us some while I try to sort out good Mr Conan Doyle's books, please?" Helen calls from the top of the ladder.

"Sure, let me get my coat and I'll go. Are you going to be okay?"

"Of course I am! I need an extra shot of coffee though."

On his way back with his coat, the crashing sound of a ladder and books falling sends him tearing down the narrow stairs.

"Helen!"

Jimmy runs into the shop to find Helen splayed on the floor under the big wooden ladder with her legs tangled between the rungs.

"Helen! Love! Talk to me! Are you okay?"

Jimmy gently removes her leg from a ladder rung and lifts the big ladder off her. "Helen, can you move? Can you hear me? Are you hurt? Where does it hurt?"

"My leg," Helen moans, rolling her head back and forth. "Nothing broken. I think I'm okay. I didn't fall that far. Don't fuss." But as soon as she tries to move her shoulder, she can't help but cry out in pain. "My leg and right shoulder hurt a bit."

"No, you're not okay. You're in pain! Can you move your toes and fingers? Your shoulder looks odd. I'm taking you to the hospital."

"My shoulder hurts bad, really bad. Toes move fine. They hurt a bit too."

"Don't move," Jimmy says, covering her with his coat.

Luckily, his car is parked right behind the shop. It's a Saab 900 convertible, it's old, but it's his baby. He keeps it in decent shape and the front seat falls back quite well. Jimmy runs out, gets the passenger door open, rushes back inside and lifts her up carefully. She wraps her left arm around his neck. While she's heavier than he'd expected, he manages to carry her into the car and tenderly places her in the front seat lowering the seat back and fastening her seatbelt.

"You okay there?" Jimmy asks walking around the car.

"I'm okay, but what are you doing? We can't leave now," Helen says, as Jimmy is about to get into the driver's seat. "The back door is open! We can't leave the shop open!"

"Ah yes, of course. Where are the keys?"

"In my handbag, upstairs."

Jimmy rushes back inside, climbing three steps at a time, finds her handbag and hurries back down.

Helen uses her left hand, fishing the keys from her bag. "Twist the lock properly and kick the door a bit, it's a bit sticky and heavy."

Jimmy gets the door locked, tosses the keys into Helen's bag. Back in the car, he zooms off, reaching the Brookside hospital in less than 10 minutes after breaking all speed limits. He jumps out of the car and runs inside. "Please help, my girlfriend has been injured."

"How badly injured? Can she breathe on her own? Can she walk, talk?"

"She can't walk, but her talking and breathing is okay. She fell off a ladder. Her shoulder and leg are injured."

An orderly takes a wheelchair and follows Jimmy back to the parked car. He lifts Helen gently into the wheelchair and starts chatting to her.

"What happened? Where does it hurt?

While Helen explains what happened to the orderly wheeling her in, Jimmy walks to his car to park it properly.

"She's in excellent hands, don't worry," the orderly calls after him.

After parking his car, Jimmy walks back and asks the reception where to find Helen. He's told to wait while she's examined and treated.

"Is it going to take long? She's going to be okay, right?"

"Come back in an hour or so. She should be fine, though."

Jimmy drives back to Faukon Abbey. At first, he thinks about going back to his office, but instead he drives to his own flat and calls Terry to get more information about the cyclist. No answer. He putters about his flat for a while not able to concentrate on anything and drives back to Brookside instead.

The receptionist tells him to go to the third ward on the second floor.

He finds the ward. After walking past the other patients, he finds Helen in a hospital gown, right arm in a sling and bundled up in a bed. She's checking her phone.

"Hey! How are you feeling? Jeez! You gave me a proper scare falling off like that!" Jimmy says, leaning towards Helen, giving her a one-armed hug and a kiss on the cheek. "Did they patch you up properly? How long are they keeping you? Are you hurting?" He pulls a chair up closer to the bed and sits down.

"Not hurting now. They gave me meds for that. Apparently, I was lucky. I landed mostly on my shoulder, so my shoulder got dislocated and they pulled and manipulated it back into place."

"Oh ouch, ouch! Pulling it back into place HURTS! Poor you!"

"Yeah, that really hurt! I think I even screamed a bit, but now it's okay. Not much pain anymore. The other thing is my ankle. Apparently, I twisted it when it got caught in the ladder rung. Although they agree I landed on my shoulder, they still think I hit my head a bit too, so they keep coming by like every 15 minutes and shining lights in my eyes, and asking if I'm feeling sick and what day it is."

"You're in good hands and you're okay. Holy Maloney, that fall could have killed you!"

"Right, well, it didn't, I'm fine. But about the shop ..."

While Helen keeps talking, Jimmy's attention moves to listening to someone else - about killing someone in the bathtub. But as he's holding Helen's hand he can't just jump up and see who's talking. By the time he gets up, the speakers have gone. Helen has been trying to explain how to lock up the store, put a sign on the door and call her parents. He directs his attention back to her.

The fall impacts Helen's and Jimmy's holiday plans as Helen is now going to stay overnight in hospital and, even after she's out, she shouldn't be travelling anywhere, at least not for a week or two. *Saved by the bell*, Jimmy thinks and immediately scolds himself thinking just that. *She could've been killed for chrissake!*

Helen calls Ingela. No response. She texts her and asks if she can tend the shop for her for a day or two while she's in hospital.

Oh, no! Not you too, Ingela texts back. *I'll come soon.*

"What does she mean, not you too?" Helen asks.

"I don't know for sure," Jimmy says.

"You mean something has happened to Ryan?"

"They found a dead guy and a bicycle in a ditch just about five to six miles out. Terry and everybody else were there. Terry refused to tell me who the dead guy was."

"Oh my God. No, no! I hope it wasn't Ryan. Please God, no! Ingela's been so happy since she met him. Oh gosh, what a terrible thing! I hope it's not Ryan. He's such a nice guy too. Did Terry say anything about what had happened to the dead guy?"

"No, I couldn't get him to tell me anything. They had to inform the next of kin first."

"Yes, of course. Now who'd that be? Ryan's only lived here for what, four or five years or so? His folks don't live here as far as I know, do they? I think Ingela said something about Ryan being an orphan." Helen scrunches her eyebrows. "Do you know anything more about him?"

"Not really, no. The only times I've met him have been with you and Ingela. He seemed a bit shy. We didn't really talk that much."

"Yeah, not sure if he's actually shy but he's a bit hard of hearing, lost hearing in one ear, I think. He talks little because of that, I suppose. Apparently, he'd caught measles, or is it mumps, when he was in the reserves or something. Army reserves, I think Ingela said. Or maybe it was an explosion, not sure which."

"Mumps," Jimmy says. "Mumps as an adult is bad, causes all sorts of issues in men. And the army has a lot of explosive things." He shifts his seating. "This chair is rather hard to sit on. Are you allowed to have coffee and eat something?"

"Yes, please! I'd like coffee and if they have any cupcakes or muffins or something to eat, I'd love some."

"Okay, I'll see what I can find."

"These cupcakes aren't half bad, but this coffee is terrible." Helen says.

"It's not that bad. I've had worse. The coffee at Gwedrow is like someone took a coffee bean, shoved it into a dirty old coffee pot and swirled it around in tepid water," Jimmy says.

"Eww, that bad eh, you poor thing. You shouldn't make me laugh. Not good for my shoulder. Surely it wasn't that bad?"

"Well ..." Jimmy smiles.

Ingela finds them. She looks so frail and thin, her blond hair a tangled mess. Her normally big blue eyes are now red with swollen eyelids behind her glasses, her face blotchy. Jimmy jumps up and gives her a hug. He pulls her towards Helen who tries to give her a one-armed hug.

"Sit, sit down. It's Ryan? Have they found him?" Helen asks.

"He's dead. Ryan's dead," Ingela whispers. Big tears flow down her cheeks.

"Oh no, oh no! I'm so sorry," Helen and Jimmy say in chorus.

"What happened to him?"

"I don't know, the police said they found him. They don't tell me anything." Ingela's crying silently, gulping in big breaths and is clearly on the verge of a breakdown. Helen looks over Ingela's bowed head. "I think you should drive her to her mum's. She's in shock. She needs her mum."

"My mum is outside; she drove me here. I just wanted to come and see that you're okay," Ingela says. "I wanted to come here to see if they could show me Ryan, but they didn't allow me." Ingela bursts into tears again. "It's so terrible. He was so happy and looking forward to his tour, even though the weather was bad."

"I'm so sorry. Is there anything Jimmy or I can do?"

"No. But I don't think I can take care of the bookshop now." Ingela looks downcast. "I'm so sorry, but I think I'd be really useless right now."

"Oh gosh, no! Don't even think about it. Go home with your mum, let her take care of you for a while!"

Jimmy puts his arm around Ingela's shoulders and walks with her.

"It's devastating, it hurts so bad, I know. It's terribly painful to lose someone you love. I lost my mum. I know it hurts. Let me walk you back to your mum. And let me know if I can do anything to help."

"Oh, Ingela, call me, anytime," Helen calls out. "I'm so sorry, it's just so dreadful."

After depositing Ingela back with her mum, Jimmy walks slowly back to Helen's bed.

"That's so terrible. Poor Ryan and poor Ingela," Jimmy says, shaking his head. "She's totally heartbroken."

"She's such a dear and I feel so sorry for her. She's had a rough time meeting any guys. Once she met Ryan, she was so happy, and I thought she and Ryan were going to get married and have at least a dozen kids. They both love kids. Ryan was an only child, said it was lonely so he always wanted to have them, and Ingela loves kids. She's always with them in the library. Oh God, this is so terrible. Ryan was such a nice guy." Helen's eyes fill with tears. Jimmy grabs a paper hanky from his pocket and hands it to her.

"Come now, come now." He holds onto her while she sobs quietly.

"It's just so horrible. He wasn't old, he was still young. It's not fair! Ryan was too young to die."

He hands her another hanky. She blows her nose, wipes her eyes, and draws a deep breath.

"Jimmy, could you go to the shop and put a sign up that we'll be closed until Wednesday, please," Helen says. "Have to keep it closed until I get back. I don't know anybody else I could trust. You have your work to do too."

"Yes, of course."

"And find out what happened to Ryan!"

After dealing with the bookstore, Jimmy drives home and thinks about killing someone in the bathtub and what he'd heard in the hospital. He plonks himself down in front of his laptop and sets out to find out more details about Marion Rivers and her death. Slim pickings in that. He tries to call Terry, no answer.

Jimmy continues searching the internet. *Curious about Terry and Greene going to see Geldenhuis. Why'd they do that? Just because he's her neighbour? Hmm, that doesn't hold water.* He chuckles at his own pun. But there was something about that Geldenhuis guy.

He searches for info on Geldenhuis, reading news articles from South Africa, and then he spots an old article with the name Geldenhuis which mentions the word bathtub in a South African paper. He locates the paper's website, finds out it's still running and emails the editor asking for details about the article. *Geldenhuis and bathtubs, eh? Now that is a bit curious.*

Jimmy scrolls and searches, and finds an old story about one George Joseph Smith, and the 'Brides in the Bath' murders. According to that story, George Smith, who had multiple aliases, married a few women around the country. He was convicted of killing at least three of them in the early 1900s and had been hung for his crimes in Maidstone, in August 1915. There had been another story about it in 2010. Interesting, very interesting indeed. *Geldenhuis said he'd been married. Is the wife still alive? The neighbours talked about him and Marion. Curious indeed*. He checks his watch and sees it's visiting time at Brookside.

Jimmy's eager to tell Helen what he's found but when he gets to the ward, she is talking to her parents on Skype and asks him to come back tomorrow instead. Jimmy nods and drives to *The Whistle & Tin* to get something to eat.

After ordering a plateful of vegetarian meatballs - a delicious contradiction in terms, and getting a pint, he finds a table in a corner. Terry is sitting on his own looking worn out. Jimmy joins him. Terry sadly confirms that it was indeed Ryan Bolan who was found in the ditch. They both take a swig of the beer. Their meatballs arrive. They're both feeling rather down in the dumps and eat in silence. Ryan Bolan had been young guy just cycling about because he liked doing it, he had a great girlfriend whom he loved, and a future, and now he's dead, through no fault of his own. It's just wrong that he's now dead. After they finished eating, Jimmy quietly asks if he can print this, since Ingela's already been told but Terry insists that he'll have to wait until final identification.

To add to the gloom and doom, Jimmy tells Terry about Helen's accident. When Jimmy offers to get another pint, Terry declines and drives instead home to call Christine. Jimmy is left to nurse his beer alone. Even the weather is gloomy.

Monday, 9 February

The Abbey Chronicle, Page 1

Faukon Abbey police received a call on Saturday at 11 a.m. from a cyclist, who reported seeing what looked like a person and a bicycle in a ditch about five miles from Faukon Abbey. Emergency services attended, but tragically, the cyclist was found to be deceased. Faukon Abbey police attended the scene, closed the road, and have launched a full forensic examination. Police are now appealing to any witnesses who may have been in the area to come forward. Please contact the nearest police station or call 111 111 111.

DI Peter Greene and DC Terry Ford

Terry has barely made it to his desk in the morning before his phone rings.

"Hello, hello?" a male voice shouts at the other end.

"This is DC Ford, what seems to be the issue?"

"Are you the one who was here talking about Marion Rivers?" the loud voice continues.

"Yes, sir." Terry moves the phone away from his ear.

"You said to call if I remembered anything, and I just remembered something."

"Yes?"

"That Golden hue guy, the one living next to Marion? He was there on the day she died."

"When was that?"

"Don't know for sure when he came, but I saw Marion calling for him. I think he was about to leave again?"

"What time was that?"

"About noon or thereabouts."

"Did he stay?"

"He went in with 'er, stayed 15 minutes or so, and left."

"Did you see Marion after that?"

"No, let me think. No, I don't think she came to the door."

"And you're sure that this happened last Wednesday?"

"I maybe old, but I know me days. They always deliver me meals on Wednesdays and the woman who delivers was late coming. So, I was looking out the window waiting for her."

"I see. Thank you, sir. Anything else you remember?"

"Nah, meal lady came a bit after, so I saw nothing else until I heard the ambulance later. Woke me from me nap, it did."

"Thank you, sir, for calling."

"That damn dog again!" The phone goes dead.

Terry massages his ear and shakes his head.

"You heard, sir?"

"Yes, I think we'd better talk to Mr Geldenhuis again. Golden hue, eh? Didn't he say he was at work in his office all day long?"

"Yes, he did."

Peter and Terry drive to Gwedrow Glassworks again. When they get there, the receptionist tells them that Jon Geldenhuis is in a meeting but should be free in 10 minutes. They sit down. They can hear loud voices and even yelling, coming from the same room they were in on Friday.

A tall, muscular, black man dressed in grey chinos, a blue, striped shirt and a jacket and tie throws open the door and storms out, yelling, "You're not going to get away with it. *Masende kababa wako (Your father's balls!)*. You piece of *kak*, I'll get you!"

He marches out of the building. Geldenhuis comes out, raking his slim fingers through his hair, but looking as dapper as ever. He's muttering to himself and his limp is a bit more noticeable than usual. He keeps tapping and swiping his phone, until, walking towards the staircase he finally notices Peter and Terry standing a few feet from him.

"Really? You again, what is it now? I don't have much time. Is this about Marion again? I'm always happy to help the police, but I know nothing more than I've already told you. Besides, wasn't it an accident?"

"We just want to make sure we have all the facts," Peter says. "Could you tell us again about your movements on that Wednesday?"

Geldenhuis sighs. "Okay, we'd better go in here." He leads them back to the room. "Take a seat." He closes the door behind them and starts checking his mobile, scrolls a bit and says, after sitting down, "Wednesday last week. Oh right, right, I did go home at lunch time. I was about to receive some computer equipment and, as it was supposed to rain, I didn't want it to be left outside."

"Did the equipment arrive?"

"Yes, it did."

"Did you see Marion Rivers?"

"Actually, I did. She must have seen me coming home and pounced on me as I was about to leave. She said she needed help with a quick thing. Just a small thing to fix. A shelf had fallen down in the bathroom."

"And did you help her?"

"I said I'd take a look." Geldenhuis sighs. "I went in. She went on and on again about how her son is never around to help her. For once it turned out that it was a quick job. I just screwed the shelf back in place. She thanked me and I left."

"And where was she when you left?"

"Heading to the kitchen. She had asked me if I wanted a cuppa. I said no and left. I had to get back to work."

"And what time was that?"

"12:45."

"Very precise."

"Yes, I checked my mobile as I left. I had to be at a meeting at 1 p.m. and didn't want to be late."

"How come you didn't tell us about this before?"

"You didn't ask. And frankly, I had forgotten all about it. In case you haven't heard, we have a lot of changes coming up at Gwedrow and I've been rather busy."

"And who was the person storming out of here earlier?"

"Ah yes, that's Kirwana, Julius Kirwana. Just because he's been here since the stone age, he thinks he's the one and only person who knows how to do anything in this company."

"Why was he so angry?"

"His team is going to get some new machines and he doesn't agree."

"Redundancies?"

"Yes, a couple. Which is what riled him up." Geldenhuis rolls his eyes. "He'll just have to get with the program or find another job." Geldenhuis looks at his mobile. "All clear now?"

Peter thanks him and stands up to leave.

"What kind of car do you drive?" Peter asks.

"A racing green Mini. Why?"

"And where were you on Saturday?"

"Saturday? Why do you ask? I drove back and forth to Newquay. A bit chilly for the beach so I ate the most expensive fish and chips ever. Tasted great, but way overpriced. Then I came home."

Geldenhuis stands up too and walks to the door, then stops. "Talking about driving, you really should check on how people drive around here."

"What do you mean?"

"Some idiot was speeding and tried to run me over on Saturday evening. He swerved and nearly killed me! I fell off my bicycle. Luckily, I landed in a hedge. Thankfully there was no brick wall there. After I got up, I found that my shorts were torn, but I had no injuries, apart from minor scratches. Bicycle was fine too."

"You were wearing a helmet?"

"Yes, always."

"What time was this?"

"I didn't look. After 6 p.m. or so. I was on my way home. Had to work out after eating that fish and chips."

"And where was this?"

"You know that small side street off Mason, when you turn left? Not sure of the name of it."

"Yes. Did you see who it was? Registration number?"

"Nope, it was a dark sedan. The car was filthy and it all happened so quickly."

"If you want to file a formal report you can do that at the station."

"Nah, not worth it since nothing really happened. Just thought you ought to know that there's some wannabe racing driver or, more likely, a drunk driver on the loose."

Terry and Peter walk out of the building and notice a group of men standing outside the factory building. One of them seems to be Julius Kirwana. They walk towards them and hear one of the men saying, "Oh the fuzz is here!" The men scatter, leaving only Julius Kirwana standing alone.

"Mr Kirwana. DI Peter Greene, and this is DC Terry Ford." They both show their warrant cards.

"What do you want? Did that *twat* make a complaint?"

"If you're referring to Mr Geldenhuis, he didn't say anything about you. We were merely talking to him about his neighbour."

"Oh, about Mrs Rivers, the old librarian who died last week? You think he killed her?"

"Why'd you say that?"

Kirwana's eyes narrow and his nostrils flare. "Because he thinks he can do anything and get away with it. But I know that he's a phony. He's a liar, a crook, and a war criminal!"

"A war criminal?"

"You're the cops, find out!"

A loud whistle blows and Kirwana walks away. "Ask him why he has the torture rattles!" He turns and walks inside the building. Terry starts going after him, but Peter stops him.

"He's not going anywhere. We can talk with him later."

"Torture rattles? What does he mean? What are those?" Terry says.

"Let's check them both out, but my hunch is that we have a newcomer, a white guy originally from South Africa, and a black guy, who probably came from there too. There's a lot of history there, most of it very nasty."

They walk back to Terry's car.

"Before we head back to the station let's see if we can catch up with that elusive Ben Rivers," Peter says.

They find Ben is outside washing his car. Peter seems to remember that there had been an orange mark on Ben's car. But now the car is nice and shiny all over, no dents or markings. Peter asks Ben how he got rid of it.

"Didn't see any marks, I just washed the car. It was very dirty, maybe just a dead leaf that got stuck or something?" he says.

"Or it could've been from one of those cones at the Asda parking lot," Peter says.

Ben shrugs and says, "No idea."

Peter asks Ben where he was on Saturday. While Ben hoses down the car, he says he was in Penzance. Peter continues asking Ben more about what time he had left, what time he returned home and what he had been doing there. Ben grudgingly answers that he'd been in the bookstore there for the second part of a course about writing books at Leonie Phillips' bookstore. She holds courses about writing and on how to become your own publisher and make loads of money. Ben starts with the polish and claims that because he drives a minicab he hears so many funny and sad stories that he wants to write about them and make money. It was an all-day course. He had left at about 4 p.m. Peter asks him if he'd seen anybody riding a bicycle at that time. He says no, no cyclists.

"You said it was the second part of the course? When was the first one?"

"Previous Saturday."

"That'd be the 31st?"

"Yeah."

"Same program?"

"No, then we talked about writing. Last Saturday was all about how to get published."

"Did the first course also end at 4 p.m?"

"Yes."

"And you left right away?"

"Just about."

"You must have been famished after sitting all that time?"

"Nah, we ate."

"And you didn't go anywhere after the class?"

"Nah, drove straight home."

"Both days?"

"Yeah."

Peter and Terry thank Ben and return to the office.

Tuesday, 10 February

The Abbey Chronicle, Page 3

Marion Rivers' Inquest on Thursday

The Faukon Abbey police have now confirmed that the inquest into Marion Rivers' death will be held in the Town Hall Blue meeting room on Thursday 12 February. The purpose of the inquest is to determine the cause of death. The Faukon Abbey police initially treated her death as an accident.

Dr Percy Slater, Home Office Pathologist

Slater performs the post-mortem on Ryan Bolan, the dead cyclist found on Saturday. After he has finished, he calls Peter. Terry drives with Peter to the morgue.

"And here we are again," Slater says. "Good morning to you both."

"Good morning," Peter says. "What do you have for us now?"

Both Peter and Terry take the masks offered by a tech. The smell in the room is rather overpowering.

"Breath through your mouth," the tech advises them, "and smear this under your nose. It's Vaseline mixed with eucalyptus oil."

"Now, gentlemen, it seems that this case is also a bit unclear. As you can see, he's suffered major trauma to his face. The force required to shatter his nose and forehead to that extent is likely to be greater than if he had just fallen off his bike. And when we looked at his bike, it's clear that it was hit from behind."

"So, it wasn't an accident? We have a hit-and-run?"

"Sort of."

"What do you mean, sort of?"

"Yes, it seems highly likely that he was hit by a car, then flew headfirst, landing on the rocks and mud, face-down. It is possible that he died on impact or right thereafter, as I didn't see any mud in his mouth. It could've been because of an accident. However, he also had a deep laceration on the back of his head. And he wasn't wearing a helmet. We found a helmet still tied to his pannier."

"Not making sense, Doc."

"You see, we found a small piece of crumbled spacecake in our victim's bag."

"Spacecake?" Peter asks.

"Spacecakes are cannabis edibles, sold mostly in 'selected shops' if you know what I mean, in Amsterdam," Terry says.

"Ah yes, I know about edibles, didn't know the name."

"To continue," Slater says, "he didn't have any of it in his stomach, but we haven't received all the tox screens back yet. However, if our victim here had any residue of marijuana in his system, he could very well have been cycling erratically. A driver coming from behind may not have been able to avoid him if it was dark. We've sent the bicycle to Exeter to have it analysed for possible traces from the car. Only thing we noticed was that the traces were dark in colour. Another odd thing is the helmet. It seems it didn't fit him."

"I thought all bicycle helmets were adjustable," Peter asks.

"They are," Terry says, "some more than others, some styles work better for women, some for men. Christine has one, it fits me, but I don't want to wear pink."

"I see," Peter says, "and how long has he been dead?"

"Most likely 4 to 5 days, could be a week. It's been cold and he was in the shade so he's relatively well preserved."

"That would mean he died on 31 January, as he was found on 7 February?"

"That's possible."

"And when did Marion Rivers die?"

"On Thursday 4 February, at around 3 p.m."

"And Ben Rivers called at 4.20 p.m.? So that means Marion Rivers had already been dead more than an hour by the time Emergency services showed up?"

"That's also likely."

"Thanks, Doc."

"Didn't Ben Rivers, whose car is very dark blue, nearly black, say he was driving back from Penzance on 31 January? And didn't Penzance say it was a dark sedan which hit the cyclist you rescued?" Greene says, when they get into the car.

"Yes, they did."

"Let's check it all out a bit further. Let's find out if Ben left the book club, or whatever it was, when he said he did. And if he went to a pub or somewhere else. Call Penzance and ask them to find out. Also, I think we need to get Ben Rivers' phone and financial records too."

"Yes sir."

DC Terry Ford

Terry drives to collect Ingela for the formal identification of Ryan. The techs have cleaned his face, but it's not pretty, as he had been dead for more than a week before he was found. Ingela takes one look at the face and gulps for air, tears rolling down her face. Terry puts his arm around her heaving shoulders and walks her to a group of chairs outside the room and sits her down.

"That is Ryan Bolan?"

"Yes!" Ingela nods, big tears running down her cheeks. "You should have listened to me! You could have found him in time. He shouldn't be there. You did nothing, you, you, you..." She sobs, trying to wipe fluid from her nose, and hiccups.

"I'm so sorry," Terry says, "we all are. But I have to tell you that it seems he died on that Saturday when he was on his way back. He was close getting home, as he was found a few miles away."

Ingela blows her nose. "Do you think he suffered? All those injuries to his face."

"The doc said no, it would have been instantaneous, or just about."

"What happened to him?"

"We don't know for sure yet. It looks like a car hit him and sent him flying headfirst into a ditch."

"A hit-and-run accident?"

"As it looks now, that seems to be the case."

Ingela's sobs have quietened down, tears still streaming. Terry gets her a paper cup with water.

"Drink quickly, it's good for hiccups."

Ingela downs the water and hiccups again.

Terry goes to refill the cup. Ingela sips the water, her unseeing eyes fighting the tears, fixed on the now darkened window.

"Are you okay to answer a few questions?"

Ingela nods.

"We'd like to know where Ryan was staying after he had left Penzance. Do you know?"

"I don't know. I don't." Ingela's voice breaks. "I didn't talk to him. I worked late at the library and only when I was leaving, I noticed I had missed a call from an unknown number."

"What time was the call?"

"I don't know. I only saw it when I was leaving."

"Did the caller leave a message?"

"No, no message. I called the number but there was no answer. I thought it must have been a wrong number." She draws a deep breath again. "I can't bear to think it might have been Ryan and I didn't talk to him!" Ingela gulps for air and presses her handkerchief against her eyes.

"So sorry to bother you like this, but did Ryan have any friends here in Faukon Abbey or elsewhere he could have talked to about where he was going or where he planned to stay?"

"Don't know. Maybe he talked to the guy who was replacing him? When I called the hotel before I reported him missing, they said they hadn't heard from Ryan either."

Terry can hear the distress in Ingela's voice. "Why are you asking these questions? Have you found any relatives yet?"

"We just like to be thorough. Thank you again. And I'm so sorry for your loss."

Terry drives Ingela back to her mother's house and returns to the hotel, only to find out that the guy who was replacing Ryan Bolan is probably asleep at home, as he, like Ryan, works the night shift. He drives back to the station.

Back at his desk, he finds an email from one of Slater's techs. After the techs had gone through everything collected from the site, they had found Ryan's mobile in his pannier and managed to power up the phone. Luckily, the panniers are waterproof. They had also managed to trace his pin code and had gained access to the phone. The tech sent Terry phone numbers, as well as emails, from the previous week. Either the phone was new, or Ryan hadn't been big on communicating by phone, as there were only five phone numbers and ten emails and only one SMS.

Terry dials the last number Ryan had called on Saturday 31 January and gets lucky. A girl answers. Terry doesn't tell her that Ryan is dead, just asks if Ryan is there. Nope, he'd left over a week ago, she says. Terry thanks her and ends the call. Since there's a possibility of drugs being involved, Terry walks downstairs to talk with DS Sarah Tremis who keeps an eye on drugs in Faukon Abbey and the Dartmoor area.

"Spacecake, you say?" Sarah Tremis says.

"That's what Slater called it."

"We rarely see that here. It's more something people buy in Amsterdam. They go there, get some and eat it there. Too risky to bring it over and get caught in customs, you know, dogs. But if Slater said so, seems someone had managed to bring it over anyway. And you think these friends where your dead guy stayed are in Bodmin?"

"That seemed to be the last place he stayed. Here's the phone number."

"Okay, let me get hold of the Bodmin team and they can go there to talk to these friends. Could be it's a once-off thing, could be it's something organised. We better find out."

"Thanks. Could you tell the team to ask whether they are indeed friends of Ryan Bolan and, if they say they are, also inform them that he's dead? I'd also like to know what date and time he left there, as well as what kind of shape he was in when he left."

Two hours later Terry gets a call from Sarah. The Bodmin team had traced the number and had gone to the location. It was student housing for art history students on assignment in Lanhydrock. All the students claimed they knew nothing about any drugs. They acknowledged that Ryan had been there. He had left on Saturday 31 January around noon or thereabouts, after a late breakfast.

"Did the Bodmin team believe them about the drugs?"

"You know how it is, it's difficult to say. Nice enough group, Bodmin said. They were invited inside. There was no telltale smell wafting about, all the students seemed to be clear-eyed, and they appeared genuinely shocked to hear about Ryan. Bodmin said they gave the students your phone number and told them to call you if they wanted more information about Ryan."

"Thanks, I may also call them again."

As soon as Terry ends the call with Sarah, his phone rings.

A girl asks nervously, "Is it true that Ryan is dead? Ryan Bolan? Can you tell me, please? I got your phone number from a copper who came here."

"You're calling from Bodmin?"

"Yes."

"I'm afraid that is the case. I take it you're a friend of Ryan's? And that he stayed with you?"

"Yes, he crashed on our sofa here. There's five of us.

"And when was that?"

"About two weeks ago, for one night. They didn't tell us how he died. Can you?"

"It seems a car hit him and the driver fled."

"Oh my God, no! That's terrible! Poor Ryan!" Terry can hear her crying. She blows her nose.

"Maybe he'd been cycling a bit erratically and the driver didn't see him in the dark. Is that a possibility, you think?"

"This is so wrong! He shouldn't have died! He'd been telling us, we used to know him way back in Exeter uni, you see, how he'd found this great gal, Ingela. He was so happy. We talked about getting together maybe to go surfing in May or something. He'd bring Ingela. Poor girl, so sorry for her."

"Sounds like you were celebrating?"

"Yeah, we were happy for him, yes."

"I'm trying to find out how Ryan died, so, if there's anything you can tell me, if he could have been cycling erratically that would be most helpful."

A bit of a pause on the other end. Then Terry hears a deep sigh.

"Yes, he could've been. He was still a bit loopy in the morning."

"Why was that?"

"A friend of ours had been in Amsterdam, for a friends' stag do and brought home two spacecakes. We don't do drugs, I swear! We don't! He brought those two back as he thought it would be cool just to try them once. I swear, none of has ever done any drugs. We're into art, not drugs!"

"I get it, I get it. You just wanted to try. What happened?"

"It was late Friday afternoon when Ryan came around and asked if he could crash on our sofa overnight. And of course, he could. We hadn't seen him for ages, so he was more than welcome. We sent out for big pizzas, got beers and wine too, had a good old time. Then someone thought about those spacecakes. Since we didn't really know anything about them, we cut them in pieces, and each took a piece. We first had one piece, didn't seem to do anything, then we took another one. And then it sort of hit us after a while. We were all giggling and laughing our heads off. It was so strange. Quite bizarre really. It was like I was outside myself looking around at a bunch of silly asses laughing their heads off. Scary and way weird. I think we all crashed like before midnight. I don't remember going to bed but I woke up in it. We were all rather hung over and a bit loopy in the morning."

"So, Ryan left about what time?"

"Yeah, he left on Saturday. Not sure what time though. Maybe around 1 p.m., not sure, we all woke up late. He took a shower to clear his head, he said. We all were rather off. Can't really describe it. And no one really had any memory of the evening after we'd eaten that cake. Strange it was." She blows her nose.

"Do you remember anything else? Did you talk to him again?"

"No, I didn't speak to him, but I remember Ryan called here. I think it was Mike who answered. Maybe around 5 p.m. or a bit later, it was dark. Don't know. Ryan was asking if he had left his extra battery pack for his phone here. His phone battery was dying and he couldn't find it. We all went to look for it. Someone found it and called him. Ryan said, not a biggie, he'd come again. He said the weather was miserable, but he was just about another hour from home."

"Thank you. You may be contacted by the coroner here in Faukon Abbey and possibly asked to attend the inquest."

"Do we have to tell about the spacecake?"

"You mean who brought it? It's illegal, as you know, but I don't think the coroner is interested in who brought it. It wasn't the spacecake that killed him."

"Thanks."

"One more question, when he was found, he wasn't wearing a helmet."

"Ah yes, it didn't fit, did it? Ryan said some ass had swiped his helmet in Penzance and left him with one that was too small. He was furious about losing it as it was a new one, expensive too."

"Thank you again. If you or your friends have more questions, give me a call."

Jimmy Carter, *The Abbey Chronicle*

Jimmy visits the Gwedrow plant again. This time he talks with a few workers milling about the yard and asks them about the upcoming changes, the rightsizing, possible lay-offs, and their views. They have a lot of those. A lot of very vocal opinions, very few facts though. Many scared about losing their jobs, some swear to fight.

When he's about to leave, Kirwana pulls Jimmy aside and tells him of his suspicions about Geldenhuis. He claims he'd seen Geldenhuis driving away from the plant on the day Marion Rivers died, but he hadn't known where he had gone. Kirwana also tells him about the discussion he overheard in the library and who he thinks Geldenhuis really is. This would make Geldenhuis a prime suspect in Marion's death. No, he doesn't want to talk to the police. They had already been there and asked questions. He doesn't like cops.

Jimmy calls Terry and says that he has had an anonymous tip that Geldenhuis was seen at Marion's place the day she died. Terry thanks him and wants to know who provided the info. Jimmy says he doesn't know, the person didn't identify himself.

"Uh-huh, right."

"So, you're not going to check it out?" Jimmy asks.

"What else did you hear?"

"Did you know that Geldenhuis could be a war criminal? A torturer in the South African forces during the war?" Jimmy recounts the story Kirwana had told him.

"Really Jimmy, surely you don't believe everything someone tells you? Aren't you supposed to be an investigative journalist? Do you have any additional proof other than just hearsay from some disgruntled worker?"

"Well, no, not yet, but I'll find out. But if Marion Rivers, who was known to be a nosy parker, found out about Geldenhuis being a war criminal, and if he was at her place when she died, isn't that reason enough for you to check out what he's been up to?"

"Steady on. You can't print that, that's slander, you know that. But thanks for the tip. If you find out any actual factual information we'll certainly look into it. Bye."

Just after lunch Jimmy gets a call from a woman with a rather non-descript voice, cultivated, using good English, but not a native English speaker. She says she's calling from Stockholm, Sweden, and she wants to know what this Geldenhuis person, mentioned in the article about Gwedrow, looks like. The picture posted online was rather pixelated. She just wants to make sure he's the correct Geldenhuis before calling him. It is possible that there are other South Africans with that name working there, is it not?

Jimmy tells her what Geldenhuis looks like: curly, salt and pepper hair, sharpish nose, long thin fingers, medium height and weight.

"Not very distinctive, could be any middle-aged guy," she says. "Anything else?" Jimmy hesitates. "Does he have one leg shorter than the other and does he limp?" she asks.

"Yes," Jimmy says.

"And did he tell you he was injured in a riding accident?"

"Yes, he did."

She laughs. "Except the bum leg he has did not come from a riding accident, just from an accident falling off a roof and breaking it as a kid. It never healed properly and was left a bit shorter. Thanks, I know your Mr Geldenhuis. He always was a charmer, a liar, and a cheat, and he owes me. Last I heard he was heading to Canada. Good to know he is closer than that."

She thanks Jimmy and ends the call before he manages to say another word. Jimmy is left staring at his phone, wondering what that was all about.

Jimmy walks over and tells Mike about the call.

"Strange that someone would just call us and ask about someone in Gwedrow. Where was the call from? Did she say who she was?" Mike asks.

"No, and her call didn't show her number, which is odd too. She said she was calling from Stockholm."

"For all we know she could just be fishing for info for something else. You really shouldn't have told her. Who knows what he's been involved in?"

"Could be. It was rather odd to ask what he looks like, since the article about changes in Gwedrow has a photo of Geldenhuis and the plant manager, in Geldenhuis's office."

"You better do some research and find out more about this Geldenhuis guy."

And Jimmy, who loves nothing better than digging on the internet and doing research, sets about to do exactly that.

After a quick search, Jimmy finds out that there is, indeed, a Ruth Geldenhuis at the Department of Anthropology at Stockholm University. He checks her bio on the site but that doesn't tell him anything apart from her contact information. He writes it down and decides to call her.

Jimmy introduces himself as a reporter from *The Abbey Chronicle*.

"How did you find me? Why are you calling me?" Ruth Geldenhuis says.

"Jon Geldenhuis mentioned that his ex-wife worked at a University in Stockholm. Your contact information was on the uni website. I just wanted to get a bit more information about Jon Geldenhuis and our call ended abruptly."

"I ended the call as you had told me what I wanted to know. Thank you for that. I have nothing more to say. Please do not contact me again." She ends the call.

Again, Jimmy is left holding his phone. He shakes his head.

Still don't understand why she called me and what that was all about. Women!

Jimmy extends his research to South Africa, and checks newspapers there, for information about Geldenhuis. Jimmy notices that he has received a reply to the email he sent to South Africa on Sunday. It had gone into his junk mail. He calls the editor.

"Mike, another strange thing about that Geldenhuis. I talked with an old editor of a local newspaper. He told me…"

"Jimmy, unless there's some concrete proof coming up, we're not writing anything about Geldenhuis and war crimes, okay?"

"Oh, this wasn't about war crimes. This could be about Geldenhuis's father."

"Why is his father of interest?"

"He's dead for one thing." Jimmy raises his hand as Mike's about to say something. "The editor told me that Geldenhuis senior was found dead in his bathtub by his wife. A bathtub. His wife had gone shopping, and Geldenhuis junior, about six years old at the time, was playing with his toys outside. That much had been reported in the paper. What wasn't reported was the following: The father had come home from work, he was seen and heard telling his wife to get some beer, while he washed up. The neighbour had heard the father yelling that there was no soap and calling his son to bring it up for him. The boy, aged six, scurried upstairs and returned shortly after to play with his toys. What happened in the bathroom, nobody really knows. The wife found him half an hour later. There were rumours about the kid being abused and beaten by the father. Geldenhuis senior's death was ruled an accident. The boy was not questioned. Everybody was rather happy that the father had died. Apparently, he was a mean bastard."

"Right, so not only is Geldenhuis allegedly a war criminal and a spy, but now also a murderer at a young age? Really Jimmy!? We can't use any of that. Get serious and find something we can actually print!"

"But he could..."

"No! I don't care. We can't print any of that. Find something that we can!"

After work Jimmy goes to see Helen in the hospital. He brings her food from *The Whistle & Tin* and a beer for himself. Helen can't move much; she can only hobble around. While they're eating, Jimmy tells her the latest news.

"Don't quite know what to make of it and whether it's true or not, but that's what Geldenhuis told me."

"Let's hear it," Helen says, taking a small can of wine from the bedside cabinet.

"Sheesh, where'd you get that? You're not supposed to drink with those meds."

"Not telling. One small glass of wine is not going to do anything. I'm going out of my mind here, hobbling about, nothing to do, nobody to talk to."

Jimmy gets up and opens the can for her. "Hmm, since you're already wobbly, getting tipsy is not a good idea. You're to stay in bed."

"All right, all right. So, tell me all about this Geldenhuis guy."

Jimmy looks around and pulls his chair closer to her bed.

"He said he got to Sweden by receiving political asylum."

"Why'd he get political asylum? What did he do?"

"He said being an Afrikaner, as in white, and because of his high security status with the former South African government's IT organisation which tracked and targeted ANC leadership, he was a prime target for the ANC after the transition of power to Mandela and the ANC."

"ANC is who again?"

"The ANC is the African National Congress, the political party which came to power when Mandela became president."

"Ah yes, now I remember. They're still in power, right?"

"Yes. Anyway, Geldenhuis claimed that the former Swedish government saw him as a useful asset to them to track what was going on inside South Africa, so they granted him residence in Sweden. The Swedes were trying to find out if there was a connection between the South African armed forces and the murder of the Prime Minister, Olof Palme. Geldenhuis also said that he had been in the South African military as a medic."

"That sounds more like something out of a thriller. And it's not really logical either. How was he going to tell the Swedes what was going on inside South Africa if he was in Sweden? And if he was a medic in the military, how did he get into IT? Did you ask him that?"

"No, I didn't get a chance to ask him anything. He got another call and ended the meeting."

"Sorry my dear, I don't believe his story. Do you?"

"He sounded very convincing."

"Uh-uh. I think he was pulling your leg. People fabricate all sorts of stories to make themselves sound interesting."

"True, but there's another thing too. The foreman in the factory, a guy named Kirwana, big black guy, claimed that he'd heard Marion Rivers asking questions about torture rattles in the library. She'd been very distressed."

"Torture rattles? What are those?"

"Marion was overheard telling someone, not clear who, saying that her neighbour had torture rattles at his house. They look like big baby rattles, and, according to a book she'd seen, torturers used them before causing pain."

"Blimey, that sounds terrifying! I'd be concerned too! Yikes."

"Indeed. And she was talking about her neighbour, obviously Geldenhuis, who'd been seen at her place the day she died! So, my dear Watson, did he have a reason to make away with her? Being exposed as a war criminal would cost him his cushy job and more than that."

"That is scary! But I don't know. It sounds strange, though. I mean, if you're a war criminal and have kept it well hidden all this time, would you really tell your neighbour about it?"

"Oh yes, true. But from what I understand, he didn't tell her, she'd just seen those things at his house."

"Hmm still sounds odd. Not buying it at all."

They finish eating and Jimmy collects all the rubbish in a bag.

"Thank you, sweetie, this was way better than what they serve here! And you've had a busy day!" Helen leans over to give Jimmy a kiss.

"And it got even stranger if you can believe it. I got a call from Geldenhuis's ex-wife!"

"What? Weird. Why on earth would she call you?"

"No idea! Strange, eh? She wanted to know if the Geldenhuis in the article we had online about Gwedrow was her ex. When I confirmed he had a limp, she hung up. I called her back, but she refused to talk and I'm none the wiser."

"Very odd fish that Geldenhuis, for sure! Something stinks."

"And it gets even stranger based on what I heard from the neighbours," Jimmy says, and tells her what he's heard.

Wednesday, 11 February

The Abbey Chronicle, Page 1

Tragic news - Ryan Bolan found dead

We are sad to report that Ryan Bolan, a 25-year-old night porter, who had taken a week off work to prepare for an upcoming cycling event, has been found deceased following a distressing turn of events during his bicycle tour. Leaving home and his girlfriend, he set off on Monday 26 January from Faukon Abbey. His planned route was through Minehead, Barnstaple, Tintagel, Penzance, Bodmin, then back to Faukon Abbey. Anticipated to return home on

Saturday, 31 January, the last known contact with Ryan was on Thursday, 29th January.

His body was found approximately two miles before Tersel Woods. The Faukon Abbey police received a call on Saturday at 11 a.m. from a concerned cyclist who had spotted what appeared to be a person and a bicycle in a ditch. Emergency services arrived promptly, but, sadly, Ryan Bolan was pronounced deceased. Faukon Abbey police attended the scene, closed the road, and have launched an investigation.

Police are now appealing for any witnesses, or anyone with information about Ryan Bolan's whereabouts after he departed from the Hostel Egyptian in Penzance on the morning of Friday, 30 January, to come forward. Please contact the nearest police station or call 111 111 111.

DI Peter Greene and DC Terry Ford

Just after lunch, when Peter and Terry are returning from the pub, Geldenhuis comes to the police station. He sees them and says he wants to report a burglary. Someone has been in his house between the time he'd left this morning, at 7.30 a.m., and when he'd returned to collect some notes he'd forgotten, about 12.15 p.m. He's checked everything and nothing seems to have been taken, but it is clear that someone has been there and rifled through his things. Geldenhuis is now heading to a hardware store to get new locks. And this time he intends to change all the locks himself to ensure it doesn't happen again.

Peter asks, "When did you move there?"

"Close to nine months ago. "

"How come you didn't change all the locks then?"

"Didn't have time to do it myself back then and I was told that this was a low crime area."

"It is, but we always recommend changing the locks when buying a house. And you're quite sure nothing was taken?"

"Yes, I'm sure."

"If that's the case, how'd you know someone had been there?"

"Well, when I got in, I noticed my TV was in a different position to where it had been when I left this morning, and the DVD drawer was slightly open."

"And you are certain that you hadn't left either in that position last night?"

"I'm sure. I was watching TV this morning and had it turned it towards the kitchen."

"Who has keys to your house?"

"Nobody, except me."

"No housecleaner? And no spare keys with a neighbour?"

"No spare keys and I clean my house myself."

"And your house doesn't have a burglar alarm system?"

"No. I didn't think it was necessary here, as I don't really own anything valuable, apart from a couple of old TVs, a DVD player. Clearly, I was wrong."

"Very well. Since you say nothing was taken, it's not really a question of burglary, more like unlawful entry. But you can still fill out the form with as much as detail you can and let us know if you notice anything missing once you've had the time to check further."

Before they leave him to fill out the forms, Greene asks Geldenhuis about rattles.

"Rattles? What rattles? What are you talking about?"

"Torture rattles."

"Torture rattles?" Geldenhuis shakes his head incredulously. "What on earth are you talking about? Are you serious? What torture rattles? What are those?"

"We were told that you have some," Greene explains, somewhat apologetically.

"Oh, Holy Mother of God! I forget how small towns work. Marion must have been blabbering her mouth off and I suppose you've only heard about that now?"

Greene doesn't nod, but his eyes give an indication to Geldenhuis.

"This is just totally ridiculous! The rattles, as you call them, are talismans. Marion was getting on my nerves constantly asking questions. Sheesh, that woman never stopped." Geldenhuis growls. "She saw what she took to be baby rattles on a shelf in my living room. But these are a bit different as they are made of thin steel wire and, here's the kicker, they have a couple of teeth inside them. I was so damn tired of her constantly, endlessly, nonstop, asking all these questions, that I told her they were baby rattles used in Africa to ward off evil spirits and whoever touched them would catch the evil eye. She literally jumped a foot away from the shelf." Geldenhuis chuckles gleefully. "But I guess that didn't stop her from prattling about them. She really was the most tiresome person."

"From baby rattles to torture is a bit of a stretch, surely?"

Geldenhuis sighs again. "This really is mindbogglingly absurd. Let me spell this out very clearly for you. There are no torture rattles, never were. Where she got that idea from, I can't say. They are two things that look like rattles, like small maracas, made of metal string, you know? A handle and a bulbous part on the end with something inside them? I bought them in New Orleans years ago, while we, my wife and I, that is, were there on holiday. The guy who sold them to me said they are supposed to be Voodoo charms, *gris-gris*, used to alleviate pain when visiting a dentist and getting a tooth removed. I hate going to the dentist, so I thought they'd be funny and helpful as I was going to see the dentist as soon as I got back home. You rattle them while the dentist deals with your teeth. Hate to admit it, but I'm a total chicken when it comes to dentists, so anything that can help is okay by me. But my ex-wife, despite being an anthropologist, thought they were creepy and didn't want them at home. I had them at work and when we divorced, I, of course, took them with me. I think the idea is a pretty basic one. You focus your mind on rattling those things and pay no attention to the dentist, *ergo,* you don't feel as much pain. Simple enough really. And the teeth inside them are just plastic, not real ones."

"But why would Mrs Rivers think they were torture rattles instead of baby rattles?"

"I have absolutely no idea." Geldenhuis rolls his eyes, shakes his head and sighs. "How did she come up with all her other weird stories and questions? I told her those were baby rattles, that's all. Nothing about torture. Why would I say anything of the sort? Granted, she was slowly driving me bonkers, but no, no torture. Are you happy now?"

"Yes, of course. Thank you for the information."

Peter and Terry walk back to their desk and leave Geldenhuis to fill out his paperwork.

"That was a bit odd, don't you think, sir?" Terry says. "TV was in a different position? Not sure I'd remember what position mine was when I left it. Would you remember, sir?"

"No, I wouldn't. But I'm equally sure that there was something he wasn't telling us."

"If nothing was taken, why tell us in the first place?"

"Not sure, maybe he just wants us to know where he was?"

"Let's leave Geldenhuis for now. Where are we with Ryan Bolan? Any relatives, family, or anything else? Have you checked his flat?" Peter asks.

"Yes sir, no sir."

"Explain."

"I haven't found any relatives yet for Ryan Bolan. His mother died when he had barely turned 18. No father listed. No siblings. I'm still waiting to hear about his mother's parents, as they could be alive. I went to his flat. But there was nothing there. No photos, or even photo albums."

"For a young guy like that, what was he, 25? No photos of his mum? Or grandparents?"

"No sir, no family photos."

"Strange, especially since he'd lost his mother, but I suppose the younger generation keeps the photos on their phones. Let's go and have another look if we can find out anything about him. There must be something."

"I received a few emails and phone numbers from Slater's tech who had managed to turn on his phone. They didn't mention anything about photos."

"Maybe he'd just bought a new phone. Get back to those techs and have the phone returned to us."

The detectives drive to Ryan Bolan's flat near the hotel.

"Is this a rental or does he own it?"

"Don't know, sir. I haven't been able to find anybody who can answer that."

"Let's talk to the neighbours then, someone must know something for sure."

Unfortunately, each neighbour they talk to says the same thing. They didn't know Ryan; he'd kept to himself. Quiet guy, friendly neighbour, didn't cause any bother. Only one neighbour mentions something different. She thought Ryan had hearing issues. Her husband does the same thing, turns his head a bit when someone's talking to him. He had lost his hearing in the left ear and the right one wasn't that good either.

"That hearing issue," Peter says, as they're walking up the stairs to Ryan's flat, "did his girlfriend mention anything of the sort?"

"No sir."

"Ask her again. Maybe he was swerving thanks to that, what was it called, spacecake, and then didn't hear a car coming and boom, got hit."

"Right. But it would be difficult not to notice that you've hit someone. Why wouldn't the driver report it?"

"Likely because he or she was drunk, speeding or both."

The officers enter Ryan's flat. It's small, only a one-bedroom flat with a tiny kitchen.

"How long has Ryan Bolan lived here?" Peter asks.

"Four years or so."

"Very bare, don't you think? Not many items of clothing or shoes either." Peter rifles through clothes in the wardrobe. "For a young guy, it's rather clean, with little dust. Maybe the girlfriend's been here and cleaned it?"

"She mentioned he was somewhat of a pedant. Liked things just so. She said he had joked about it, saying that, as he was an only child, everything he had was his and only his, he hadn't learned to share. That had been difficult in the army."

"In the Army? He'd been in the Army? Don't they have any information about him?"

"Yes, sir. I checked. But they didn't know about him. They directed me to the Reserves. I've sent them a request. They are slow to answer."

"Better call them. They don't have many admin people. I'm sure they have some information about him or a next of kin."

"Yes sir."

Peter checks the bedside table. There's only one photo on it, in a nice, old-fashioned, silver frame, an image of Ingela. Peter picks it up and it rattles a bit. It seems there's something inside the frame. He finds the small metal pins, flips those and behind Ingela's photo there's a smaller photo, of a little boy and a woman. When he looks closer to the frame, he notices that, on the bottom of the frame, the pictures were not held in place by the small metal pins, but by a flat key.

"Terry, come over here. What do you think of these?"

"Where was that photo?"

"Behind the other photo in that frame and there was also this key. It looks like a key to a safety deposit box, doesn't it?"

"Yes sir." Terry takes a small plastic bag from his pocket and Peter drops the key in it. "I'll get on to the bank to check it out."

"You'd better ask the girlfriend if she knows anything about it. We need to find the next of kin. Did you find anything in the kitchen or the bathroom?"

"No, the fridge was just about empty except for a few beers. The freezer only had some ready-made food, and the bathroom only had a big bottle of shampoo and an extra toothbrush. Likely Ingela's."

"Right. Let's lock up here and go back."

Jimmy Carter, *The Abbey Chronicle*

At a table in the corner of *The Whistle & Tin*, three men are having a proper chinwag over a pint. Jimmy's ears prick up when he hears Ben's name mentioned.

"Oh yeah. He said she was going batty! She kept telling him she had this wonderful new neighbour and how they were going to run away together and move to Spain."

"For real?"

"Yup, that's what he said."

"But she's like old, isn't she? Didn't she retire?"

"Yeah, the old biddy retired what, a year ago, or something."

"Good for her finding someone new. I think Ben's dad died like, what, ten years ago. She was a surly old busybody, though. Always shushing us in the library. No eating, no talking, no walking fast. Poking her nose into everybody's affairs."

"Ben said she was putting her house up for sale and then going to buy a place in Fuengirola or something."

"Wow, I bet that knocked Ben for six! And now she's dead. Bad luck."

"Good luck for Ben though, now he'll get the house."

"Another round?"

Jimmy's phone rings It's Helen. They chat for a while. She's not happy being in hospital. Nobody to talk to, people snoring, impossible to sleep. He promises to stop by.

Terry walks in with a pint in his hand and flops down.

"Helen not coming?" Terry asks.

"She's still in the hospital. Running more checks, she says. Why the gloomy look?"

"Women."

"Hold that thought, I'll get another pint."

When he comes back, Terry looks at his phone with a morose look.

"What's going on? I thought you were getting married and everything's great?"

"It is. I think it was or is. Search me," Terry sighs. "Christine's been talking with to her girlfriends about the honeymoon. Now she wants to go to the Maldives for two weeks. Maldives. Where the heck am I going to get that kind of money?"

"Blimey. That's an expensive trip. Did you say no?"

"No, but I was trying to explain then she started to wonder if I didn't love her after all."

"Jeez!"

"I love her to pieces. She's the best thing that ever happened to me, but I can't afford that kind of trip. So, what do I do now?"

"Wish I could tell you. No experience in that. Helen would know. She's been to like ten weddings in the past four years. You can call her and ask. She's still at the hospital. She said earlier how bored she was, nothing to do, nobody to talk to. I can only be there so often. Her parents are coming next week, I think."

"I'll call her."

"Let me get you another pint and I'll tell you something which will take your mind off women, sort of."

When Jimmy comes back, he tells Terry what he's just heard about Marion wanting to move to Spain.

Thursday, 12 February

DI Peter Greene

After the Marion Rivers' inquest, Peter walks over to Charles Penny's office to find out if Marion Rivers had made a will. Charles Penny is the only lawyer in Faukon Abbey. Peter rings the buzzer and the door is unlocked. He walks upstairs and meets the receptionist, who is also the secretary.

"Good afternoon, what can I help you with?"

Peter shows his warrant card. "I'd like to see Mr Penny."

"Of course. Please take a seat and I'll check with him." She leaves and Peter paces about. The room is rather small. Apart from the secretary's desk, which is overloaded with folders on both sides of a computer monitor, the only other furniture is an uncomfortable-looking sofa with metal legs and very thin padding.

"He can see you now." The secretary comes back and points Peter towards the back room.

Charles Penny and Peter shake hands and Peter sits down.

"This is about Marion Rivers, I take it?" the solicitor croaks. "Apologies for my voice. I caught a severe cold a while ago and it just doesn't want to go away. That's why I haven't been able to call you back."

"Yes, Marion Rivers. What can you tell me? Was she a client of yours? Did she leave a will?"

"She was a client and yes, she did." The solicitor shuffles folders on his desk and finds what he's looking for. "It's a bit of an odd one. As you know, I can't really tell you the details, but, in this case, I think I can tell you something at least. You see," Penny pushes his specs higher up on his nose, "she, Marion Rivers that is, has named an executor, one Ingela Marsh. I've yet to get in contact with her. Maybe you can help?"

"I didn't realise Mrs Rivers was that wealthy?"

"No, she wasn't. But basically, she disowned her only son. He's apparently a bit of a wastrel and she had concerns about him. She thought little of his capabilities to deal with money. Apparently this Ingela is a quite clever girl, a bit younger than her son. A pretty little thing, albeit a bit of a mouse, or so Mrs Rivers said. I think she thought about a bit of matchmaking. Ingela's to execute the will and manage the money, and, if the son, Ben, plays nice and gets his act together, he'll get the girl and the money."

"That sounds like something right out of Downton Abbey."

"Indeed. I asked her if she had talked with this Ingela. Mrs Rivers just said, she's a good girl, she'll be fine and gave me a document on which Ms Marsh had agreed and signed that she'd be the executor for Mrs Rivers' will."

"Anything else? How much money did she have?"

"Altogether not that much. There had been a previous insurance settlement for her husband. That money, combined with additional money she'd inherited, had been invested, so, without the house, she mentioned around £500,000. Or something like that. She said she lived on her own, worked and didn't have many expenses, but of course we haven't seen the bank details yet."

"Half a million is a rather nice sum of money. What about the house?"

"Now, here's the odd thing..." Mr Penny coughs for a while, holding a big cloth handkerchief in front of his mouth and then takes a few sips of tea. "I apologise. This cough is really killing me. Now, where were we? Ah yes, the house. Can you tell me that Mrs Rivers' death was an accident? That she didn't drown herself or that no one else helped her die? My secretary said the Inquest had been adjourned so I assume you're still investigating. Was there something suspicious about her death?"

"Our investigations are ongoing, but I think I can say that we're not yet convinced she died accidentally."

"Right. Then I can tell you that you should investigate her neighbour!"

"Her neighbour? Which one?"

"There's this foreigner who had apparently wooed and courted her, and she was all aflutter talking about him. She said they were planning to move to Spain together!" Mr Penny hits the will with his middle finger several times.

"This foreigner, is he Jon Geldenhuis?"

"Yes! How a good, God-fearing, gentle, and wise woman like Mrs Rivers would fall for someone like that, I don't understand." Penny shakes his head. "She was such a lady, and so knowledgeable and always very helpful."

"You knew her well then?"

"Yes, well, I can say I knew her. We were not friends, as such, but I came to know her over the years as we served on the same church committee. She was a pillar of the community, always prepared to help those less fortunate. And she was incredibly supportive after my wife died. She was too young to die and I'm very sad about her passing." Penny blows his nose and wipes his eyes with the corner of the handkerchief. "I apologise. She was such a good woman."

"We will investigate I promise you that. Now, you were going to tell me about the house?"

"Ah yes, Mrs Rivers decided that her house was to be left to her neighbour, Mr Jon Geldenhuis. I don't know who he is, apart from what she told me. He's her neighbour and he works at Gwedrow."

"To Geldenhuis? Really? Did she explain why?"

"No, she didn't. I asked a couple of times, but her mind was made up. All she said was that she wasn't planning to die anytime soon, and her son didn't need or deserve the house. But she wanted to be prepared. She explained that her sister had died a few years back without a will, and that process is still ongoing. *Ergo,* she wanted to be prepared and write her will so that, if something happened to her, this Mr Geldenhuis could sell the property and use the money for charities they both supported or something. Before you ask, she didn't mention which charities. I assume this Geldenhuis would know."

"Thank you, Mr Penny. You said you haven't talked with Ms Marsh or Mr Geldenhuis about the will?"

"No. I asked my secretary to contact Ben Rivers, Ingela Marsh and Jon Geldenhuis and ask them to come over here on Monday at 2 p.m."

"Are all of them aware of the contents of the will?"

"I doubt whether Ben knows. Normally when someone is signed up as an executor, they're told something about the estate and how the testator wants to deal with it. But as I haven't spoken to Ms Marsh, I don't know."

"Thank you. This has been most helpful. If possible, could you let me know how your discussion with those three goes once you have met them. It may help with our investigation."

They shake hands and Peter walks back to the office.

Once Peter gets back to his office, Terry tells him what Jimmy had heard in the pub.

"Ben knew that his mother was planning to move away?"

"It sounds that way. But if she's dead, he'd inherit."

"Except, in her will, it's Geldenhuis who will get the house."

"What? For real? That doesn't make any sense at all. Why an earth would she leave her house to a neighbour instead of her own son?"

Peter recounts what the lawyer had told him.

"Well now, that explains it. Ben clearly has a motive to kill his mother, to get the house before she moves away. Except, he doesn't, if he knows about the will," Terry says.

"Right."

"But why would Geldenhuis kill her?"

"Don't know. That's what we need to find out."

Jimmy Carter, *The Abbey Chronicle*

A few minutes after Jimmy brings Helen home from the hospital, Helen gets a call from Ingela.

"She sounded so unhappy; I invited her over. You don't mind, do you?" Helen says.

"No, of course not, the poor kid is in a sorry state after Ryan."

"She mentioned something about Marion Rivers' will, and that there was something odd about it."

"Right, I'll go and get some food for us, then we'll eat and have a glass of wine when she comes over. Do you still have a bottle or two somewhere or should I stop by and get some?"

"Thank you, sweetie. Yes, please get food, and wine too. I have to brush my teeth and change clothes. I want to wash that hospital food taste out of my mouth!"

"Didn't you brush your teeth there?"

"Of course I did, but that taste kind of lingers. And here I have an electric toothbrush."

Jimmy kisses her. "Okey-dokey, just don't overdo walking about, will you? The doctor said to take it easy!"

"I'll be fine, get some nice food for us. And don't forget the wine. I may have some white, so bring red."

When Jimmy gets back, Helen is sitting on the sofa with her foot on a pillow, with Ingela next to her. Both have a glass of wine in their hands.

"Food's here! Come to the kitchen," Jimmy calls.

Jimmy and Helen listen to Ingela talking about Ryan and how she's going to have to figure out how to arrange the funeral for him. How the cops haven't found any family. Nobody even seems to know where he lived before. Jimmy has been filling Ingela's glass with wine and they convince her to sleep over on the couch so they can figure things out in the morning.

"Poor Ingela, she's been through so much!" Helen says. "That call from Marion Rivers' lawyer is just bizarre. Wonder what that's all about?"

"No idea, it's getting late. Can we go to bed, please? I have to work tomorrow. You and Ingela can continue

thinking about the sad business of Ryan's funeral tomorrow. You have your laptop up here, right?"

"Yes, let's get some sleep. At least you don't snore."

Friday, 13 February

The Abbey Chronicle, Page 3

Marion Rivers' Inquest

Inquests are not overly exciting. The coroner starts by briefly explaining the purpose of the inquest, which is to establish the circumstances surrounding Marion Rivers' death. He then calls witnesses.

The first witness was DI Peter Greene, who reported where and how the body was found. Ben Rivers, son of Marion Rivers, had called the emergency services at 4.20 p.m. on 4 February after finding his mother unresponsive in the bathtub. The paramedics and the police had arrived on the scene five minutes later. The paramedics had tried to revive her, but despite their efforts she remained unresponsive and was pronounced dead at the scene at 4.55 p.m. She was then transported to Brookside Hospital where Dr Monroe confirmed her death.

Next the coroner asked Ben Rivers to come to the front. The coroner started by offering condolences to Mr Rivers who just nodded. The coroner asked him to recount what had happened that day. Rivers reiterated what he had already told the police; how he had come to his mother's house and found her in the bathtub, not breathing. It looked as if she had slipped in the tub. Rivers continues to tell how he had tried to get his mother out of the tub, but she had been heavy and slippery from the soapy water, how it had been difficult, she had kept slipping from his grasp. He had drained the tub and finally managed to get her out and called the emergency services. Before their arrival, he had tried to pound her chest to make her breathe, but she hadn't. The ambulance had arrived in a few minutes.

The coroner then asked Rivers why he had gone to visit his mother in the first place. "She'd called me earlier that day. I was busy working and couldn't talk. So, I decided I'd drive there when I had a break to ask what she had wanted." "What time did you arrive?" "It must have been about a quarter to four, or something like that. I banged on the door, but she didn't come so I took my keys and went in." "And then what happened?" "I called for her, telling I was there. I walked about looking for her. I finally went upstairs. The light was on in the bathroom. I knocked on the door but received no response." "And then you went in?" "Yes, I banged on the door a few times more, but heard nothing so I got worried. Once or twice, I recalled how she'd taken a bath and fallen asleep, so I thought that might've been the case again. But this time she was under the water!" Rivers' voice became anguished. "When I saw her, I rushed in and tried to get hold of her and get her up. But she was so slippery, so slippery. I tried!" The Coroner thanked Mr Rivers.

Next to testify was Dr Slater, the Home Office Pathologist who had performed the post-mortem. "Marion Rivers was a 66-year-old woman who enjoyed rather good health for her age. Based on the statements made to the Emergency Team on their arrival, it was assumed that Mrs Rivers had slipped in the bath-tub, hit her head, knocked herself out and drowned. She had a contusion on the back of her head and the drowning part is correct. She drowned. However, she was still alive when she drowned since she had water in her lungs." "Could she just have been drowsy after a re-laxing warm bath?" the Coroner asks. "It's possible. However, she had multi-ple contusions on her arms and some contusions on her ankles. The ones on her ankles could have been due to having worn very tight socks before taking the bath. And the marks on her arms could also indicate that she'd been flailing and hitting her arms against something, likely the sides of the bathtub." "That would indicate she was trying to get up, but couldn't? Did she have any medicines or other substances, like alcohol, in her system which could have caused her to be drowsy?" "No, she didn't take any medications apart from occasional pain medication according to her GP. The toxicology report didn't show anything either. No alcohol or other substances. We are still waiting for additional test results." The coroner thanked Dr Slater. The inquest was adjourned as the cause of death couldn't be established at that time since doubt remained surrounding Marion Rivers' death, the coroner stated. And now the Faukon Abbey Police will have to investigate what caused the death of Mrs Rivers.

According to Marion Rivers' son, she was alone in the house at the time of the incident. The neighbours claim they did not see anyone entering the property, but is that truly the case? It is worth noting that there is an alternative entrance at the back of the house through the back garden. Is it plausible that an intruder, such as a burglar or someone else, gained access that way? Which would then lead to one possible hypothesis that Mrs Rivers heard some commotion from downstairs, tried a few times to get up, but unfortunately slipped in the soapy bathtub, falling back down. After several unsuccessful tries, she submerged beneath the water and succumbed to drowning. However, it is unknown as to whether this sequence of events unfolded, or whether some other factors were involved. We may also suggest that, as part of their inquiries, the Police investigate potential beneficiaries of her death and uncover the truth surrounding Marion Rivers' tragic fate.

DI Peter Greene and DC Terry Ford

Peter and Terry return again to talk to Ben Rivers about Geldenhuis without revealing what they know about her will. Ben is just about to leave, late for work, he says, when Peter and Terry knock on his door.

"No time to talk."

"Just a few questions Mr Rivers," Peter says.

"What's it this time? I've been telling you everything a million times over! Don't you take notes?"

"Yes, we do. We just have a few questions about your mother's neighbours. Do you know them?"

"What about them? Of course I know them. I lived there when I was a kid."

"Do you also know the neighbour on the other side?"

"Do you mean the pancake guy?"

"Pancake?"

"You must've seen him! He looks like someone rolled him flat like a pancake. Everything's starched and sharply pressed and not a hair out of place."

"So, you know him, then?"

"No, like I said, I don't know him. Never talked to him. Me mum was constantly talking about him, how I should learn from him, he's so well-groomed and all." Ben turns his head and spits. "Ptooey! The starchy one sits behind his fancy desk all day making loads of money... Me? I have to drive all kinds of people around in all sorts of weather for a pittance."

"Do you know what he does?"

"Why are you asking about him? I don't know the guy. Talk to what's her name, Maureen, she knows everything about everybody over there, the nosy parker she is. Mum said he's some big shot at Gwedrow. She kept saying he was always helpful and complained that I should've been there to help her so that she didn't need to ask others for help. I'm late."

"Thank you for your help," Terry says.

Ben glares at him, locks the door and walks to his car.

After a quick lunch, they arrive at Gwedrow to talk to Geldenhuis a bit further about his other neighbour. They hear loud shouting from the upstairs offices. The woman behind the reception desk pretends she can't hear anything and asks what their business is. Peter asks if Geldenhuis is available for a short meeting. She calls and tells him that the police are here again.

"He asks you to go up. His office is the third one on the right."

Peter and Terry walk upstairs. They hear someone bellowing, "*Jy is laer as slangkak op die see bodem. Ek is gatvol vir jou kak. Fok jou! Eet kak en vrek!*" (*You're lower than snake shit on the sea bottom. I've had enough of your shit. Fuck you, eat shit and die!*) and a door slamming. A black man storms out of one of the offices in the opposite direction and heads down to the back stairs.

When they reach Geldenhuis's office, they knock on his door. He opens it, pushing his fingers through his hair and limps back behind his desk.

"Sit, sit," Geldenhuis says, pointing to the chairs. "I assume you heard the commotion? It's nothing, I can assure you. Kirwan, the foreman, just got upset because he thinks he knows best how to run this company and he's now finding out that he doesn't. He just doesn't get it that times have changed and that this company must change with the times. So anyway, what can I do for you again, officers?"

"We'd like to talk to you about your neighbour."

"Not about Marion again? Give me strength! I have nothing more to say. I received a strange call from someone named Charles Penny requesting my presence on Monday in his office. He said something about a legacy? Do you know what that is about?"

"No, this is nothing to do with Marion or Charles Penny. We'd like to know about the neighbour on your other side. What do you know about him? And what is your relationship with him?"

"Relationship? He's a neighbour, that's all, a neighbour with extremely poor hygiene habits." Geldenhuis shudders. "I've never seen him wearing anything else but a dirty T-shirt and a pair of dirty jeans. And he reeks of old beer and cigarettes." Geldenhuis wrinkles his nose. "I take it you've met him?"

"Yes, we have. He said you've asked him, among other things, to receive packages for you?"

"I order things online and these are usually delivered during the day. Unfortunately, delivery times are very often not adhered to and I can't be off work, waiting for a parcel to arrive, so I've asked him to look out and sign for them for me, which he does."

"What do you order online?"

"I don't really see how it's any of your business. Mostly, I order technical equipment, computer parts and such. As I work with such things here, I like to try and test them to see if they all work as I need them to, before we take the items into use here."

"So why not order things to be delivered here?"

"I don't want to spend my evenings here. It's easier for me to do it at home. And why is this any of your business? It's not illegal to order online. I order the parts and pay for them."

"Do you pay him for that service?"

"No, he gets a bottle of Scotch from me now and then."

"And that's all he does for you?"

"He may have done some gardening work for me. My garden is not a garden, according to Marion. She was of the opinion I had to trim shrubbery and all that. I'm not into gardening, so I asked Preswick last year to clean it all up, which he did. What is this about? Has Preswick done something? He hasn't died too, has he? Why are you asking me about him?"

"We just like to be thorough. Did you notice whether he was at home when you went back to work the day Marion Rivers died?"

"I would surmise he was. He doesn't seem to spend his time anywhere else. I wouldn't know."

"Did he get along with Marion?"

"I have no idea. You'd have to ask him."

"You didn't see or hear them interacting?"

"No. And now I have to ask you to leave unless you have something more important as I have work to do."

"Thank you. One more question. Did you plan to move to Fuengirola with Marion?"

"What??" Geldenhuis had stood up, ready for them to leave, however, hearing Peter's question he falls back into his chair with an astounded look on his face. "Are you mad? For real? Why an earth would I do anything of the sort!? What is this? Comic relief? Of course not! No, absolutely not! I would never ever move anywhere with Marion! Does that answer your question?"

"She apparently claimed that the two of you had been discussing that."

"What? But that's utterly absurd. No, we never discussed anything of the sort, I can assure you. Why would I do anything like that? Holy Mother of God. Someone's been pulling your leg. And for the hundred millionth time, I didn't have any relationship with Marion Rivers. Nor was I ever planning to have one. She was an old woman who lived next door; a neighbour, a nosy parker, a busybody. That's it." Geldenhuis shakes his head. "I can't believe this. Where do you get this stuff?" He gets up again, walks to the door opening it. "And now I really must ask you to leave as I have work to do. Good grief!"

Peter and Terry walk back downstairs to the car.

"Do you believe what he said, sir?"

"Actually, I do. I just don't see him having a relationship with someone that much older. It's possible, but…"

"But what about him getting the house?" Terry asks.

"I don't think he knew anything about that. Someone in his position probably has enough money anyway. Inheriting a house from a neighbour would only mean a hassle with taxes and, in the end, you'd likely end up owing money."

"I didn't know that."

"My wife inherited a small farmhouse from a distant relative. We had to hire a solicitor, a surveyor, and all sorts of other people to deal with it. It was sold, of course, and, in the end, we had to pay a lot of death duties. After we paid all those other people for their services too, we ended up with enough money to pay for a dinner with wine for the two of us, and that was it."

"Sorry to hear that."

"Do we have Ben Rivers' phone records, as well as his mother's, yet?"

"No sir."

"Try to get them expedited. I'd like to confirm exactly when Marion Rivers called her son. And what about both of their financials? Do we have those?"

"No, we don't have those either. I've sent a request, but the banks are not very speedy with their responses."

"Hmm, they usually are when they want your money. Humph! Let's try to get both of those expedited as well. That'll give us a better picture of the situation."

"Do we need to check Geldenhuis as well?"

"On what grounds?"

"Isn't he a person of interest?"

"Yes, but that's not enough to get that information. And I really don't see him drowning Mrs Rivers."

"No?"

"If he was going to kill her that was a messy sort of way to do it, right? No, he would've used poison or something."

"But sir, he had the opportunity, he was there. Maybe he's cash-strapped? Didn't he say he had recently divorced? He could have expensive habits. Or maybe he just couldn't handle her constant requests for help? He went there, she needled him for something else, and he snapped, pushed her in the bathtub and she hit her head and drowned?"

"Hmm, could be. But she was naked when found. He went there to fix the shelf. I just can't see him undressing her, and then pushing her in it and leaving. And timing too."

"Maybe she really tried to entice him. Didn't you say the neighbour claimed Mrs Rivers was going gaga over him?

She could have just had her dress on her, when he got to the bathroom, she removed it and...?"

"And what?"

"I don't know, sir. But I'm sure he's hiding something. Just don't know what it is. We only have his word that she was still alive when he left. Maybe when he went there, she was already running a bath, took her clothes off and he knocked her in the tub?"

"Hmm. Very well, fill in the form for his financials and phone records. I'll see if I can convince Mullan that we need them."

Peter walks into his office and tries to think how he can explain the matter of getting Geldenhuis's phone and financial records to Chief Detective Inspector Bill Mullan, his boss. He doesn't believe that Geldenhuis is actually the one who killed Marion Rivers. It makes little sense. But Geldenhuis was there, had the opportunity and who knows, he may have even had a motive. People hide things, they lie, and deceive. They have secrets. In Geldenhuis's case, he might lie about a lot of things, but he didn't seem to be a killer. But, who knows, people do strange things, for strange reasons. And he did protest, a lot.

Saturday, 14 February

***The Abbey Chronicle*, Page 3**

No solution, not even a suspect in the Marion Rivers' case

As we previously reported concerning Marion Rivers' inquest on Thursday, there now appears to be something suspicious about her death. Her son found her dead in her own bathtub. But what have the Faukon Abbey police done to catch the suspect? It seems nothing much has been done. May we offer some avenues for investigation?

When it comes to a sudden death, aided by someone, that someone is most often someone known to the victim and the reason for doing away with a victim is usually related to money or personal relationships. We're convinced Faukon Abbey CID knows all this.

If we follow the money, then who has something to gain from Marion Rivers' death? She lived in a nice, terraced house which she owned. The house is most likely in good condition, it also has a well-kept, good-sized garden. On the current market, its estimated worth is likely £150 000 or thereabouts. As she was known to be prudent with her money, it is possible she had savings from after her husband passed away as well. All and all, even after death duties, still a decent sized inheritance for her only son. It's known in the community that Marion Rivers and her son had a strained relationship. Ben Rivers has also admitted to that. After Mrs Rivers retired, she frequently mentioned plans to sell her house and move to Spain. If she did that, then there would be no inheritance.

By his own account, as stated during the inquest, Ben Rivers went to his mother's house during a break at work. She had called him earlier. He went to her house to find out what she had wanted. That was at about 4 p .m. according to his statement at the inquest. However, we have information stating that he had been seen there much earlier, around 1 p.m. Why was he there at that time and why wasn't that mentioned during the inquest?

Another person who had been seen visiting Marion Rivers that fateful day was her next-door neighbour, Jon Geldenhuis. Mrs Rivers was seen, around 12 p.m., coming out of her house, talking to Mr Geldenhuis who was outside his own house. Mr Geldenhuis followed Mrs Rivers inside her house, stayed there for 20 minutes or so and left. Mrs Rivers wasn't seen alive after that. We want to note that we haven't been able to discover any reason why he would want to harm Mrs Rivers. If anything, we have been told that he had been a friendly neighbour to her. And, as far as we know, he has nothing to gain from her death either. But what was he doing there while he was supposed to be working at his office in Gwedrow? Why didn't that visit come out during the inquest? At any rate, he may have seen or noticed something.

A third person was also seen skulking around in the back gardens of both Marion Rivers and Jon Geldenhuis. However we haven't been able to establish who that person was. Maybe it's time for Faukon Abbey police to investigate?

Sunday, 15 February

DI Peter Greene

Late on Sunday afternoon, Peter is cooking a lonely supper for himself when the doorbell rings. He goes to the door and there's Maggie. They haven't spoken since he left her place in Penzance two weeks ago after a huge fight. Peter just stands there looking at her and she stands there looking at him and neither one says anything for a while. *Why is she here? She looks great! But what does she want?*

Peter recovers first.

"Come in, come in, let me take your coat. I've just made a Spanish omelette, come into the kitchen, I'll get you a plate. There's plenty."

Peter takes her coat and hangs it on a hook by the door. Maggie hasn't said a word yet, she just follows him into the kitchen. Peter takes out a wineglass from the cupboard and pours a glass of wine for Maggie. "Here, have some, sit, sit."

He walks around the kitchen finding a plate, a fork and a knife and brings them and the pan to the table, sets the plates and the cutlery.

I really should renovate the kitchen, Peter thinks, looking around the kitchen, looking at her, swirling the glass in her hands. Why is she here?

Maggie takes a sip of wine.

"What brings you here?" Peter asks. "Are you on your way to London?"

"No, I don't know," Maggie says quietly, "I don't know why I came." She takes another sip of wine. "I don't know what I'm doing here."

"Well, at least you can eat and then we can talk, right, if that's what you want? How have you been?"

Maggie tastes the omelette. "This is good, really good." She eats a bit more and sips some more wine.

They eat in silence, not a real companionable one, but not really an uneasy one either. Something in between, like an old couple who have run out of things to talk or fight about a long time ago. They keep stealing glances at each other when each thinks the other isn't looking. They sip wine, eat, chew and still, they don't say a word.

God, I've missed her, Peter thinks, but we're so different. Different in every way. She, a rich dad and high-class background. She went to uni, runs her own B & B and me, what am I? Just a small-town copper who thought he'd got the girl.

They finish the omelette. Peter clears the plates. He brings a brie and a wedge of old Cheshire cheese on a plate, finds some crackers, and brings those to the table. He pours them both more wine. They nibble on cheese and neither one says anything.

Why is she here? Do we really need to talk? Didn't we say everything there ever was to say two weeks ago? Oh God, I've missed her. But still. It was just a damn walk. A bloody long walk! From Penzance to Newlyn and back. A lovely day, albeit a bit chilly. It was only after we got back it turned to rain and sleet. She kept pointing out each and every restaurant on the way back, saying how nice it looked. And then, no warning, after we got back to her place, she just exploded for no good reason whatsoever! Yelling about how I didn't listen to her and how we should've stopped to eat. But how the hell should I've known! She said nothing about eating, just kept prattling about how nice that restaurant was and this restaurant looked! She said nothing about being hungry! I knew nothing about those restaurants so why would I've said anything? How the heck should I've known she was hungry and wanted to eat, why couldn't she just say so? Women! God, I've missed her. She looks great. But what the hell was all that about? Can't understand. I could've used a sit down, my right foot had started aching, but no, she just kept trudging on, pointing to that pub or this restaurant and saying how nice they looked! And based on that, I was somehow supposed to know that she was hungry. I'm not a bloody mind reader. Thought it was all good after I went and got the fish and chips. The fish was good, wine too, talking about this and that. All was calm. Then I say Elm House and she explodes and everything went to hell again. Why? Can't deal with women like that. Hmm, maybe that's why she's here now, Elm House? She looks good, a bit sad though, why is she here? God, I've missed her, but after all that??

The cheese is gone, no crackers left. Peter looks at the wine bottle, nearly empty.

"Do you want some more wine or something else to drink? I think I have some whisky?"

"Whisky."

Peter finds the whisky bottle, brings two glasses to the table, and pours two fingers' worth for them both. They both take a sip.

"I didn't ..."

"I'm here ..."

They both start talking at the same time. And for the first time since Maggie came, they actually look at each other for a long while.

"Maggie, I'm so sorry for leaving like I did. And for not calling you."

"I'm sorry too, Peter, I shouldn't have thrown all the things that had gone wrong in my life before I even met you at you! None of it was your fault, but it just came out. It was wrong, I was wrong, and I'm so sorry!"

Peter takes her hand and holds it, looking deeply into her eyes.

"I've missed you," he says softly.

Maggie's eyes light up. "Oh, I've missed you so much!"

Peter walks around the table. She stands up, moving into his open arms, in a warm embrace. They stand there, holding tight to each other, happy just to be there in the moment, and yet afraid to lose each other again.

"Come, let's go and sit on the sofa, it's more comfortable." Peter grabs the bottle, and his glass and they walk into the living room.

"Gosh, I've missed you," Peter says again, "can you stay? Are you on your way to London?"

"Yes, I can stay, and no, I'm not on my way to London. I came to see you."

Peter pours them another two fingers' worth each, and they sit down. Maggie finds a comfortable corner, pulling one leg up, facing Peter.

That sounded ominous, Peter thinks. *Now what?* But he says nothing.

"I've thought about what you said," Maggie says, "about Elm House."

"Oh?"

"The B & B isn't doing that well at the moment. Not sure if it ever will. There are now just too many competitors nearby. They have money to throw at fancy TVs in every room, hire a French chef to come and cook and arrange tours, etc."

"That sounds expensive."

"It is. I don't make enough money to pay for that and I don't have enough money saved for those things, and the bank won't loan me anything. Luckily, Lizzy is all set, so I don't have to give her that much money anymore. She sold the flat in Exeter. Did I tell you about it?"

"No. I take it she got good money for it?"

"Yes, she did. It's a fantastic location, as you know. Anyway, Elm House. I'm not sure why I just exploded like I did. I'm so sorry." Maggie pauses to take a sip of whisky and looks at Peter. He gives her shoulder an encouraging squeeze. "I never lived there. That house doesn't mean anything to me. After I talked with Robert Hughes, you remember him, right? He's now in charge of the author retreat. I decided to come here and see what the job is all about. I'm meeting Robert there on Monday at 1 p.m."

"Yes of course I remember him. He's sharp. He'll hire you for sure! He knows you; he knows you can do the job and he'll be happy to have someone like you there to do it."

"I'm a bit nervous. I haven't seen him for ages. And I'm not entirely sure what the job is really all about."

"You'll get the job! Cheers!" Peter clinks his glass against Maggie's. "And you came here hoping I'd be at home and that you could stay here until tomorrow?"

"Stupid, I know, but yes." Maggie sits up straight. "Can I stay here? I could go to the hotel or *The Whistle & Tin*, if you'd rather not have me."

"Don't be silly, of course you'll stay here! This sofa is amazingly comfortable."

"Oh, really?" Maggie looks at him, the corners of her eyes crinkling. She smiles.

"Come over here, and I'll show you just how comfy it can get," Peter says, pulling her close.

She snuggles closer to him and he kisses her.

Monday, 16 February

The Abbey Chronicle, Page 3

Ryan Bolan Inquest

The Faukon Abbey police have now confirmed that the inquest into Ryan Bolan's death will be held in the Town Hall's Blue meeting room on Wednesday, 18 February. The purpose of the inquest is to determine the cause of death.

DI Peter Greene and DC Terry Ford

Late in the afternoon, a young woman, all dressed in black, with black hair and a thin silver ring pierced through left nostril is standing by the desk when Peter walks by.

She looks frantic, twisting her hands.

"Can you please help? I think something must have happened to Mark. Please!" she says.

"Of course," Peter says. "Let's get a bit more information. Who is Mark and why do you think something has happened to him?"

"His name is Mark Woods. We work together in Gwedrow. He's an IT tech like me. He hasn't shown up at work and hasn't answered his phone and he's not been online at all during the weekend. Something must have happened to him! Please, I need your help."

"And what is your name?"

"I'm Izzy."

"Are you just a colleague or...?"

"We're friends, we work together. Please can you help? Something's deffo wrong."

"Of course, tell me, why do you think something might have happened to him? Couldn't he simply have gone away for the weekend? Be visiting his family? Gone to London?"

"No, no! He lives alone. He doesn't have any family. He has health issues! We're on the same groups online and play online games. Mark hasn't shown up at all during the weekend. That's not normal! He's usually online or, if not, he leaves a message there. Now there's no message, he doesn't answer his phone, I tried to ping him too, no answer. I've been to his place several times, but nobody answers the door. Something's wrong; really wrong!"

"Give me a minute," Peter says and walks to the back office, returning with a community police constable and Terry.

"Izzy, these officers will go with you to check on your friend Mark. Just let them know where he lives."

Izzy drives in the Panda with Terry and the PC to Mark's place, a small terraced, rental ground-floor flat in Mason Woods. On arrival, Terry asks Izzy to point out which door belongs to Mark and tells her to stay in the car while he rings the doorbell. Nothing. The constable bangs loudly on the door, nothing. Terry walks to the next door and rings a bell there. An older woman opens the door.

"Hello, I'm DC Terry Ford." He shows his warrant card. "We're conducting a wellness check on your neighbour, Mark Woods. Have you seen him today or this weekend?"

"No, haven't seen him at all."

"When did you last see him?"

"Friday morning when he left for work."

"You didn't see him come home?"

"I wasn't at home on Friday, went to Exeter, came back on Saturday."

"Thank you, would you have keys to his flat or is the landlord here?"

"I have his keys. Let me go and get them. Has something happened to him?"

"We don't know."

She gets the keys for Terry. Terry and the constable bang on the door one more time. Still no answer. Terry opens the door.

"Hello Mark," Terry calls out. "I'm Terry Ford, from the police, we're here to help. Hello?" He and the constable walk inside to a small hallway.

One black shoe on its side has been left in front of the door, the other one lies further down the hallway. They look in the kitchen. Nobody is there so they walk on further.

"Mark, are you here? Are you okay?" Terry calls out again.

The officers walk into the bedroom, it's empty. The constable opens the door to the bathroom.

They find Mark, his eyes closed, dripping wet and fully clothed, crouching under the shower, his arms around his knees. As soon as Terry approaches, Mark opens his eyes and tries to focus.

"Don't come near me, I'm dirty. Don't come here!" Mark cries out in anguish.

"We're here to help," Terry says.

"Don't come here, don't come here! I'm dirty!" Mark draws a breath.

"Okay, okay," Terry says. He takes a few steps back and turns to the constable. "We need an ambulance, quickly. Call and explain. I'll try to talk to him." Terry returns to the bathroom. Mark hasn't changed his position.

"Izzy was worried about you, that's why we're here. We're getting help for you. It's on its way. Things are going to be okay; you'll see. They'll help you."

No answer from Mark, except a muffled cry. "I'm dirty, I'm bad, don't come near me."

The emergency team arrives only a few minutes later, and Terry leaves them to it. He goes to talk to Izzy who got out of the Panda when the ambulance arrived and tries to come inside. Terry blocks her and walks her back to the car. She tries to sneak in under his arm, but he keeps walking her back.

"Is he okay? What's going on? I knew something'd happened to him. Tell me what's wrong with him? Is he injured? Has he hurt himself? Tell me!" Izzy cries.

"We found him, but we don't know yet what's wrong. He's alive, that's all I can say. The ambulance will take him to the hospital where they'll help him."

"What do you mean hospital? It's something serious then? Did he fall?"

"I'm sorry, but I don't know. The emergency services are here to help him. Best let them do their work. That way Mark gets the help he needs."

While they are talking, the ambulance driver goes inside with a gurney. Shortly after, they come back out, with Mark on the gurney.

"Mark!" Izzy shouts, "Mark!" She tries to run to the gurney, but Terry stops her.

"Why can't you let me see him? Let me go. I want to see that he's all right!"

"Better let them take care of him. Once he gets to the hospital, they have visiting hours and you'll be able to see him there," Terry says, while the ambulance drives away. Terry looks around and sees faces in the windows and quite a few people standing outside. The neighbours have been watching it all.

"Let me lock Mark's place up and we'll drive you back to Gwedrow, if that's where you want to go."

Izzy slumps down in the back seat looking like a rag doll with all the stuffing removed.

"I should have been there! I should have stayed and helped him," Izzy says half-crying.

Terry walks back inside. He checks the bathroom, and the constable checks the windows to ensure that they are all closed, the water and the stove are turned off.

They drive to Gwedrow where they leave Izzy.

Terry goes back to his office.

"Oh Terry, did you find Mark Woods?"

"We did," Terry says. Peter looks up from his desk. "Was he okay?"

"No, it was odd, very odd." Terry explains how they found Mark.

"Sounds like he must have had a shock or a bad panic attack or something. Good to hear he's being taken care of now."

"Let's hope so. She was so worried."

"Panic attacks can cause all kinds of strange things. Very good that you got him help. Now, back to our normal work. Did we get the financials and phone records for Ben and Marion Rivers yet? And Mullan didn't want to approve getting Geldenhuis's records yet. He wanted something more tangible to prove they are needed."

"Let me check if we have them yet," Terry says. "Geldenhuis is apparently missing."

"What you mean missing?"

"Izzy, the girl who came about Mark, said Geldenhuis wasn't in the office today."

"Does she work for him?"

"Yes, she does. She also blamed Geldenhuis for what happened to Mark. Geldenhuis was nowhere to be seen before she came here for help. According to Izzy, Geldenhuis had gone to the server room on Friday early afternoon. Geldenhuis had been livid. She had heard him yelling at Mark on the phone (they share an office) about how the server room is a total mess, no cables are properly labelled, equipment on the floor, loose cables. She had asked Mark if he wanted her to come and help, but Mark had said no, and he'd gone downstairs. And now Mark's in the hospital, she said, and blamed Geldenhuis for it."

"Having your boss yelling at you is certainly not an uplifting experience, but it's usually not a reason to end up in a hospital. Maybe Mark had a terrible weekend or something?"

"You didn't see him, sir. He was in an awfully bad way. I've never seen anybody like that."

"He's well cared for now, I'm sure. They can help him in Brookside or get him help, if not. We can't do anything for him. Once he recovers sufficiently, we can talk to him and find out what happened. Let's get on with those financials and phone records, please."

DC Terry Ford

Terry gets a call from the coroner. He'd sent the coroner a list of Ryan Bolan's friends in Bodmin with whom he had stayed overnight. The coroner says, that, with the help of the Bodmin team, he contacted the friends on Skype. The friends had felt very guilty about the spacecake but, since they clearly knew it was a tricky legal situation, they didn't want to say anything more about it. After contacting Dr Slater, the coroner agrees not to mention the spacecake at the coroner's inquest at all.

Terry says he'll let Ryan's friends know. They'll likely be very happy to hear that they don't have to appear as witnesses at the inquest. However, they'll have to deal with the Bodmin police about the spacecake issue later on.

Tuesday, 17 February

DI Peter Greene and DC Terry Ford

Terry rings Peter's doorbell at 7.30 a.m.

"Good morning, sir, I tried to call you. We just got a call to say that Jon Geldenhuis has been found dead in the server room in Gwedrow. Mullan wanted to make sure we both go there as soon as possible. Slater is on his way there now."

"Good morning. Geldenhuis is dead? What happened? Give me a few. There's coffee in the kitchen, go and get yourself some, you know where the mugs are."

Terry walks to the kitchen. Maggie, her hair tousled, feet bare and wearing a too-big bathrobe comes in.

"Oh, hello Mrs Warner. Good morning. That's your car outside?"

"Good morning, Terry," Maggie says. "Coffee?"

"Yes, please."

She takes two mugs from the shelf, pours coffee in both, grabs a mug and walks out of the kitchen. "Bye, Terry."

"Bye," he says.

Wow! Boss and Maggie are together again. Hopefully, he'll be less grouchy this week, Terry ponders while he tries to find the sugar.

Peter comes into the kitchen just as Terry is finishing his coffee.

"Okay let's go," Peter says. Maggie comes into the hall, fully clad this time. Peter gives her a quick peck on the cheek and says, "Bye, I'll see you later. You are staying, right?"

Maggie nods, and says, "I'll call you later." Peter pulls on his coat and gives her a quick shoulder hug, whispering something in her ear. "Okay." She smiles.

"Actually Terry, you go ahead. I'll take my car and see you there."

Terry drives to Gwedrow and parks next to a Panda and an ambulance. Peter arrives shortly after. A crowd of workers is standing outside. A constable standing by the door waves to Terry and Peter, "Server room, to the right, at the end of the hall, sirs."

The gurney they're carrying rattles as the ambulance team exits.

"Not our case after all, too far gone."

Peter and Terry walk down the corridor to get to the server room. Terry hands Peter a pair of gloves and pulls on his own. Slater's two techs are already taking pictures. PC Bertie Lawson is dusting everything for fingerprints. They pass two rows of server cabinets with blinking lights.

Slater waves to them from the back of the third row where he's crouching next to the body.

"Morning. What is this, Midsomer?" Slater asks. "Three suspicious deaths in 10 days."

"Good morning, Doc. What's suspicious about this one?" Peter asks. He's holding his hand in front of his nose and breathing through his mouth.

"The likelihood of getting hit on your forehead, getting hit in the back, and then dragging yourself a bit, only to fall down and die on your back is a bit slim. As you can see, the markings on the floor show clearly that the body has been dragged here. I can't rule it out that he did it himself, but I find it improbable."

"So, what hit him?" Peter asks.

"Not sure yet, something sharp on the forehead. The back of the head was caused by a different object, not clear on that yet either."

"When did he die?"

"Not this morning, or yesterday either. No *rigor mortis* anymore, so not today, but then the temperature here is cool, so that has had an impact as well. I'll know more when I can check him out a bit further."

"Thanks, Doc. On Friday afternoon he was apparently heard yelling at someone," Peter says, turning to PC Lawson, "Who found him?"

"A young lady with very black hair and clothes. She's outside. Her name is Izzy. She'd gone to the server room and found Geldenhuis. She knew he was dead and ran out to call the Emergency services."

"Anything else Doc?" Peter asks.

"No, I'll keep you posted."

"Thanks."

A mobile phone rings. Everybody pats their sides and pockets until Slater reaches behind the dead man under a cabinet and finds a mobile on the floor. It keeps ringing. An image of three cartoon rats is showing on the screen. Slater hands the phone to Peter who answers, "Hello?"

"Your package is here. It's starting to rain," a barely audible male voice says on the other end.

"Thanks," Peter says. The phone goes dead. Peter looks at the phone and the image of the three rats, one white, one black and one green rat, fades. He tries to poke it, but nothing happens.

"Terry, can you find out who the caller was?" He hands the phone to Terry.

"It seems to require a pin code, sir. Without it, we can't access the information."

"But you can receive and answer calls without the pin?

"Yes. But you can't make one without it."

"I see. Could he have a second mobile? This one doesn't look like the one he was using when we saw him, does it, Terry?"

"No, it's a different one. The other one was smaller. Many people have one for private and one for business."

"Anything in his pockets, like keys to his house? Mobile? Wallet?"

"We'll tag and bag the lot, sir, and go through his pockets, too," a tech replies. "But no keys or mobile yet."

"Maybe those are in his office. Bertie, you'd better go to Geldenhuis's office to check it out. Dust for fingerprints. And find his keys to his house too. It's the third office on the right."

"Izzy?" Peter says turning to Terry. "Isn't that the girl who came to us about this friend of hers, Mark something? You went to his house and found him yesterday?"

"Yes sir, same girl."

"Rotten luck, she has! Poor kid, first her good friend, and now her boss."

Peter and Terry find Izzy and Linkled outside in the hallway.

"I'm Detective Inspector Peter Greene, and this is DC Terry Ford. I'm sorry but we need to ask you both a few questions. Is there somewhere where we could talk, please?"

"Yes of course. Follow me," Linkled says, leading them to the same room in which they had previously met Geldenhuis.

"Could you let me know who found Mr Geldenhuis's body?"

"I did," Izzy says.

"Could you tell us what happened this morning, please? Take your time."

"I went to the server room to check for a back-up. It looked like it hadn't run, so I had to go down there to see it myself."

"And then you found him?"

"No, I sat down and worked on the terminal in the corner, fixed the back-up and then I heard a phone ringing." Izzy draws a deep breath. "I recognised the ringtone. Been into enough meetings with Jon, so I knew it was his. Thought he must be somewhere in the back. But he didn't answer the phone, so I went to look."

"And you saw him?"

"Yes! He looked awful! I knew he was dead, and that damn phone just kept ringing and I couldn't see where it was!"

Linkled pats her, somewhat awkwardly, on the back. Terry has found some water bottles on the side table and brings one for Izzy. She takes a big swig and starts hiccupping.

"Take your time, no hurry, take your time," Peter says.

"I can take over," Linkled says. "I was just coming to work when Izzy came flying out of the server room, in shock, saying, 'He's dead, he's dead, he's dead!' The receptionist came in and I asked her to look after Izzy while I went there to look. I opened the door, and I had to hold my nose. Then I saw him."

"You didn't touch anything?"

"No. Didn't need to. He was dead, I could see that. I came out, closed the door and called you."

"Izzy, did you notice the smell when you came into the server room?"

"Yeah, it smelled a bit. But I didn't think much of it. You see, last summer, we had guys fixing things, and it was so warm, and they used to go to the server room to cool off. When Geldenhuis saw that he went ballistic and threw them out!"

"But that was last summer. Any repair guys now?"

"No, I just thought Mark had forgotten one of his sardine sarnies there and it'd gone bad. He used to bring his lunch there." She shoots a sideways glance at Linkled, sniffs a bit and wipes her nose with a rumpled-up paper handkerchief. "Mark always covered everything with kitchen paper, there's a roll behind the monitor and he was very careful to make sure he didn't spill anything. Jon would have skinned him alive if he did! But I thought he might have forgotten his sandwich bag there over the weekend or something. Did he have a heart attack?"

"We don't know yet, I'm sorry to say. It seems, however, that he's been dead for a while. Did either of you go to the server room yesterday?"

"No," both Linkled and Izzy say.

"Who has access to the server room?"

"It's restricted, so only Geldenhuis, Mark and Izzy, and of course I have access to it," Linkled says.

"Nobody else?"

"No, the code on the door was, in fact, changed what, two weeks ago, was it?" Linkled looks at Izzy.

"Yes, on the first, at Jon's request. Unless you know the code, you can't get in."

"Thank you both. Just to ensure nobody else had access we need take your fingerprints so we can eliminate you. PC Lawson will take those."

"I noticed that there are cameras there too?" Terry says.

"Yes, we installed those after Jon started here," Linkled says. "He was a stickler for security."

"Do you have the recordings?" Terry asks.

"I'm sure we do, but I wouldn't know where. Izzy, do you know?"

"Yes, those are kept by the RM Corp. They aren't kept here."

"Ah yes, of course, you're right. I forgot. I'll let them know you'll be requesting those," Linkled says.

"Thank you both," Peter says.

Izzy and Linkled turn to go, but Peter stops him.

"Mr Linkled, could you take us to your personnel office, please? We'd like to know, unless you know already, who the next of kin is for Mr Geldenhuis."

"Indeed, yes of course. Let's go upstairs," Linkled says. "He was divorced. I remember him telling me that. He moved to Exeter from Sweden after the divorce. I don't know if he's met anybody here, nor do I know of any relatives or family he may have. He's only been with us here in Faukon Abbey as an employee less than a year. He used to work for us on a project and he did an excellent job. Our previous IT manager retired and Jon seemed like a good fit, so we offered him the job. He's been doing great since he came here. This is so terrible! I just can't take it in that he's dead. How long was he there, do you think?"

"I'm sorry we don't know. All the doctor said was that it probably happened during the weekend. Was he in the habit of coming to work on the weekends?"

"He's a person who wanted to get things done and wanted them just so. It's indeed highly likely he could've come here to ensure whatever was supposed to be done was getting done. I'm sorry I don't know all the technical details of the big IT change project, but the project was doing well, all going according to the plan. We had a meeting about it on Friday. Izzy or Mark can tell you more about it."

"Thank you, we'll talk to Izzy again. Also, we may need to remove items from his office. We'll drop a receipt for those at the reception when we leave. When it comes to the server room, it's going to be off-limits for a while until we've had a chance to check it all out and find out what happened there."

"Yes, of course, I understand." Linkled knocks briefly and opens a door to an office.

"Lisa, these gentlemen are from the police. They'd like to talk to you about Jon Geldenhuis. I'm sorry to let you know that Jon was found dead in the server room this morning."

"Oh my God! I knew something was going on down there, but nobody said anything! How terrible. Was it a heart attack?"

"We don't know yet, but we'd like to inform his next of kin. It would help us if you could let us know if you know who that is."

"Oh gosh, this is so terrible! Of course, yes, let me look. I'm sure he wrote something in his papers when he was hired. Oh God, I can't believe this!" Lisa moves about the room, pulling one drawer after another open, until she finally finds the correct one.

"Ah yes, here's his paperwork."

"Could we get a copy of this one please?"

"Yes, of course," Lisa says and walks over to a copy machine in the corner. "Here you go."

"Thank you. If we have more questions, we may contact you again."

"Yes, yes, of course. This is just so terrible." She plops back down into her seat.

Terry and Peter go to Geldenhuis's office.

The office is very tidy. Oddly though, Geldenhuis's bicycle is in the office, behind the sofa. Peter opens the desk drawer. Nothing much there: a notepad and a couple of pens. The laptop is on the desk.

"We need to take that with us. I assume his calendar was on it since there's no paper one."

Bertie grabs a plastic bag and puts the laptop in it and tags it.

Terry finds Geldenhuis's short leather jacket hanging from a hook behind the door. He feels in the pockets and finds what appears to be a huge incisor with a ring of keys dangling from it. "I think these are the keys to his house. No mobile though. What about his wallet?"

"Not in his jacket pocket."

"We need to get to his place. Do you have his mobile phone number?" Peter asks Terry.

Terry fishes his own mobile out of his pocket, scrolls a while and finds the number. A phone rings and Peter locates a computer bag deep under the desk and finds the mobile.

"We'll take this mobile with us. Bertie, do you have a bag for these too?"

Terry comes over with the keys.

"What is this huge thing?" Ford asks.

"Looks like a big tooth. Or maybe the tip of a deer horn. No idea," PC Lawson says.

"Could be the tip of a reindeer horn. Didn't he live in Sweden? They have those there," Greene replies.

Peter asks Ford to bag the keys and the mobile after Bertie has checked both for fingerprints. On their way out, Peter stops in front of the windows to Geldenhuis's office.

"The blinds are still closed. Was his door open or locked? It seems he wasn't here yesterday unless he was in the habit of closing them every evening?" Peter says.

"The cleaner unlocked the door when she came in this morning. All the managers have lockable doors," Bertie says.

"Terry, you'd better stay here. Get the receptionist to ask Linkled if we can use a meeting room as an interview room. Start interviewing everybody who was here this morning. Get the uniforms to help you. We need everybody's information. Bertie and I will drive to Geldenhuis's place and see what this package thing is all about. I'll take Geldenhuis's mobile with me in case there are other calls."

"Also, we need find to out if Ben Rivers was seen here. He has the most to gain, I would think, if Geldenhuis is out of the game."

On his way to his car, Peter takes a look at the paper the personnel office had given him. Jon Geldenhuis had written down his ex-wife, Ruth Geldenhuis, as his next of kin. There's a phone number included, in Sweden. Once he gets into the car, Peter calls it, but it goes directly to voice mail. He leaves her a message asking her to contact him at her earliest convenience.

Peter drives with Bertie to Geldenhuis's house.

They enter his house which looks like a mirror image of Marion Rivers' house. The kitchen is very different, however, there's only a short wall and a counter between the kitchen and the lounge. Very modern. White cabinets, black and white checkerboard floor. Peter and Bertie walk upstairs. Two bedrooms, the bigger one is clearly the one in use. It has a wardrobe and *ensuite* bathroom with a shower, no bathtub.

"What is that?" Bertie asks, pointing at what looks like two flat shelves standing upright on two metal feet.

"Oh, that. Gosh, only seen those in hotels years ago. It's a trouser press," Peter says. "You open it, put your trousers in and close it. Nicely creased trousers."

"Wow," Bertie says, "fancy!"

The other bedroom, a smaller one, contains only a pull-out sofa and a small table. The third bedroom has a tightly closed door with a lock. As soon as Peter tries the handle, Geldenhuis's mobile peeps. They try all the keys on his keyring and finally find the correct key.

Peter remembers the call about a package, but there's no parcel in the entrance and none to be found inside. The office is very utilitarian, with pale grey walls and dark wooden flooring. It's very clean, containing a desk attached to the wall with shelving and a chair. Peter calls Bertie in to check the drawers, dust the office for prints and then bag the laptop for the IT tech to check it all out.

Peter walks around Geldenhuis's house while Bertie is engaged in dusting for prints, taking pictures and documenting. Jon Geldenhuis's place is organised, as in very organised. Books stand up straight, mugs' ears all face in the same direction, the surfaces are clean, there is no dust anywhere, no dishes in the sink, and the dishwasher is empty. Peter checks out the kitchen cupboards, all the food items are in clear containers, all labelled. In another cupboard shelf one pull-out clear container which has some jars of jam and marmalade, another shelf has one with some canned soups and cans of tuna all with labels turned the same way sorted by size, while a shopping list is pinned to a board inside a door. There are only a few items in the fridge, including an unopened bottle of white wine and a few beers. A lonely life by the look of it. The TV is turned slightly towards the kitchen, so presumably Geldenhuis had been watching it in the morning.

Bertie comes downstairs. "Anything else?"

"No, not right now. Let's go." Peter's phone rings. "Bertie, can you ensure everything is locked? And that everything is turned off?"

"This is Peter Greene, Faukon Abbey police," he says, answering his phone.

"So, what has he done now?" a woman on the other end says. "He stood me up and now he is in your custody and wants me to bail him out? You can tell him that is not going happen. And where did you get this phone number? From that sleazy newspaper guy?" She ends the call before Peter manages to say a word.

Peter shakes his head and drops the phone in his pocket. "Okay, let's go."

They get back to the station and Terry arrives a few moments later.

"By the way, has your pal Jimmy said anything about Mrs Geldenhuis?"

"No, not to me anyway. Why?"

Peter tells Terry about Ruth Geldenhuis. "You need to talk to Jimmy."

He calls Ruth Geldenhuis from his office phone.

"Mrs Geldenhuis, this is Detective Inspector Peter Greene from Faukon Abbey police. Please don't hang up, we'd like to talk to you."

"So again, what has he done now?"

"Jon Geldenhuis is your husband?"

"He is my former husband, my ex. We divorced years ago. Why are you calling me about him?"

"You mentioned he stood you up. When was that?"

"We were supposed to meet on Saturday, but that sleaze-ball stood me up, as usual. I have stopped counting how many times I have waited for him to show up! What has he done now? Is he being chased by some angry husband?"

"You live in Sweden, correct? Was Mr Geldenhuis supposed to come and see you in Sweden?"

"No, I'm attending a conference in London this week. I came early. He and I have some unresolved money matters, so I came to Faukon Abbey to see him."

"When was this?"

"What is this? What has he done now?"

"Please, could you just answer when and where you were going to meet him?" An audible sigh is heard.

"All right. On Friday, he was supposed to come to the hotel where I was staying. He said he would come at 7 p.m."

"And he didn't show up?"

"No, I already told you so. I waited and waited. Now, what is this?"

"I'm terribly sorry to tell you but your ex-husband is dead."

"What? Why didn't you say so? What happened? An accident? What? When? How?"

"That's what we're trying to establish. He was found earlier this morning. You mentioned you are in London this week? We'd like to talk to you further. Would it be possible for you to come to Faukon Abbey?"

"My God, what happened to him?"

"We don't know yet. Is it possible for you to come here, we'd like to talk to you?"

Another sigh. "I don't know. This is quite shocking."

"I understand."

"Let me check. My conference lasts until the end of this week, and then I was planning to meet friends for the weekend in Norfolk. I will be back in London on Tuesday 24th, one day for shopping in London and then I have a ticket to fly back on Thursday 26th. I guess I could come to Faukon Abbey next Wednesday."

"Very well. Please let us know what time you'll arrive and where you'll be staying."

"I think I can stay in the same hotel I stayed in before, what was it called again, Livingstone? No, Levington. I'll call them." She ends the call.

"We need to check with the Levington when she came here, at what time, and when she left," Peter says.

"She sure was angry at him!"

"Indeed, furious, by the sound of it. She said nothing about how she came here from London. Check the railway and buses too."

"She could have driven here, rented a car."

"Yes of course, but she's Swedish. I doubt she'd hire a car and drive here, especially coming from London and driving, as they claim, on the wrong side and in harsh weather. It was raining cats and dogs on Friday afternoon."

"I'll check it out, sir."

"Enough for today. Let's go home."

Jimmy Carter, *The Abbey Chronicle*

After he gets to work in the morning, Jimmy calls Gwedrow again and asks for Geldenhuis. He'd called on Monday as he'd wanted Geldenhuis's reaction to the article published on Saturday. But Geldenhuis wasn't in the office.

The receptionist tells him that sadly, Mr Geldenhuis can't take any calls as he was found dead this morning. Jimmy grabs his jacket, bolts out of the office and drives to Gwedrow. But he doesn't get through the gates as only employees are being let in. He has to turn around and drive back. When he returns to the office, he sees Mike standing by the window.

"He's dead!" Jimmy hollers when he gets inside.

"Who is?"

"Jon Geldenhuis!"

"What happened? Accident? When?"

"Don't know, don't know, don't know!"

"What do you mean you don't know? Some reporter you are! Go and find out. Call your pal in the police."

"I have. I just got back from Gwedrow. I went there after I was told by the receptionist that Geldenhuis was found dead. But they didn't let me in. All I have for now is that he was apparently found dead this morning, in Gwedrow."

"And what do the police say?"

"Nothing, they just confirmed that, yes, he had been found dead. Didn't say where or what had happened to him. But it must be something suspicious if the cops are there. If he had fallen down the stairs or had a heart attack, the ambulance would be there. So, it must be something else."

"Then do your job and find out!"

"Are we going to post that he was found dead right away?"

"No, not until we have more facts. You know how coppers get touchy about telling the next of kin first, which is understandable, it's their job."

"Right. Should I call that Ruth Geldenhuis?"

"No, let's wait with that too. Just find out what happened to him and compile what we know about him. In hindsight, that article of yours on Saturday puts us in a rather bad light."

Jimmy feels quite deflated.

"I'll go and get a coffee, want some?"

"No."

Jimmy goes to *Mocha* to get coffee and a donut. While he's waiting for it, he calls Helen, but her phone is busy. So he sends a text instead, telling her that Jon Geldenhuis is dead.

Back at his desk he calls Terry Ford who finally answers his phone.

"Hi Terry, just wanted to have a bit more information. Is Jon Geldenhuis really dead? And if so, can you tell me what happened to him?"

"Hi Jimmy, can't talk with you. I can confirm that Jon Geldenhuis is dead, but you can't print that yet. We have to find the next of kin first, as you well know."

"Come on Terry, you can tell me a bit more than that. Since you guys went there it can't just have been an accident."

"Geldenhuis was found this morning and, for now, we're investigating his death. We don't know anything more than that as yet."

"Oh man, surely you can say more than that?"

"Sorry Jimmy, that's all for now." Terry ends the call.

"Damn!" Jimmy sets out to do more research.

Wednesday, 18 February

Dr Percy Slater, Home Office Pathologist

"Good morning, Doc, what was so urgent that you wanted us to come?" Peter asks.

"I wanted you to have the information about Ryan Bolan before I shared it with the coroner. I've received the test results from Exeter."

"How did he die?"

"More interesting might be the fact that the Exeter lab had investigated a bicycle accident which had put a guy in hospital a couple of weeks ago. The lab found the same paint residue on the bike in Penzance and Ryan Bolan's bike."

"So that means the same car had hit two cyclists?"

"That's how it looks, yes. Mind you, the paint is a common black one sold mostly to car repairers and used by those who choose to paint their own cars. So, it is also possible that the paint residue came from two cars with the same paint. Especially since the locations are different, but then you're the detectives. The bicycle in Penzance belonged to the cyclist Terry and Christine rescued."

It wasn't me, I wasn't me, thank God, it wasn't me, my car hasn't been painted. Peter thinks for himself.

"Thanks, Doc. Terry, as I recall, Penzance didn't have any traffic cams which were usable?"

"Yes, I mean no, they didn't. I'll check with Penzance again and see if they have any more information," Terry replies.

"Thanks, Doc. We'll get on now." Peter turns to leave.

"Hold on, I haven't told you about Ryan Bolan yet."

The officers turn around.

"As you know, we found some spacecake in his bag. But, according to the test results, he had only a minor amount in his blood. That means two things: he wasn't a regular user of cannabis and he had only ingested a little of it."

"That could mean that he wasn't cycling erratically? Instead, the car was driving badly, hit his bike and sent him flying into the ditch."

"Yes, that seems to be the most reasonable answer. Of course, he could have been swerving for other reasons, say to avoid an animal or something, making it difficult for the driver to avoid hitting him."

"Didn't you say Ryan also had a gash to the back of his head?" Terry asks.

"Yes, that's also something for you to think about. One of our lab techs went back to the site and found this." Slater uncovers a granite rock the size of large fist. "See this here," Slater points to a sharp edge of the rock, "it has blood residue on it which is a match for Ryan Bolan's."

"That's the one he was hit with?" Peter says.

"We can't be entirely sure if he was hit with it, or if it fell on him. When descending from the road to the ditch, a lot of the rocks on the side are rather loose and can roll off on their own."

"How likely is it that the rock fell on him? Any fingerprints?"

"You're the detectives, but, considering the depth of the laceration, it suggests a force somewhat greater than just a rock rolling on its own and falling on him. But I can't be sure. And no fingerprints." Peter was about to say something, but Slater waves his hand. "In Exeter, they are assessing that aspect with computer models. So, give it a bit of time, and then we'll know more. "

"Thanks. Anything else?"

"No."

"Then we'll get on with this and see you at the inquest."

The officers walk back to their car.

DI Peter Greene and DC Terry Ford

"Terry, can you get hold of that guy who reported finding Bolan. You interviewed him on-site, didn't you?"

"Yes, he was in a bit of a shock after finding a dead body there. Especially since the body had begun to smell quite a bit too."

"I can imagine. But did he say he had touched anything or done anything?"

"No. All he said was that he had seen the wheel in the ditch, stopped, then seen the rest of the bicycle and the body there. He hadn't even gone down in the ditch to him. No need for that. He called the emergency services and stayed there until they came. I talked with him after I got there, but he had nothing more to tell."

"Hmm, talk with him again. Maybe he noticed something else and didn't mention it as he didn't think it was relevant."

"I'll call him. Not sure if he's coming to the inquest. He's a student and lives in Exeter."

"Good. And talk to Penzance about the traffic cams. It could very well be that Bolan and your Penzance cyclist were hit by the same car. Any information from them could be vital. Exeter should be able to provide more details about the paint so we can narrow it down. Contact them and ask them to send us all the details they have. Share with Penzance and ask them to find out on their end about the paint, and if it's something sold around there, and if so, to whom and when. We need to ask questions around here too for the same thing. And I want to check all the traffic cams we have coming from that direction between 31 January and 3 February. Talk to Sarah Tremis.

Her team can help. They know about the roads, traffic, and cameras too."

"Yes sir. Anything else?"

"No. I don't think we both need to be at the inquest. You can drop me off at the station. Bertie and I'll go to Gwedrow to talk to, what was her name, the girl who found Geldenhuis? Izzy?"

"Her name is actually Miriam Lumberton, but apparently everybody calls her Izzy."

"Good, I want to know if she knows where the cameras are in that server room. Linkled promised us the camera info too."

On the way to Gwedrow Peter gets a call from Bill Mullan who had received a call from Gwedrow's manager Linkled. Peter calls Slater.

"Hello Doc, Peter Greene here. I just got a call from Mullan who had had a call from Gwedrow. They need urgent access to the server room. Are your techs finished documenting and collecting everything? Linkled has, per Mullan, insisted that, without access, their business is going to be hugely impacted."

"Oh, hi Peter, good timing, I was just about to leave for the inquest. Yes, I think we're finished there. Just wait and I'll check." Peter can hear some muffled talk. Slater comes back. "I'd like to keep that one section, where the body was found, off limits, for maybe a day or so more, but they can get access to the rest of it."

"Thanks. I'll let them know. Bertie and I are heading to Gwedrow. We'll cordon off that part. Terry is going to be at the inquest."

Peter and Bertie arrive at Gwedrow and the receptionist calls for Izzy. She comes in with Linkled.

"Could you take us to the server room please?" Peter asks. Bertie removes the tape, forbidding access, from the door and the keypad. Izzy glances inside her arm and punches in the keys to unlock the door. Peter, who stands behind her sees what's on her arm and the keys she punches in, and they don't match.

They all go in. Once inside they stop.

"We're mostly finished here, but we need to check a few more things in the section where Mr Geldenhuis was found and we'll keep that section off-limits for now," Peter says.

Linkled looks at Izzy and asks, "Do you need anything else? Are you okay? Do you need access to that area?"

"No, it's fine. The racks there are old back-up servers. It's fine," Izzy says.

"Do you need anything from me?" Linkled turns to Peter and Bertie.

"No, thank you, not for now. But we need to talk to Izzy. I assume she can tell us about the camera recordings?"

"Fine, fine, if you must. But please know she's our only IT person now, with Mark sick and Geldenhuis gone, and we have a business to run."

"We'll try our best not to keep her longer than necessary."

Peter and Bertie walk to the back section where Geldenhuis had been found. Bertie checks about to find a place to fasten the tape crosswise, blocking access to that aisle. Peter walks about and looks all around, in the ceiling, to see if there are cameras.

Izzy stays near the entrance, in front of a monitor, typing furiously on a keyboard.

"If you're looking for cameras, they're hidden."

"Indeed I was."

"You won't be able to see anything, though. The entry camera there," she waves her hand pointing at the ceiling, "only records who comes into the server room. The other camera there is supposed to record at a very narrow angle to show if anybody touches the server racks, but it's not working yet, as we haven't got all the racks in."

"Do you have access to those recordings?"

"No. The RM Corp manages the cameras. I think I mentioned that yesterday."

"Yes, indeed you did. We have yet to receive the recordings. Sounds very advanced for a small room like this," Peter says.

"It was Geldenhuis's idea. Before him we had nothing. People used to come to the server room to cool off in the summer, like I said. When Geldenhuis came along, even before he became the boss here, he convinced Linkled that access control and security was necessary. So his company got a deal out of that."

"Who has access to this room now?"

"Geldenhuis, Mark and me. Linkled knows the codes, but he's never here. So now it's just me."

Izzy had been typing frantically while they were talking. She hits one final key and a few lights blink above and a low whirring sound is heard.

"Finally!" Izzy says. "We can go now."

Bertie finishes taping and they all walk out.

"I guess you want to talk to me now?" Izzy asks.

"Yes, we do. Is there somewhere where we can talk?"

"Do you want some coffee? Angie, is the disaster empty?" Izzy calls to the receptionist.

"Yes, looks like it."

"Ok we'll take it. I'll just get some coffee for us first."

"You go in, I'll bring coffee." Angie says.

"Thanks! This way," Izzy says, and leads them to the same conference room where they had previously met Geldenhuis.

"Disaster?" Peter turns to Izzy.

"Well look at it, it's pretty bad, don't you think?" Izzy waves her arm at the room and smirks. "Gwedrow has four meeting rooms, this one is D. Sit, sit. What do you want to know? Do you know what happened to Geldenhuis? Was it a heart attack? Do you have any news about Mark? They're not telling me anything." Izzy draws a deep breath and plops herself down.

Bertie has taken out his notebook.

"I'm sorry, I understand you're worried, but I have no information about Mark. All I can say is that we haven't been allowed to interview him yet."

"Yeah, they told me he's asleep. But how can he be asleep for over 24 hours?"

"Unfortunately, I don't know anything. Maybe they've given him some medication? Are you okay to talk to us now?"

There's a knock at the door and Angie comes in carrying a tray with three mugs of coffee, a small jug of milk, sugar, and a few digestives on a plate. She places the tray on the table and leaves. They all take a mug. Izzy grabs a digestive and dunks it in her coffee. Peter sips his coffee.

"How long have you been working here?" Peter asks.

"I came here after uni, 2010. They offered me a job, so I came."

"Do you like it here? Do you have family here?"

"Nah, my family, such as it is, moved to France when I went to Cambridge. Dad took an early retirement and fancied wine. So, he and his wife have a B & B and a piece of '*terroir*' as he insists on calling the small stony plot to grow grapes." Izzy rolls her eyes. "My mum died ten years ago."

"No other family?"

"No, I had a grannie who lived near the moors when I was a kid. We used to go there every summer. I liked it."

Izzy looks at her mobile. "I don't think you came here to talk about my family."

"You said that the only ones who have access to the server room are you, Geldenhuis and Mark. Linkled too, you said?"

"Yes, Linkled has the access code in a sealed envelope in a safe behind his desk."

"You were here on Friday? Did you go to the server room?"

"No, I didn't. I mean I was here, of course, but I didn't go to the server room. We had loads of deliveries, new equipment coming in, a couple of new racks. Mark was there. Geldenhuis ordered him to set things up, tag, cable and clean. I had other things to do."

"What did you think of Geldenhuis?"

"Jon was sort of okay, for an old-timer. He knew his stuff. He was a bit of a jerk, though, and he was a first-class nitpicker."

"How do you mean?"

"You've seen him, right? I mean when he was still alive?"

Peter nods.

"Well then you noticed his chinos and shirt sleeves had such knife-edge creases they'd cause injury!" When Peter nods, Izzy continues. "Geldenhuis said he liked precision, just so. Well-organised and orderly. And he meant ORDER in capital letters."

"What did you think of that?"

"I like things being in order, but Geldenhuis took it to a different realm. Heaven forbid if the cables were not tied just so, or marked properly, he'd make a proper stink about it."

"Was he equally picky towards everybody?"

"Yes, well no, yes sort of."

"How do you mean?"

"He was picking on Mark more than me, being a female, so he didn't want to be a total pig about it. Mark got yelled at a lot, for not being fast enough. And he was on the receiving end of major scorn for his food habits. Jon was a serious health nut. Mark's really clever, he knows the job and he's the sweetest guy I've ever known, but he likes his Jaffa cakes."

"You didn't like Geldenhuis?"

"Jon was a bit of jerk, like I said. But I didn't have any beef with him. He knew his stuff and I agreed with his aim to bring things into the 21st century here."

"Are there some people who didn't like his ideas?"

"Kirwana hated Geldenhuis and his proposals. The union rep didn't exactly love him either."

"Why do you think they didn't?"

"Union guys could lose jobs. Not sure why Kirwana hated him." Izzy frowns. "It wasn't like his job, or his team would've been impacted by much at all. But he really seemed to hate Geldenhuis. No idea why. They often yelled at each other in Afrikaans. Everybody heard them.

Only word I understood was *kak*." Izzy grins. "It means poop, the impolite version. They both used it, a lot."

"Anything else you think we should know."

"I don't know, since you haven't told me what happened to him. Did he have a heart attack or something?"

"We don't know yet. Who will take over Geldenhuis's job?"

"It won't be me!"

"Oh? Why not?"

"I don't need the headache and I'm not the managerial type. I assume Linkled will talk to the same firm that brought us Geldenhuis. They already do a lot of other things for Gwedrow, so I'm sure some equally properly starched and ironed type will show up here soon."

"You won't miss Geldenhuis then?"

"He wasn't around long enough for me to really get to know him. I was in his team, but Mark and I mostly did as we were told, dug up old files and specs, and he took those and went through them. He had plenty of meetings with his pals from his old firm and Linkled."

"What about Linkled?"

"He's okay. I'm not sure how much he actually understood about all the stuff that Geldenhuis was proposing, but he wanted the company modernised and Geldenhuis promised to do just that. So Linkled let him do it and went off to play another round of golf."

"He likes golf, eh?"

"Yeah, he thinks we don't know where he goes but..." Izzy raises her shoulders. "Look, I need to get back to work."

"Yes of course. We'll get back to you if we have any more questions. You mentioned that Linkled has the recordings from the server room cameras?"

"No, Linkled doesn't, but he can request those recordings to be sent to you."

"Understood. Thank you," Peter says. "Just one more question, if I may? I saw you looking at your arm when you punched in the code to the server room, but the numbers on your arm didn't match."

Izzy chuckles. "Gotcha there, didn't I? I have a set of numbers and then I have one in my head that I use to deduct from those numbers. That then becomes a code."

"I see," Peter says, "thanks."

"It's not rocket science, just a bit of security thinking, that's all. Learned that from Jon actually. I got to go now."

"Yes. Thank you for your time."

Peter and Bertie walk past the receptionist, Angie.

"Could you tell us about Geldenhuis's calendar on Friday?"

"Last Friday you mean?"

"Yes. Did he have visitors?"

Angie clicks her computer a few times.

"He had meetings most of the day. You were here too, I think?"

"Yes. Any other visitors?"

"There were quite a lot of things going on in the afternoon. Not sure. They were bringing in loads of boxes to the server room through the side door. Geldenhuis and Mark were running about and getting things in place. It was very busy."

"So, apart from us, nobody else asked to see him?"

"No, I don't think so." She crunches her brow. "Actually, maybe there was someone."

"Yes?"

"I think it was on that Friday, but I could be wrong. There were so many people running around, it was hard to keep track. But I think it was on Friday. There was this woman. She came in and, before I had a chance to ask her what she wanted, Geldenhuis came from the server room and saw her. She saw him. They both stopped moving, like it was a surprise or something. He waved his hand and she walked to him. Then they walked towards the server room."

"What time was this?"

"Not really sure. I think it was after you'd been here."

"Did she have an appointment with him?"

Angie checks the computer again.

"Nope, no appointments in his calendar. He had the whole afternoon blocked off for that big delivery. He could've had an appointment, not everything shows up, could've been a private meeting or something. I don't think so, though. He looked rather surprised to see her."

"How long was she here?"

"No idea. I didn't see her after that. She could have walked out through the other door at the end of the building which was open anyway."

"What did she look like? Young? Old? Anything you remember? Did you hear them talking?"

"Didn't hear them at all. And I didn't really look at her. She wasn't young, though, I think. I only saw her for a short while. She looked like she'd been walking on the moors. She was wearing a parka and a red woollen cap."

"Anything else you remember about her?"

"No, not really. I didn't really pay any attention. But it was Friday afternoon, for sure, as I was busy trying to finish so I could leave by 4 p.m."

"Were there a lot of others still here?"

"The delivery guys were running in and out, carting stuff. Mark was here. Geldenhuis, of course, not sure about Izzy. I think Linkled had already gone, most of the admin staff too. But I don't see when people come in or go. They normally come in through the doors at each end of the building." She points to the doors. "Only the visitors come through the front."

"Thank you. If you remember anything else about that Friday, please let us know. Could you check if Mr Linkled has time to see us now?"

"He said to go right up. His office is at the end on your right."

"Mystery woman, eh? Who would that be?" Bertie says, as they're walking up the stairs. "Maybe he had a girlfriend?"

The Abbey Chronicle, Page 1

Jon Geldenhuis, head of IT at Gwedrow Glassworks has died

We're sorry to report that Jon Geldenhuis, the newly appointed head of IT, was found deceased yesterday morning at Gwedrow Glassworks. The Emergency Services arrived at the scene within minutes, but he was declared deceased at 8:55 a.m.

The Faukon Abbey CID are investigating.

DI Peter Greene and Terry Ford

Peter drops off Bertie at the station and picks up Terry to drive to Jon Geldenhuis's house.

"Anything interesting at the Bolan inquest?" Peter asks.

"No, nothing really. As expected, it was adjourned to give us more time."

"Good, we need to know about the car paint."

They enter the house and Peter notices the TV is now facing the sofa.

"That's odd, the TV's been moved," Peter says.

"Not you too, sir? Noticing TVs now?" Terry chuckles.

"Ha ha, hilarious! I was actually looking at it yesterday when Bertie and I were here, and I could have sworn it was facing the kitchen. Let me call Bertie to see if he took a picture of the room." The officers stop in the middle of the room while Peter makes his call. "I was right. Bertie says his photo confirms it. The TV was facing the kitchen yesterday. Someone's been here."

"But who and why? Geldenhuis is dead. And what's with the TV?"

"No idea. It looks like an ordinary TV to me. While we wait for Bertie to come around with the fingerprint kit, let's find that garage. You have all Geldenhuis's keys? Do we know which one is his?"

"No, sir, I don't know which one it is."

The go through the garden, very carefully opening the door and the gate to make sure no possible fingerprints are disturbed, to the row of garages on the other side of the alley. They try the keys to all six garages in the row. Finally, next to the last in the row, closer to Mrs Rivers' house, they find the correct one. Inside there's Geldenhuis's racing green Mini and, in the back of the garage, a big flat box leaning against the shelving.

"I suspect that's the box the caller yesterday was referring to."

"So, someone else has keys to the garage too?"

"Looks like it. We need Bertie here too."

The garage is like Geldenhuis's kitchen, well organised, with tools hanging on pegboards, labelled boxes for small items, shelves for oils and a plastic basket for rags. Both Peter and Terry look at the pristine order, compare it to their own and sigh.

"That guy was super organised! Man, this is great! I've been meaning to get one of those pegboard and box combos for my own garage for ages. Wonder where he bought it?" Terry says.

"No idea. But we're not here to admire it. Wait a minute, this looks like a door handle." A door can be seen, just about concealed by the shelves and painted to blend into the background.

"And there's a code lock for it too."

"So, no key that fits it to open it?"

"No sir."

"Obsessive about order and secret doors with code locks? We need to get Bertie and that IT tech, what's his name Robbie, here. Geldenhuis's office was locked and bolted and connected to his phone too. Let's close this place for now and come back here tomorrow. What the heck was Geldenhuis up to?"

Thursday, 19 February

The Abbey Chronicle, Page 2

Ryan Bolan Inquest

The coroner held an inquest into Ryan Bolan's death yesterday. Ryan Bolan, a 25-year-old night porter, had taken a week off work to prepare for an upcoming cycling event. He was supposed to return to Faukon Abbey on 31 January. Instead, he was found face down in a rocky ditch about two miles before Tersel Woods on 7 February by a passing cyclist who had spotted a bicycle upside down. When he saw there was not just a bike, but also a person there, he called the Emergency Services.

What was initially thought to be an accident, or maybe a hit-and-run, now possibly appears more sinister, since paint residue from a car was found on Bolan's bike.

The Home Office Pathologist, Dr Slater, who testified at the inquest, stated that Ryan Bolan had a deep laceration at the back of his head which may have caused his death. What may have inflicted this has yet to be determined. The inquest was adjourned to give the police time to investigate.

DI Peter Greene and Terry Ford

Terry and Peter drive to Geldenhuis's place once again. Bertie, and Robbie, the IT tech, travel in the other car to crack the code to the door inside the garage. The IT guys have been investigating Geldenhuis's work laptop, but it's all work-related, nothing private. The other laptop found in his home office has strong password protection and they haven't been able to crack it yet.

They get into the garage but, as soon as Robbie sees the lock, he says he can't crack the code on that door, that's a top security one. You want to get inside; you need to break it. Bertie looks around for tools. Robbie notices the cardboard box as it has the name of a big data equipment manufacturer on it and opens the top of the box. "Nice! Top-notch!" he says.

"What is it?" Peter asks.

"It's a blade server to be added to a rack. I suspect that a room with that much security on the door is likely to have a few server cabinets," Robbie says.

With no way to know for sure, Peter decides to use brute force to get the door open. Bertie finds a crowbar, and Terry and Bertie set to work. Half an hour of hefty cracks with the crowbar, and the door opens to reveal two server cabinets and a desk between them with a monitor and a keyboard. Robbie plops himself down.

"Can you access it?" Peter asks.

"Not sure if I can, it has isometric access, so it needs Geldenhuis's fingerprint, I think. Not sure if I can crack it."

"Police! Stop what you're doing! Keep your hands where I can see them!"

Peter, Terry and Robbie turn around. Bertie stands frozen on the spot in the corner with the fingerprint brush in his hand.

"Peter?" says the older of the two police officers who have entered the room. "What the heck are you doing here? Breaking and entering is against the law, you know."

"Miles? What are you doing here?"

They all shake hands. Peter tells them about the death of Geldenhuis. The officers from Exeter tell them why they are there.

A concealed camera near the ceiling by the shelving, they point out, had alerted their unit yesterday to a possible break-in. As they could not get hold of Geldenhuis, DI Miles Miller and DC Albert Storm came to see if the burglars would try again. And when they did, and got in, the police came in too.

Peter leaves Terry and Robbie to sort out whether they can gain access or not, and if not, to figure out how to close the door again, while he talks to the Exeter police. They sit in the Exeter police officer's car located around the corner, not visible from the houses. Peter tells them that Geldenhuis is dead, likely murdered, and wonders why they hadn't called Gwedrow. Miles Miller tells him what's on those servers—porn, loads of porn, and most of it—child porn. They had not provided the porn, of course, neither had Geldenhuis. Instead, he'd been asked to set up the servers as a sting operation to catch a group of paedophiles. His site and servers provided a presumed well protected site for those who wanted to upload their illegal videos and images, and for those who paid to view them and to chat about it. Geldenhuis kept logs concerning who did what, or rather his computers did. Everything on his servers was backed up to secure servers with the police. Obviously, those who used his servers, used many different kinds of covers to hide their true identity, but it was still easier to trace the users through this set-up compared to tracking them on sites online. The plan was for him to run it for a year, to allow irrefutable evidence to be gathered and to ensure prosecutions. Miles had a team in Exeter who traced the individuals logging onto Geldenhuis's site and gathered information. His team also collaborated with other similar ones around the country, as well as in other countries. It's a big operation and a very hush-hush one, he tells Peter, which is why they couldn't call Gwedrow. Geldenhuis had a different mobile for this, but he hadn't been answering. Now they knew why. After their talk, Peter and DI Miller walk back to the garage.

Terry comes out of the room. They had carried the server box inside, next to the server cabinet. Bertie is dusting everything for fingerprints and Robbie hasn't gained access.

"Terry, you'd better call for a locksmith. We must make sure that the lock on the garage door is changed. Someone brought that box in here, so someone else has keys too."

"No need for that, Miles Miller says. We'll bring our guy here and empty it all out. Let me make a call."

"Sorry Miles, but this is part of my murder investigation, you can't do that yet. Once we're done with it, you can clear it all out."

"But we need access to those servers, and we need them to continue to operate," DI Miller says.

"I understand. Since we now know what's on them, I don't think we need to get access to the servers. But we need to have our own guy here to dust for fingerprints and all that. Shouldn't take long."

"All right, all right. We'll wait until tomorrow," DI Miller says, and turns to walk out of the garage.

"Wait!" Peter says. "You said you knew we tried to get in here yesterday. Can you send us the video or access to it so we can see who's been coming in and out of here. Are there any other cameras here?"

"Yes, there's one outside too."

"Can we get those too, please?"

"I'll get the IT to give you access to them, but I need to clear it with the Head first. You may need to have Bill Mullan call Superintendent Cable to get the access."

"Thanks, I'll talk to him."

"Robbie, you can stop trying to get access to it," Peter calls, "we don't need that anymore."

"Oh good, I was going mad seeing those damn rats and not getting anywhere."

Terry calls the locksmith and Bertie keeps dusting everything inside the room, the garage and the car for fingerprints. Peter asks them to find a few broad planks of wood or shelves and nail those over the door to keep it closed. Terry stays to wait for the locksmith and Peter drives back to the station to talk with Mullan.

"Oh, there you are, come in. I just got a call from Superintendent Cable."

"That was quick. I only left Geldenhuis's house 15 minutes ago."

"What you mean Geldenhuis? He's dead. Murdered, it seems."

"Sir, you said you talked to SI Cable."

"Yes, he wanted to inform us about a sting operation of theirs which may have had some interference. A suspected burglar had tried to gain access to their sting ops site."

"Yes, sir, I see sir, and where is this site?" When Mullan reads the address, Peter realises it's Geldenhuis's garage.

"I see. sir, I have a confession to make. The culprits trying to break in were PC Bertie Lawson and I."

"How and why did you get the idea to break in?"

"Sir, we didn't know what was in there. The site you described is the garage which belongs to Jon Geldenhuis, the Gwedrow IT manager found murdered on Tuesday."

"He was running a shady site and got murdered?"

"Not sure yet. We met with DI Miles Miller from Exeter there today. Miles told me all about their sting operation." After Peter has finished sharing with Mullan what Miles had told him, Mullan asks, "Was Geldenhuis killed because of it?"

"We don't know yet. I left Terry, Bertie and Robbie to document and check for fingerprints. Terry is getting a locksmith to ensure we get new locks on both Geldenhuis's house, back door, and his garage. They're to nail down the door to his server room."

"Good, good. Anything else?"

"Miles mentioned that they'd placed cameras both in and outside the garage. I've asked him for the footage. He said Cable might call you about it."

"Ah yes, of course. Obviously, we need to see it. I'll call him back."

"Thank you, sir."

Friday, 20 February

Dr Percy Slater, Home Office Pathologist

Dr Slater performs the post-mortem on Jon Geldenhuis. Both Peter and Terry attend and again put on masks. Geldenhuis had been dead a few days. According to Slater, it seems, he had likely died on Friday evening or Saturday. The chill in the data centre had slowed down the process, making it difficult to pinpoint the exact time.

"What caused his death, Doc?" Terry asks.

"He died of fatal *occipitocervical* dissociation injury," Dr Slater says.

"Occipito what?" Peter asks.

"It's also known as internal decapitation."

"Decapitated? His head seemed to be well in place when we saw him. Still is, by the look of it. How was he decapitated?" Terry says.

"I said internal decapitation, which happens when the ligaments connecting the spine to the skull are severed."

"So, while he looks normal, head together with the rest of the body and all, internally, his head isn't connected to his body?" Peter says.

"That is so."

"What caused it?"

"Trauma. It seems he was first hit with something, which then caused him to trip backward, hitting his head on a sharp edge."

"Must have been some blow to trip him like that," Terry says.

"Not really. His left leg was shorter, likely due to a poorly-healed childhood injury. I take it he had a limp?"

"Yes, he did."

"That could've impacted his balance when something hit him on the forehead. See the laceration here, not a big one, a bit of an odd shape?"

"So, he trips backward and falls, hitting his head on a sharp item?" Peter asks.

"Indeed. We checked those old computer cases they had there. You may have noticed them? Grey metal ones, with very sharp edges. We found one which had traces of blood on it which belonged to Mr Geldenhuis," Slater says.

"And that caused him to die?" Terry asks.

"Yes, causing near instantaneous death."

"Hold on... As I remember, there were no computer cases where Geldenhuis was found," Peter says.

"Indeed, those old cases were in another corner."

"You mean someone first hit him with something and then dragged him to hide his body behind those cabinets?" Terry asks.

"You're the detectives. All I can say is that it is very unlikely he could have moved from one side of the room to where he was found."

"Thanks, Doc. So, it's murder?" Peter asks.

"I didn't say that. I would call it suspicious for now."

Peter and Terry thank the doctor and drive to the office.

DI Peter Greene and DC Terry Ford

Peter and Terry bring Julius Kirwana in for questioning. He now claims Geldenhuis was a famous torturer in South Africa during the war in Angola. They had already brought him in on Wednesday, but he had refused to say anything more without his lawyer present. Since he works at Gwedrow and had been seen arguing with Geldenhuis on multiple occasions, Greene wanted to hold him for the murder of Geldenhuis, but they had to wait as they didn't have any actual evidence yet. Today, his lawyer, Jacob Smithers, who had been the lawyer for Christina Granger and who Peter had previously met in London, comes with Kirwana.

Kirwana is upset and again claims he had recognised Geldenhuis as a torturer who had been operating during the Angolan Bush war. Or he had been the medic who revived the tortured afterward. Either way, Geldenhuis was a war criminal. When asked why, Kirwana says it's those small rattles made of twisted thin metal thread Marion was talking about in the library. The torturers made those kinds of rattles which contained the tortured people's teeth!

"According to what Mr Geldenhuis told us, those were voodoo rattles he had bought in New Orleans years ago."

"The man was a war criminal, I'm sure of it! If he wasn't the torturer, then he was a medic who revived the tortured afterward. Either way, Geldenhuis was a war criminal!"

"No need to shout Mr Kirwana. The fact is, Mr Geldenhuis is now dead and can't defend himself. And we must investigate his death," Peter says.

"Well, I didn't kill him! I'm happy someone did, but it wasn't me and you can't pin it on me."

"You've been seen multiple times arguing with Mr Geldenhuis and now you claim he was a war criminal; it seems you have an excellent motive."

"It wasn't me!"

"Can you tell us where you were from Friday afternoon until Sunday morning?"

"I was in Exeter. I'd gone there to watch a rugby game with my buddies. Came home on Sunday."

"We need to know the names of those buddies. Also, do you have any tickets?"

Jacob Smithers confers with his client. After some quiet discussion, Kirwana takes up his mobile and starts rattling off names and phone numbers.

"Those are my buddies. You can call any one of them and they'll tell you I was there! Can I go now? And here's the ticket I had for the game."

Terry takes a photo of the ticket Kirwana shows on his phone and asks for it to be sent to him.

"Is my client free to go, Detective Inspector Greene?"

"Yes, he is, for now. We're going to check his whereabouts and confirm."

As soon as the door to the room opens, Kirwana rushes out. Jacob Smithers stays behind to collect his papers.

"Isn't this a bit outside your normal work, Mr Smithers?" Peter asks.

"Indeed, it is, indeed it is. You see Kirwana spoke to a friend who then called my mother. You may have heard of her? She writes to *The Guardian* about human rights?" Jacob Smithers says.

"Mariah Ocumba Smithers is your mother?"

"Yes, she is. After my father was killed when I was three, she grabbed me and we fled South Africa. Friends in Stockholm helped us and we ended up in London."

"Boxton, Smithers and Gillen?"

"Yes, Timothy Smithers is my step-uncle as my mother married Jonah Smithers."

"I see. Now tell me, was Geldenhuis really a war criminal?"

"I'll check with my mother, but I very much doubt it."

"When you find out, please let me know."

Peter walks back to his office, still convinced Kirwana killed Geldenhuis. They just needed more evidence.

Jimmy Carter, *The Abbey Chronicle*

Ingela, nearly out of breath, her face flushed, comes to visit Jimmy in the office. She's upset and wants to talk. Jimmy tries to calm her down and gets her some water. Ingela gulps it down and tells Jimmy that she's now required to execute Marion's will.

Marion had asked her about being the executor a year or so ago and she'd said yes, without really knowing what it entailed or what it was all about. And neither of them, of course, expected Marion to die anytime soon. But now Marion is dead, and, according to Charles Penny, it's up to her to deal with Marion's estate, except she doesn't know what to do and she's not sure if she wants to do or know either. On top of it, Marion's son, Ben, has been very nasty about it and threatened her as soon as she got out of Penny's office.

Mike brings Ingela a cup of tea and asks her to tell them more.

Ingela sips her tea and tells them that, since that Geldenhuis person is dead, there were only two parties meeting with Penny. Ingela and Ben, and she's the executor of Marion's will.

"How did Ben take that?" Mike asks.

"Ben got mad! And it got even worse when I told him he wasn't to get any money until we know what happened to Geldenhuis. Ben started yelling and screaming that I was stealing him blind. That it was his money, his mother, his house. That I had no right to any of it!"

"Oh, that's awful!" Jimmy says.

"I didn't sign up for this! I only signed the papers because Marion insisted and I don't know how to deal with any this, and I have Ryan's death to think about too." Ingela starts crying.

"So sorry to hear about all this. Didn't Charles Penny help?"

"No," Ingela says, and blows her nose. "What am I going to do?"

"You can resign your duties as executor," Mike says. "It's perfectly possible. All you have to do is to talk to Penny and he'll figure it all out."

"Really? I can do that?"

"Yes, you can, legally."

"Oh, you're a lifesaver!" Ingela hops up and gives Mike and Jimmy a hug. "Thank you, thank you! You guys are wonderful!"

The Abbey Chronicle, Page 3

248

Jon Geldenhuis Inquest

The Faukon Abbey police have now confirmed that the coroner's inquest into Jon Geldenhuis's death will be held in the Town Hall Blue meeting room on Wednesday, 25 February. The purpose of the inquest is to determine the cause of death.

Sunday, 22 February

The Abbey Chronicle, Page 1

Unsolved deaths in Faukon Abbey as police investigations appear stalled

Faukon Abbey is reeling from a series of unexplained deaths, leaving its residents unsettled and demanding answers. Marion Rivers, Ryan Bolan and Jon Geldenhuis all met tragic ends under suspicious circumstances. No arrests or identified suspects. The lack of progress has heightened concerns among the community.

Marion Rivers was discovered lifeless in her own bathtub. Despite three potential culprits, Faukon Abbey police have provided no substantial updates. Could her death have been caused by a killer copying the infamous 'Brides in the Bathtub' murder method?

Ryan Bolan, on a cycling tour in Devon, suffered a fatal blow to the head after being sent flying into a ditch by a car. Initial theories of a hit-and-run were dispelled at the inquest, but the Faukon Abbey police have remained silent on any breakthroughs.

Equally disturbing is the discovery of the lifeless body of Jon Geldenhuis, the head of IT at Gwedrow Glassworks, in the server room there just days ago. Insider sources suggest that his death did not occur naturally, raising suspicions of either an accidental mishap or a deliberate act. Many individuals allegedly had access to the onsite data centre, which boasts an array of security measures including cameras and access controls. Despite these safeguards, the Faukon Abbey police appear to be groping in the dark, struggling to shed light on this enigmatic case.

We can posit at least two plausible motives for someone seeking to harm Mr Geldenhuis. Firstly, the ongoing restructuring at Gwedrow Glassworks, as relayed to us by Mr Geldenhuis himself, is set to have an impact on manufacturing operations. As expected, not everyone on the manufacturing side is embracing the changes, with multiple heated confrontations between staff members and Mr Geldenhuis reported. Could mere verbal altercations have escalated into something far more sinister? Additionally, Mr Geldenhuis's ex-wife has mentioned unresolved financial disputes with her ex-husband, hinting at yet another possible motive. It is worth noting that Mrs Geldenhuis was recently seen visiting Faukon Abbey over the weekend.

Three unexplained deaths in as many weeks, and anxiety for their own safety has grown among the residents of Faukon Abbey. And yet the silence from the Faukon Abbey police remains deafening.

<u>About the Brides in the Bathtub murders:</u> In 1914, a tragic case of a bride drowning in her bath in Highgate, London, caught the attention of the public and the police. The victim was Margaret Lloyd, and her death prompted Mr Charles Burnham, the father of one of other victims to go to the authorities. The investigation led to the discovery of a complicated case of bigamy and murder, with a man named George Joseph Smith at the centre of it all. Smith had married seven women between 1908 and 1914, conducting several bigamous marriages.

George Smith, a con artist, lured single, vulnerable women into marriages, then took out large life insurance policies on their lives. After a while, he would murder his wives, making the deaths appear to be tragic accidents. He had a way with women, which he combined with ruthlessness in acquiring their money. When he appeared in court charged with murdering Alice Burnham, Bessie Munday and Margaret Lloyd, it was revealed that he had murdered his victims by drowning them in the bathtub. Detective Inspector Neil demonstrated, together with Home Office Pathologist Bernard Spilsbury, to the jury, the method of drowning Smith had used on his victims, by raising their knees while they were in the bath. Smith's trial took place in June 1915. The jury took only 22 minutes to return a guilty verdict and George Smith was executed on Friday the 13th of August 1915, at Maidstone prison.

Monday, 23 February

DI Peter Greene

Peter's Monday doesn't start well. Thanks to Jimmy's article on Sunday, he's called in to talk to his boss, DCI Bill Mullan.

"Sit! I take it you've seen Jimmy's article?" Mullan barks.

"Yes, sir, I saw it."

"Where does he get his information from, Terry, or someone else?"

"Terry swears he hasn't told him anything. In fact, Jimmy was telling Terry about the Brides in the Bathtub killings."

"Mrs Rivers was hardly a bride!"

"True, but according to Slater, the method—lifting and holding her ankles or knees up—is indeed feasible. And she was, according to multiple witnesses, sweet on Jon Geldenhuis. So much so that she had claimed she'd sell her house and move to Spain with him."

"But he's years younger than her, was working, a big shot in Gwedrow, why'd he go off with her? Did you ask?"

"We did. He said all that was utter nonsense."

"Did you believe him?"

"Yes, I did."

"Fine, and now he's dead too. But who killed her? And who killed the others?"

Peter's forced to tell him he's not any closer to finding out who killed Geldenhuis, Ryan Bolan or Marion Rivers.

"At least Exeter seem to have kept their part under wraps. So, Jimmy knew nothing about that?" Mullan asks. "Let's keep it that way."

Peter trudges back to his own office.

Damn Jimmy!

DC Terry Ford

Terry drives to fetch Ken Preswick for an interview to talk about the 'services' he provided to Geldenhuis and to get his fingerprints.

"Why do I have to come with you? Why you want me prints? I know me rights, I've done nothing wrong!"

"It'll only take a moment; we want to eliminate you from our inquiries concerning Mr Geldenhuis's death. Is there a problem?"

Preswick grumbles but finally grudgingly agrees and they drive to the station. Bertie takes his fingerprints and Terry continues to ask questions.

"He took me prints. Can I go now?" Preswick says, wiping his fingers on his jeans.

"We have a few more questions. As he was your neighbour, surely you want to help us out?"

Preswick sits down and grunts, "Like I have a choice."

"When we talked with Mr Geldenhuis, he mentioned you used to take care of packages he ordered?"

"Yeah, I did. He's always working, busy guy, and I'm at home, so I took the boxes and put them in his garage to keep them from the rain."

"Did you do anything else for him?"

"I cut shrubs and cleared out rubbish from his back garden. He didn't like doing it, so I helped him out."

"You were a good neighbour?"

"Yeah."

"Since you took boxes into his garage, you had keys for that too, correct?"

"Yeah, I changed the locks right after he moved in, so I had his spare keys. I used to do a bit of locksmithing." Preswick chuckles.

"And I assume you got paid for it?"

"When he moved in, he didn't know anything, so I helped him out, and he paid what I charged."

"You were paid well?"

"Nah, I didn't charge him that much, but I bought the locks and did the work, so I had to charge for it."

"And he didn't ask how much?"

"He was in a hurry to get things done, so he paid what I asked. I only asked a few more quid. I had to go and get the locks, travel time and all that."

"You changed all the locks, both garage and his house too?"

"Yeah."

"Then, what were you doing in his house after we'd found him dead?"

"I didn't know he was dead, did I? I just went there to look for some DVDs. He had some by the TV. He'd promised I could have 'em."

"Had you seen him during the weekend?"

"No, he said he'd be busy when he told me about a package."

"But you only received the package on Tuesday, correct?"

"Yeah."

"So, when did you last see Mr Geldenhuis?"

"I saw him on Friday morning. He said he'd be working all weekend and that he was expecting a package."

"Did he say when the package was supposed to come?"

"He didn't know. He said he was angry. It'd been delayed a few times already, so he asked me to keep an eye out for it."

"And when did it arrive?"

"On Monday."

"You just said you received it on Tuesday. When did the package arrive?"

"It came on Monday. Sorry, it was Monday, not Tuesday."

"What did you do?"

"I called him."

"On Monday? Did he answer?"

"No. I left a message and took the box into his garage."

"Was that usual that he didn't answer his phone?"

"Yeah, he was often busy, so I left messages."

"Did you hear from him on Monday, or did you see him?"

"No, so I called again on Tuesday. Then he answered."

"But you had already put the box in the garage on Monday and called him, so why'd you call him again about it on Tuesday?"

Preswick doesn't answer.

"Was he supposed to call you or pay you?" Terry asks.

"He'd promised to bring me a bottle of MacGregor. But he didn't come on Monday, so I called him."

"And on Tuesday you went to his house?"

"He didn't come on Tuesday either, so I went there to look for those DVDs he'd promised me."

"Did you find them?"

"No."

"Did you find the bottle?"

"No."

"You didn't take anything from there?"

"No."

"Where were you on Friday the 13th?"

"Where I always am. At home."

"You didn't go out?"

Preswick doesn't answer.

"You were seen in town that Friday," Terry says.

"All right, all right, hold your horses. I went to the pub for a pint. Not a crime, is it?"

"You didn't go to Gwedrow?"

"No, why'd I go there? I wanted a pint, nothing there."

"We'll have to check this out."

"Do you know what killed Geldenhuis yet? Somebody kill him?" Preswick asks.

"Why do you think that?"

"He was a bit healthy to drop dead. So, someone could've done him in."

"You didn't like him?"

"Nah, he was okay. Marion was gaga over him."

After Preswick left, Terry goes upstairs back to his office. Bertie comes in and shows him a paper.

The fingerprints which had been found under the shelf in Marion Rivers' bathroom belonged to Ken Preswick.

"Sir, Ken Preswick's fingerprints were not only in Geldenhuis's house, they were also found in Marion's house."

"Maybe he'd changed locks for her too?"

"Yes, could be, but sir, Preswick's fingerprints were on that shelf we found on the floor!"

"Maybe he had been there too to put that shelf in place. Didn't Geldenhuis say he had done that?"

"Yes sir, but some of Preswick's fingerprints were on top of Geldenhuis's prints."

"Good job Bertie. But we need more evidence. Those prints could be old. Terry and Bertie, go to Marion's house, re-check the entire bathroom, also other places like the kitchen, all doors, even her home office. We need to find evidence that Preswick has been there. Once we know, we'll get him back and ask him why."

Tuesday, 24 February

DI Peter Greene and DC Terry Ford

No family members of Ryan Bolan have been located. His mother is dead, with no father named on his birth certificate. His maternal grandparents are also deceased. Since the father is unknown, there's no way to find out anything from that side. After the judge's approval, Terry gets access to the bank safety- deposit box using the key they found behind the photo. The box doesn't contain much, only his military reserve service book and his will. In the will, he leaves his flat, and everything else, to Ingela.

Terry takes the contents and the will back to the police station. Peter asks Bertie to dust them for prints and then to contact the coroner.

"Bolan's flat's pretty nice, don't you think? She'll make good money selling it. He didn't have much in his bank accounts, though, but no debts," Terry says.

"Are you saying she had a motive for killing him?" Peter's eyebrows shoot up.

"No sir, I'm not! I don't think she knew about the will. She wanted him to be found. She loved him. Surely you don't think she killed him?"

"No Terry, I don't think she killed him either. But where money is involved, you never know. Check where she was when Ryan Bolan was killed."

"Really sir? She didn't kill him!"

"I'm sure she didn't, but someone did. She has a car and you told me she drives fast, so we must make sure we've ruled everyone out."

Terry and Bertie drive to Marion's house to look for any evidence that may have been missed previously. Terry checks upstairs, including the bathroom, again. Bertie focuses on downstairs and then checks the garden too. Bertie didn't see any traces of fingerprinting dust on the pile of compost and fertiliser bags on the patio. It had rained after Marion's death, but the bags are partially under cover and look dry. As ordered, Bertie checks the top two bags and dusts them for fingerprints.

Wednesday, 25 February

DI Peter Greene and DC Terry Ford

Peter arrives at the inquest for Jon Geldenhuis just as the coroner is announcing the inquest verdict as open, giving the police more time to investigate. The inquest is only attended by a few people. Peter sees Linkled and Izzy from Gwedrow walking out together. Slater must have left earlier as he isn't there. Terry sees Peter and walks towards him but Peter waves him on and walks over to the only woman still seated, middle-aged, with short, blondish hair, wearing a dark coat. She is dabbing her eyes and blowing her nose.

"Mrs Geldenhuis?" Peter says.

"Yes," she says, "how did you know?"

"I'm a detective," Peter smiles. "Peter Greene, Faukon Abbey CID."

She turns, with a small smile lighting up her face. Her blue eyes are somewhat blood-shot and puffy. "But, actually, it is Johansson, Ruth Johansson. I took my name back after the divorce."

"Very well, Ms Johansson, could you come with me, please? We'd like to talk to you, as I mentioned on the phone, and we also need to take your formal statement."

"Of course. Do you know who killed him yet?" She stands up and gathers her things, checking around that she's left nothing on the bench.

They walk to Peter's car.

"You're Swedish?"

"Yes."

"Jon Geldenhuis was South African. It's quite far from Sweden. How did you two meet?"

"We met half-way, you could say, in Israel, in Eilat. He and his friend, a German guy, were running a windsurfing school there, and I was taking a course at the university in Jerusalem. A friend and I decided to go to Eilat during the Easter holiday. We got lucky and managed to get a tiny room in a hotel by the beach." She draws a deep breath and bites her lips. "On the first day at the beach we found the windsurfers. They had a small hut, a lot of boards and sails. It looked interesting, neither of us had done it before so we decided to go for it. Besides, the guys there were only interested in windsurfing, not us. On the other section of the beach, we got accosted by every male around! What is it with those southern guys, they go wild about blonde-haired girls and think we all want to jump into bed with them immediately? I don't understand that! Just because we are blondes, wear a bikini and are from Sweden doesn't mean we're some sex-crazed whores or something!" She draws a deep breath. "Sorry. Anyway, that is where we met Jon and Hans, I think the German guy's name was. Jon showed me how to balance on the board. They had this small training board, on the beach, placed on a giant spring. As soon as you stood on it, it wobbled wildly. And of course, I fell, and fell, and fell a few times more." She smiles wistfully. "But Jon was an excellent teacher and I learned. He was nice and funny. Next day we returned to try it in the water. We learned. We stayed on their part of the beach to avoid the other guys prowling about. And we had fun. In the evenings, we sat on the beach, talked about this and that and nothing at all, ate freshly grilled tuna and drank wine. And drank arrack with coca cola too." Ruth purses her lips. "We saw little of the rest of Eilat. By the time we were to go back, the guys had decided to come to visit us in Jerusalem." She blows her nose again. "We had fun in Eilat. One of the best holidays ever. I can't believe he's dead," she says wistfully.

They arrive at the police station and Peter takes her to an interview room.

"Can I get you something to drink, coffee, tea, water?" Peter asks.

"Coffee please."

Peter goes to get the coffee and meets Terry.

"I just saw the first part of the tapes from Gwedrow's back door, I think Mrs Geldenhuis went there that Friday!" Terry says.

"Are you sure?"

"It looks like her, but the picture is quite blurry, so not entirely sure if it is or not."

"Good thing she's here. We'd better ask her." Peter takes the coffee, Terry grabs some digestive biscuits and they walk to the interview room, which is now empty.

"Where'd she go?" Terry opens the door and looks around. Just then Ruth Johansson comes back.

"Sorry, I had to visit the WC," she says, and sits down.

"When we talked on the phone, you said that you had spoken to Jon Geldenhuis and you had agreed to meet after he finished working on Friday?" Peter asks.

"Yes, well, as I said we had a bit of unfinished business. I saw his picture in your local paper online. Or rather, it mentioned his name. The picture was rather pixelated. I was not sure it was him, so I called the newspaper, and they confirmed it was Jon. We had had some financial disagreements."

"What kind of disagreements?"

"After that summer in Israel and, after a long-distance relationship for a few months, he moved to Sweden, and we got married. After a few years of living in a cold climate, I guess he got bored or something and he cheated on me, constantly. I told him off, he promised no more, and all was good, and then he found yet another one." She draws a deep breath. "We fought a lot. After each affair he promised he would never do it again. It was wearing me out, though. I still loved him. He had a great sense of humour. We travelled quite a bit and had fun together. I was busy with my work at the university, he kept job-hopping. We lived in Stockholm where we had a nice flat. But I was getting fed up with all the fighting and was thinking about divorce. Then my father got sick and died suddenly. I had to go to Lund. It took a while to sort things out there. I had time to think, and I decided to file for divorce. As we didn't have children, it was a straightforward thing. He agreed. I flew to Stockholm to pack what I wanted to keep, put it into storage and then flew back to Lund to finish up there. He was supposed to sell our flat. He did. He even seemed to get a good deal for us, but the way things often go in Stockholm, the price agreed and signed on is sometimes different to the actual money paid. We did the final closing completely by phone. He and the buyers were in Stockholm sitting in the bank there, I was in Lund in the same bank's branch. The papers were signed, the keys exchanged, and half the money came into my account. All was good. Jon and I said our goodbyes. Then, about a year or so later, I was in the neighbourhood of our old flat and met one of the old neighbours. And to my surprise, I heard from her that the buyers and Jon had had a side deal. Meaning the price that they paid to the bank was low and Jon got the other part of the money for himself! I could not believe it! I was furious! I wanted my half of that money.

But by then he had moved out of the country, and I had no way to find him. I searched on the internet now and then, but until he popped up here in Faukon Abbey a few weeks ago, I had seen nothing about him for over two years. So yes, we had disagreements!"

"How much money are we talking about?"

"About 400 000 kronor! It's about 33 000 British pounds, I think. Not an enormous sum, but even so, for 200 000 Swedish kronor I can buy a car in Sweden. So yes, I wanted the money."

"When you called him, he agreed to meet you?"

"Yes. I just said I was coming to London and Faukon Abbey wasn't that far out, I'd like to see him."

"What was his response?"

"He just said, cool, and asked what date and time I would arrive. Told me to book in at the hotel Levington as it was near his work, and he would see me after work. We said little, as he said he was terribly busy."

"Did you talk to him when you arrived in London or at Faukon Abbey?"

"No, I just sent him an email notice confirming our meeting."

"Did he reply?"

"Yes, he accepted it."

"And when you arrived at Faukon Abbey?"

"I went to the bar in the hotel, had a drink and waited. And waited! Had another drink. And again, he had stood me up! I was so angry! I got my coat and went for a walk.

It was dark, but there are streetlights. I was so mad at him. Coming all this way and what does he do, the same as usual, he's a no-show."

"Did you go to Gwedrow?"

"You mean the glass factory? Yes, I went there. There was nobody around. I walked back to the hotel."

"And you didn't see your ex-husband or hear from him?"

"No."

"You didn't try to call him again?"

"It was Friday evening and then the weekend. I didn't have his personal phone number, only that of his office. I called again on Monday when I had a break during the conference. They said he wasn't in the office."

"He didn't call you back?"

"No. When you called, I thought he was in jail or something. I was so angry."

"That's all for now, Ms Johansson. Thank you. DC Ford will get your statement and, after you have read it and signed it, DC Ford will take you back to your hotel if you so wish."

"So, this means you haven't caught whoever killed him yet? He was murdered, right?"

"It's a suspicious death, yes."

"Do you have any suspects?"

"We are still investigating. We'll let you know as soon as we find anything. By the way, did you and Mr Geldenhuis go to New Orleans?"

"Yes, we did once, years ago." Ruth Johansson looks puzzled.

"Did your husband buy some voodoo rattles there?"

"Rattles? Ohhh you mean nasty metal things, look like maracas but have teeth in them?"

"Yes."

"Yes, he bought two of those. Horrid things! I couldn't understand why he wanted them. He claimed they were for an office party. Why are you asking about those? Surely he wasn't killed because of them, was he?"

"They came up during the investigation, that's all. By the way, I mentioned that Jon Geldenhuis had cited you as his next of kin, didn't I?"

"Yes, you did, but what does that mean? Why would he do that? We've been divorced for a few years now."

"I can't answer that, Ms Johansson, but what being his next of kin means is that, unless he has made other arrangements, like written a will, there may be money coming to you. Also, funeral arrangements, I would think. Unless he had any other family?"

"You mean I may get the money? And have to deal with his funeral?"

"I can't say. I expect that you'll find out."

"Does that mean I have to stay here? Who will contact me? Jon didn't have any family left, I think. His father died when he was young, his mother died when he went to uni. I think he had an older brother and a sister, but I have never met them, and I have no idea if they are even alive."

"You never went to South Africa?"

"No, Jon never wanted to go there. I wanted to see it. It's a beautiful country, safaris, and good wine and all that. He absolutely refused."

"Thank you. We will keep in touch. We have your contact details and I suspect you'll also hear from Gwedrow and their lawyer."

She sinks down on her seat.

"Oh my God, he really is dead! I... I... This is too much!" She buries her face in her hands, sobbing.

"I am so sorry for your loss. I'll leave you now with DC Ford. He can bring you some more coffee or water if you like."

***

Terry returns to the office after he has taken Ruth Johansson back to her hotel.

"You got her statement?" Peter asks.

"Yes. She signed it."

"Did she say anything more?"

"No, she went to her room. She sobbed most of the way. Taking it rather hard."

"She said she'd loved him, but divorced him because he'd cheated on her. Looks like she still had feelings for him."

"Seems so. Nice lady."

"Did you check with the hotel about her whereabouts?"

"Yes, the receptionist confirmed what Ruth Johansson told us. But when I asked the barman, he said he'd seen her out walking before she'd come to the bar for a drink."

"He was sure about that?"

"Pretty sure, he said. He was on his way to work when he'd seen her."

"What time was this?"

"About 4 p.m. His shift starts at 4.30 p.m. on Fridays."

"Did you contact Ruth Johansson about that?"

"I tried to call her, but her phone was off, both the hotel phone and her mobile. She had said she was going to get some sleep. Worn out she was, poor thing."

"Right, we need to check with her and the barman first thing tomorrow morning. And check the timing on those camera records as well."

"You don't think she had anything do with his death, do you?"

"At this stage we must keep an open mind and investigate. She wanted the money, that's motive. If she really was there, then she had the means, too. And he was killed by someone throwing something at him, and then banging his head down. Easy enough for a woman to do when he's already down. Don't you agree?"

"But she was genuinely heartbroken about it all!"

"Be that as it may, we must do our job. For all we know, she may be an amateur actress."

Thursday, 26 February

The Abbey Chronicle, Page 1

Jon Geldenhuis's Inquest

An inquest into the untimely death of Jon Geldenhuis, 50, the Head of IT at Gwedrow Glassworks, was held yesterday. As expected, the inquest was short and to the point. After testimonies by the Faukon Abbey police, detailing how, when and where he was found, the Home Office pathologist, Dr Slater, who had conducted the post-mortem, testified that Mr Geldenhuis had suffered a fatal *occipitocervical* dissociation, commonly referred to as internal decapitation, resulting from severe trauma. Ligaments connecting the skull to the spine were severed, leading to instantaneous death. His testimony prompted the coroner to issue an Open verdict, marking the death of Mr Geldenhuis as unexplained at this time, and thus allowing the police additional time for investigation.

As Mr Geldenhuis had resided in Faukon Abbey for just on a year, questions arise as to who would have wanted him dead and for what reasons. Two obvious questions emerge: who stands to gain from his death? And who might have had other motives? The police have conducted multiple interviews, but no charges have been filed thus far.

Through our own investigation we can offer potential insights. In terms of beneficiaries, little information is available regarding Mr Geldenhuis's financial situation. When he moved to Faukon

Abbey, he purchased a property in Glowburn Terrace, for £145,000, just over a year ago. However, surprisingly, he was reportedly listed as a beneficiary in the will of his neighbour, Marion Rivers, inheriting her house. Considering these assets, Jon Geldenhuis's estate may be valued at approximately £300,000. Though not a vast estate, people have been killed for far less than that.

In the absence of a will, two individuals could potentially benefit from the death of Mr Geldenhuis. Firstly, his ex-wife, reportedly named by Mr Geldenhuis as next of kin to his employer, has indicated she had some unresolved financial issues with him. It also appears she was present in Faukon Abbey at the time of his death. Secondly, Marion Rivers' son, Ben Rivers, who was mostly excluded from his mother's will, may also benefit from Mr Geldenhuis's passing.

Additional motives must also be considered. As previously highlighted, Jon Geldenhuis played a prominent role in the modernisation of data systems at Gwedrow. The company's restructuring efforts, right-sizing aimed at optimising operations through automation, have caused multiple heated disputes. However, whether any of these disagreements escalated to the point of causing the death of Mr Geldenhuis remains uncertain. Presently, all eyes are on DI Greene and Faukon Abbey CID. The third unexplained death in as many weeks has shattered the tranquillity of Faukon Abbey, leaving its residents on edge.

DI Peter Greene and DC Terry Ford

When Peter gets to the office in the morning and checks his email, he finally gets a bit of good news. Forensics from Exeter confirm that the traces found on the two bicycles belonging to Ryan Bolan and Lucas Hart, who was hit in Penzance, bear remnants of the same paint, not just same kind of paint but the same one. Jon Geldenhuis's bike which had been found in his office in Gwedrow, also carried traces of the same paint. Now they just need to find the car which had hit them all. Easier said than done, but Peter is convinced that the car in question belongs to Ben Rivers.

Peter requests an urgent search warrant for Ben's house and for his workplace, the taxi station, as there is a car maintenance space there, where the drivers can clean and repair their cars.

Friday, 27 February

DI Peter Greene and DC Terry Ford

After receiving the approved search warrants for Ben Rivers flat, garage and minicab site, Peter sends the uniforms with Terry to do the search together with the Exeter techs. Bertie is sent to the minicab site to do a search.

Exeter techs are going over Ben's car, taking pictures and scraping off small pieces of paint in the front of the car. Terry does a full search of his flat and garage. Bertie checks the minicab maintenance and storage shed where he finds a can of paint which the other drivers there say Ben used for his car. He'd told them he'd needed to repaint parts of his car after he had hit a customer's fence pole. Bertie bags and tags the paint can and drives to Ben's house. After a quick check by Exeter techs, they confirm that the paint is of the same kind used on Ben's car. They take the paint with them so that the lab can determine if it is the same paint from his car which was also found on the two bikes, as well as Geldenhuis's bike.

Monday, 2 March

DI Peter Greene and DC Terry Ford

"Sir, sir," Terry calls out excitedly, as soon Peter enters the office. "Bertie found fingerprints and I found something interesting at Marion River's house."

"Good morning to you too. Let me get a cup of coffee and then you can tell me all about it."

As soon as he's back Terry launches into an uncharacteristically rapid speech.

"Sir, Bertie found fingerprints on those chicken manure bags by the patio. And we have a match for them. And I found something else too. So now we can nail him!"

"Nail who, Terry, who?" Peter interrupts. "If the fingerprints belong to Ben, we already knew he brought those bags there. Didn't we check those bags already?"

"No sir, Bertie noticed we hadn't. The prints belong to Ken Preswick, sir."

"Preswick?"

"Yes sir, and his prints were partially on top of Ben's prints."

"Explain where the prints were found, please?"

"Bertie looked at the bags and, as you may remember, the bags were placed so that they were partially under the roof, so they didn't get wet. On the sides of the bags all the prints were Ben's, like he'd carried them there and put them down, which he said he'd done. But Bertie noticed that the topmost bag looked like it had been pushed aside a bit. It was close to the patio door too. So, Bertie brushed the underside of the corner and the top for prints. And Ken Preswick's prints were there. It seems like he'd tried to move the top bag a bit."

"So, you're suggesting that Preswick was there after Ben had brought those bags there? Do we have anything from him saying he'd been there?"

"His prints were also found on the patio door, both inside and outside."

"But didn't he say he had changed the locks for her which means his prints would have been there? And why didn't we see those before? I thought we had checked all of those?"

"We did, but we didn't have his prints for comparison. Since we now have Preswick's prints, it turned out they were his. Preswick's prints were also on the shelf in the bathroom, as I mentioned earlier. Geldenhuis said he'd put the shelf back on the day Marion Rivers died. And yet, we found Preswick's prints on top of Geldenhuis's prints."

"Well done. That's good! We're getting somewhere. Now we just have to talk to him again. Although, I fail to see why he would've wanted to harm Marion Rivers. He wasn't sweet on her, was he? They were long time neighbours. He'd helped her with the locks and garden work, hadn't he?"

"I think I may have found the answer to that part." Terry was beaming.

"What now?"

"When I went back into the bathroom, I looked under that bathtub too. I thought we might have missed something and indeed we had!"

"And what had we missed?"

"There was this postcard, sir." Terry hands Peter a double-sized postcard inside a transparent plastic evidence bag. On it three cartoon rats - black, white, and green - printed in colour on the front. "It's addressed to Ken Preswick. Not his name, but that's the number of his house." Terry points out.

"Now why'd Marion Rivers have a postcard belonging to him?"

"It gets better, sir."

"You mean those rats?" Peter turns the bag. "Now where have I seen those before. Why do those look familiar? Are Preswick's fingerprints on that card?"

"No prints from Preswick, only Marion's and some others. We suspect those are from the post office and others who have handled it."

"Now I remember, didn't those same rats pop up on Geldenhuis's phone when it rang at Gwedrow?"

"Indeed, they did. We also saw the same rats jumping and running about on that monitor in Geldenhuis's secret garage operation."

"Oh, so there is a connection. Damn it, I've seen those rats before somewhere else too! Let me get another cup of coffee. Now why'd Marion Rivers have Preswick's postcard? Could it be that the post office just delivered the card to the wrong address? When was that card delivered?"

Peter goes downstairs to get another cup of coffee. When he gets back upstairs Terry shows him a picture on his phone.

"Remember this, sir?"

"Where was that?"

"Warner's flat in Exeter."

"Really?"

Terry nods.

"Oh, now I remember," Peter says, "that guy in London whose breath was equally as bad as Preswick's, in a flat below Granger's and who took care of his post, had those same three rats flashing on his computer monitor too. I noticed it when he went to get the keys. I thought little of it then, it was just three rats, jumping up and down. Odd colour too, green, I thought. But now I need to talk with the Exe team. Maybe Preswick is one of their 'helpers' like Geldenhuis?"

"You don't really believe that sir, do you? Preswick isn't a very savoury character. He has no education to speak of," Terry says.

"What has education to do with it? It's true he may not be the best smelling person around, but maybe he was their decoy. You know, to catch a fly you need to spread some muck."

"Could be, sir. I just don't believe that he'd be one to help them out. He's the kind who only helps himself. Unless of course they have something on him?"

"Beliefs don't count, Terry, we need solid facts. I'll call Miles and, in the meantime, compile everything we have about Preswick. I mean everything; all statements, interviews, and everything else we know about him. We need to have our story absolutely clear; everything checked twice, before we bring him back here again. And check with the post office whether they can tell you when that card was delivered and by which postman. He may remember the card."

Terry sets out to collect all the information they have while Peter calls Miles Miller in Exeter.

After lunch, Peter goes to talk with Mullan.

"Peter, good, come in, I was just about to ask you to come. I had an interesting talk with the Chief Constable. This whole business involving Geldenhuis is far, far bigger than we thought. It's all part of an international operation both on the continent and in America too."

"Indeed, sir."

"We must work closely with Exeter. You know Miles Miller there, don't you? Coordinate with him. Make sure he gets all the help from us he needs. I want those nasty paedophile bastards and all who engage in that filth caught!"

"Sir, yes, indeed. But we have a bit of a situation. We suspect that Ken Preswick, who's Geldenhuis's neighbour, may have killed Marion Rivers."

"Marion Rivers? Surely she had nothing to do with those pedos, did she? And this Preswick, is he involved in this pedo ring too? Didn't you say he was helping Geldenhuis with things?"

"Yes, Preswick was accepting packages for Geldenhuis, but that's apparently as far as it goes. Instead, according to Miles Miller, Preswick is a big consumer of what's on Geldenhuis's servers."

"Well then, Miller can come over here and take him to Exeter."

"Yes sir, but if Preswick killed Marion Rivers, shouldn't we get to question him first?"

"Oh, I see what you mean! Murderer or a pedo or both? Do you have any evidence he killed Marion Rivers? And why?"

"Not sure why yet, but it seems Ms Rivers somehow got hold of a postcard which was addressed to Preswick. This one." Peter hands over the evidence bag with the postcard.

"Killed over a postcard? With three cartoon rats? Surely not."

"I suspect that is the case, sir. You see, Geldenhuis's system was set up to look like a computer game where the three rats are supposed to be spies as they can go underground undetected. It's just a front. If you try to sign up to play the game, all you get is an error page saying the game is still in the works or something. All very hush-hush to ensure that the actual users feel they're safe while watching their dirty files."

"Like any other organised crime."

"Indeed. In order to get one of those postcards, Preswick had to sign up for them."

"So?"

"Only those who knew the correct way to sign into the pedo server, the one in Geldenhuis's garage, could get access to all the files. And they, like Preswick, could then sign up to receive those postcards with rats whenever someone had made a bigger upload of new material. The postcards look harmless enough and, on the computer, it all looks like a game, so nothing's really suspicious."

"Pretty good covert thinking there."

"Yes, Geldenhuis was rather good at setting it all up and keeping it going. Miles was plenty pleased with him."

"So, Preswick had signed up to get the card. Where does Marion Rivers come into it? Didn't you say she was smitten by Geldenhuis? Was Preswick jealous or something?"

"No, nothing like that. At least I don't think that's the case. I think it's more mundane, just a human error. The postman dropped the card in Ms Rivers' letterbox instead of Preswick's. Maybe Preswick somehow got wind that the card had gone to her. The camera from Geldenhuis's garage shows someone looking like Preswick going towards Marion's house. This was after Ben Rivers had delivered sacks of chicken manure on her patio. Maybe he thought she wasn't at home. He let himself into her house. Went upstairs, only to notice she was taking a bath."

"Where was the card found?"

"In the bathroom, behind the bathtub. It looks like it could've fallen down from a shelf in the corner, as the shelf itself was on the floor too when she was found."

"Now why'd she have the card in the bathroom? It wasn't sent to her?"

"Not sure. Terry is checking with the post office when that card was delivered. They usually deliver post around 1 p.m., but we're waiting to talk with the postman on that route to find out if he remembers anything."

"That still doesn't explain why you think he murdered her? Do you have any evidence apart from that card?"

"Preswick's fingerprints were found in her bathroom on a shelf. Geldenhuis said that he'd put that particular shelf back on the wall on the day she died. That was at lunch time. She was found dead at 4 p.m. Maybe she was on her way upstairs to run a bath when saw the card on the floor in the hall. She picked it up and absentmindedly put it on the shelf in the bathroom while turning on the taps to run water for her bath. Maybe she thought those rats were cute and didn't even look at the address."

"That still doesn't explain why he'd kill her. It was just a postcard. There's no text on it, just those rats. What was his motive?"

"Right. Mrs Rivers was known as a nosy parker, always keeping an eye on things. She was a librarian, very keen on telling people she knew how to find out information about them. She also had, as Charles Penny said, a good moral character. It could be Preswick thought he'd been found out. I don't know. But I think we have a case."

"Very well. Coordinate with Exeter. We need to nail this Preswick and others like him. Lock them away for good! Anything else?"

"Yes, it seems there's a connection to two previous cases as well. A Warner case and a person found in the Granger case."

"Good. Get that to Exeter as well. Did Preswick kill Geldenhuis too?"

"He has an alibi. We'll continue with that one."

Tuesday, 3 March

DI Peter Greene and DC Terry Ford

"Good morning, all." Peter is in a good mood arriving at work.

"Good morning, sir," Terry replies. "We've now brought in both Ben Rivers and Ken Preswick for questioning."

"Good, good. Do they both have their legal reps here yet?"

"Ben Rivers has. Ken Preswick hasn't said a word yet."

"Okay, let's start with Ben."

After over two hours of questioning Ben about the death of his mother, as well as the death of Ryan Bolan, Peter stops the interview for a short break.

The officers get some coffee before returning to their office.

"I just don't think he killed his mother. What do you think?" Peter asks Terry.

"No, I don't think he killed her. But I'm sure he killed Ryan Bolan. He just keeps claiming it was an accident. That it was his mother's call that distracted him."

"You have his phone records, right? Do we know exactly when his mother called him?" Peter asks.

"Yes, we have the records, but Slater couldn't tell when Ryan died so not sure how that would help?"

"We know when Ryan left Bodmin? And didn't you figure out how long it would take him to cycle to where he was found? So, compare those and see if they match."

"Ben denied it was his car caught on the cameras in Penzance. Unfortunately, the images weren't clear enough to implicate him."

"True, but if we combine the phone record with Ryan's cycle and assume that Ben was speeding, we'd have a reasonable timeline we can provide as evidence. And then there's the possibility that it was Ben who hit that other cyclist in Penzance too."

"Right."

Terry clicks on his computer to find the phone records among the evidence.

"Indeed sir, his mother did call him, but it was earlier in the day. Ben's book-writing event ended about 4 p.m. he said. After that he went to the pub. His mother called him at 4.45 p.m. Christine and I found the cyclist in the shrubbery in Penzance around 5.30 p.m. So maybe Ben was distracted because of his mother's call and hit THAT cyclist? Ryan left around 1 p.m. or thereabouts from Bodmin. He wasn't pedalling fast as it was cold, rainy, and he was likely feeling the effects of the spacecake and may have been hungover from the evening before. He'd also stopped at least once to call about his charger. Sometime between 6 and 8 p.m. Ben hit Ryan Bolan and killed him. We didn't see any skid marks on the road where Ryan was found, but then he was only found a week later."

"Good, now we have a firmer timeline. Since you checked all the cameras everywhere, did any of them show when Ben got back to Faukon Abbey?"

"Not sure, I'll check again."

"Get Bertie Lawson to do it. We need to talk to Preswick."

Peter and Terry walk downstairs to question Ken Preswick. Preswick has been sitting in the interview room for several hours. The officers sit down and start the recording.

"Why am I here? I've been sitting here for hours! Can't even smoke! What is this? You've no right to keep me here," Preswick shouts and pounds his fist on the table.

"Mr Preswick, we have brought here you to be questioned under caution. You have the right to legal representation. If you don't have a representative, one can be appointed for you. Do you understand?"

"Yeah."

"Do you want to have a legal representative present? And if so, can we call one for you?"

"Nah, let's get this over and done with so I can go home."

"For the recording, please state clearly, do you want legal representation with you? Yes, or no?"

"No, I already said no. Don't want one. What's this about?"

"Where were you on Wednesday 4th of February between 2 p.m. and 4 p.m.?"

"Where I always am, at home."

"Can anybody vouch for you?"

"Of course not! I live alone, don't I?"

"You didn't go out at all that day?"

"No, I already said that. Can I go now?"

"No. You've signed up for *Underseen Underground*, correct?"

Preswick pales visibly and shifts his position before answering.

"So, what if I have? It's just a game! What's it to you?"

Peter puts the postcard with the rats on the table.

"But it's not a game, is it? And you know it's not. And we know it's not."

"I'm not saying anything more. I want a rep here."

"Very well. Do you have someone you want us to call for you?"

"No, just get me one."

"That was quick," Terry says as they walk from the interview room.

"Indeed." Peter walks over to the desk and asks for a duty legal representative for Ken Preswick.

Bertie comes upstairs.

"Did you find Ben Rivers' car on any camera?" Terry asks.

"Yes and no and maybe."

"What's that supposed to mean?"

"I looked at the camera footage for that evening between 6 p.m. to 9 p.m. For a Saturday evening there wasn't that much traffic coming from that direction. Unfortunately, it was a dark night with poor visibility and Ben Rivers' car is a common model. It's also dark blackish blue, like many others. I narrowed it down to eight cars between those times. I looked at the registration numbers but, as mentioned, it was dark, and the streetlights were not all bright enough to get good visibility."

"And?" Peter says.

"I narrowed it down to three. We see all three cars coming around 7:30 p.m. from Tersel Woods' direction. The good news is that one of them could belong to Ben Rivers, the bad news is that the registration numbers are only partially visible, so it's not possible to tell."

"Can you make out any more details? Driver visible?"

"Sorry, too dark."

"Then check the registration numbers, try to narrow them down and see if you can find who was out and about that night. Get someone from Traffic to help you narrow those down. Terry and I will continue our interview with Ben Rivers."

"Mr Rivers, you said you were at a book-writing event in Penzance until 4 p.m.?"

"I've already said that a thousand times!"

"Indeed. And after the event you went to the nearby pub for something to eat?"

"Had to eat something."

"Were you drinking?"

"I had half a pint, what of it?"

"So, you're saying you weren't drunk?"

"I wasn't drunk. Look, I already told you this earlier. Why do I have to keep repeating the same things over and over again? Don't you guys take notes?"

"We do. When it comes to the phone call from your mother, what time was that?"

"I don't remember exactly."

"We've checked your phone records. As you can see from this list, your mother called you at 4.45 p.m. on 31st January."

"If you say so."

"Where were you when she called?"

"In my car."

"You mentioned earlier today that you were distracted by your mother's call and thus didn't pay attention and hit Ryan Bolan, sending him flying to the roadside."

"Yeah?" Ben's legal representative nudges him and they confer quietly while Peter and Terry wait.

"I wasn't exactly distracted by the call, but more by what she said. I kept mulling over that in my head."

"What did she say?"

"She said she was going to sell her house, marry that Goldenhue guy and move to Spain with him! She was clearly going bonkers, losing it. I was trying to call her back because what she was saying was just insane! So yes, I was distracted and didn't see the guy on the bike. I'm sorry, but it was just an accident."

A knock on the door and Bertie stands there waving a paper. Terry goes and gets it and shows to Peter.

Peter puts the photo on the table. The registration number plate is a bit fuzzy, but a corner of the car has a visible dent.

"That's not me! It's not my car! You can't even see the registration number. It's not me."

"Ben Rivers, I'm arresting you for dangerous driving and on suspicion of the murder of Ryan Bolan. You do not have to say anything, but it may harm your defence if you do not mention, when questioned, something which you later rely on in court. Anything you do say may be given in evidence."

"It was an accident! I didn't kill him! It was an accident," Ben keeps yelling.

Terry and Bertie take Ben Rivers with them. His legal rep follows them.

Peter goes to talk with Ken Preswick. His legal rep has just arrived.

Peter restarts the recording.

"So, Mr Preswick, can you now tell us more about that so-called game which sent you postcards like this?"

"Okay, okay, so it isn't a game. What if I can tell you more about it? Details and such?"

"That would be good. There's a team in Exeter who would be interested to hear what you can tell them."

Preswick smiles broadly.

"Righto, let them know I know a lot of things that went on with it and I'll tell them all. Then I can go home now as I didn't really do anything with it myself?"

Preswick is about to stand up, smiling at his rep.

"Not so fast. I'm not interested in your activities connected to that site. I want to know why you killed Marion Rivers?"

Preswick slumps back into his seat.

"I didn't kill her. She was a nosy bitch, but I didn't kill her. Why would I?"

"That's what I'd like to know too. She was your neighbour for many years. You even helped her occasionally, so why would you kill her?"

"But I didn't."

"Then please explain why we found this postcard under her bathtub? The side of which has your thumbprints on it?"

Preswick swallows hard.

"I've helped her with repairs, so my prints are all over."

"Indeed, you've mentioned that. But explain why your prints were found on two items which were brought to Marion Rivers' house on the day she died? You previously said you had been at home all day?"

"I don't know. I wasn't there."

"We have a witness who saw you entering through the back gate to her house on 31 January about 2.45 p.m. And the same witness saw you coming out again, at 3 p.m., carrying what looked like a wet rag."

"They're lying! I never was there! I was at home! It was Ben."

"We found that wet rag, which was one of Mrs Rivers' towels, in your garden shed."

"So what? She gave me all kinds of old rags."

"Except those towels were part of a set she'd bought only a few days earlier."

"She was a nosy old bitch! She was always going on about how she knew things and how she knew everything about everybody!" Preswick bangs his fists on the table again.

Peter stands up.

"Ken Preswick, I'm arresting you on suspicion of the murder of Marion Riv..."

"Wait, wait! It was an accident, I swear. I didn't kill her; it was an accident!" Preswick is sweating and the smell is spreading in the air. Peter sits down.

"Then you'd better tell us what happened. Was it about this postcard?"

"Yeah, kind of." Preswick confers with his rep who nods several times. "Okay, yeah."

Peter sits quietly and waits. There's a knock at the door. Terry comes in and gives Peter a folder.

"Mr Preswick, start from the beginning."

Preswick sighs.

"If I tell it all, it's going to look good, right?"

"Yes. Telling it all now is going to be considered."

"Okay, so, since you know about the rats. Yeah, it's not a game, it's just a front for a porn site."

"How did you get into it?"

"Geldenhuis. He told me about it. Said he could fix things so that I didn't have to pay the fee to get to it, if I helped him. Expensive site too, I couldn't pay for it. He always had a lot of stuff coming in and he needed someone to look after it before he got home. But I only saw the regular porn, I swear, not the filth with the kids! I'm not a pedo! Didn't even know about the pedo stuff on there until recently."

"How did you find out?"

"You could sign up to get notified when there were big uploads of new files. They did those when they had a big batch of them, quality control, they said. They are videos, all made by regular people, not films. Anybody could upload their own videos there and then you'd pay to see the better ones. They sorted them too. You know women, big tits, small tits, butts, full frontal action, and so on."

Peter waves his hand. "We get it."

"You sign up and you get a postcard so that you'll know. It was a new thing, you know." Preswick adds. "Can I get some water?"

Terry gets up and brings back a six-pack of small bottles of water. He gives one to Preswick who downs most of it, spilling some. He wipes his chin with the back of his hand.

"So, you signed up?" Peter asks.

"Yeah, I did. Geldenhuis said I wouldn't have to pay if I did."

"Right. And Marion Rivers?"

"She wasn't in on it! What do you think? That holier-than-thou nosy parker, always poking her nose into other people's business, sniffing about like a damn dog looking for a bone. Always meddling, asking questions, blathering!" Preswick gulps the rest of the water and slams the bottle on the table.

"But she found out about it?"

"That damn postcard! The postman delivered the card to her!"

"Wasn't it addressed to you?"

"No, that's the thing! There's no name on it, just the house number and addressed to the Occupant. It's for security, kind of."

"Then what happened?"

"Marion comes knocking on me door and shoves a card in me hand. 'Rats for a rat! Yours, I think,' she sneered."

"And then?"

"And then nothing. She left."

"So how did this one end up in her bathroom?"

"That's a different card."

"The other cards came to you correctly?"

"Yeah. So, I thought it was all sorted with the post office. Geldenhuis said so too."

"And then this one?"

"I was looking out the window when I saw the postman. He'd stopped and was sorting post in his hand. I saw he had that postcard and I thought he'd come to my house. But no, he shoved it through her letterbox with some other mail. Can I have some more water?"

Peter gives him another small bottle. Preswick takes a sip.

"This was on 4 February? What time was it?"

"Yeah, the mailman was late, it was about 2 p.m. Ben had been at the back and brought her bags of manure or something. But he didn't go inside so I thought she wasn't at home. He usually goes in. He doesn't just come and leave things. I thought she'd gone out. Maybe gone to the library again." Preswick drinks some more water. Looks at his rep, who nods again. "If she hasn't been such a nosy bitch this wouldn't have happened!"

"What happened? You went to her house?"

"Yeah. I figured she wasn't at home, so I went to look. I grabbed the extra keys and went over there. There was nothing on the floor by the door." Preswick blows his nose. "I thought maybe she put it in the kitchen, looked, not there. So then I thought maybe she had put it in her 'office' upstairs." Preswick makes air quotes. "I heard nothing, so I thought she wasn't at home. I went upstairs." He draws a deep breath.

"But she was."

"Yeah, she was. Standing in the bathtub, in the middle of the day! Stark naked she was too; the door was open. She didn't see me at first. Then she turned her head, saw me, covered her tits, and fell. Right in the tub. I goes to look. She's under water. The postcard is on the shelf right there, so I try to reach out to snatch it, but she comes up and tries to kick me, so I grab her foot to stop her kicking. I hold it, she keeps kicking with the other foot, so I take that one too and hold it. Must've been her thrashing about caused that damn card to fall."

"And then?"

"I let go of her feet. She'd stopped thrashing. And I got down on the floor to look for the card, but it must have wedged itself between the wall and the tub. Couldn't get to it so I left."

"You took one of her towels?"

"Yeah, she'd splashed so much water on me, so I took one."

"And what about Mrs Rivers?"

"She was in the water."

"Did you look at her?"

"Yeah."

"Was she breathing?"

"Don't know. I left in a hurry."

"You didn't try to get her up?"

"Help that nosy old bitch who'd promised to ruin my life? She was going to tell your lot that I was a pedo and a molester of small kids, should be thrown in jail, shouldn't be allowed to live in a decent neighbourhood! I'm not a pedo. I saw some videos, but I didn't watch them!! I don't do kids. I like women with big tits!"

"When did she tell you that?"

"It was a while after I got a few more cards. She'd done her snooping about and found the game website. Not sure how she figured out it wasn't a game; she didn't tell me. She just came one day, banging on my door and telling me how she was going to ruin my life. She never liked me."

"When this card went to her you saw your opportunity to do away with her?"

"No, No, No! I just told you what happened! It was an accident. I didn't mean to kill her. She fell, hit her head."

"But you didn't help her up?"

"Of course I didn't! I wasn't supposed to be there, for God's sake. I saw her naked! She would've crucified me for touching her holiness! It was an accident. She slipped. I just held her foot to keep her from kicking me. That's all! I didn't kill her. I didn't even know she was dead before Ben and your lot showed up."

"Very well. Anything else you want to add?"

"It was an accident, I swear. I didn't kill her! She died on her own. I'm not gonna say I'm sorry that she's dead, she was a bloody meddlesome old bitch and she was gonna ruin my life, but I didn't kill her! I swear. It was an accident. You got to believe me."

"We'll stop here for now and get you to Exeter so you can tell them all you know about the rats."

Bertie comes in. Terry and Bertie take Preswick away. His legal representative follows them.

Peter walks to Mullan's office to update him. Mullan congratulates him.

"But what about Geldenhuis? Did either one of them kill him?"

"Preswick has a solid alibi for that time. After what Ben told us about his mother's plans, moving to Spain with Geldenhuis, he certainly had a motive for getting rid of him. Especially if he also knew Geldenhuis was going to inherit her house and he'd be left with just a little bit of money. We'll tackle him about that tomorrow. I don't think he did it, but we don't really have that many other suspects."

"What about the ex-wife?"

"She may have been at Gwedrow too, but I just don't see her killing him. He was worth more to her alive than dead. She didn't know about the possible inheritance and all that. She was genuinely shocked about his death."

"You're sure you don't just have a soft spot for a pretty lady?"

"No sir. I just don't think she did it and we have no evidence that she did."

"*Apropos* pretty ladies, how's your Mrs Warner doing?"

"She's doing well. I was planning to take a few days off later to take her to Paris."

"Paris? Romance in the air then?"

"No sir, just to get away for a few days."

"Sort out the Geldenhuis murder and you and Terry can take a week off."

Thursday, 5 March

DI Peter Greene and DC Terry Ford

Peter and Terry are on their way to Ken Preswick's house. They meet Miles Miller's team from Exeter. Miller's team has already searched and removed the server and other equipment from Geldenhuis's garage and his home office.

Preswick had sung like a canary Miller tells Peter and Terry. His team had questioned him, under caution too, for hours, and Preswick was telling all he knew. And it seemed he knew a lot. The question now was, how was it possible that he knew that much? Peter pointed out that Preswick didn't work and that he stayed at home all day long. They haven't really been able to establish where he got his money from. His parents had left him with a bit of money, but he hasn't worked for several years.

Miller's team gets the door open and they all march in. The smell hits them. Loads of rubbish in the kitchen and, when Terry opens the fridge door, the smell nearly knocks him out. Peter and Miles go round opening all the windows.

Miller's team is there to collect anything and everything related to the pedo/porno game and the paedophile users. Peter and Terry want to find the second postcard and anything else that could be related to Mrs Rivers.

Terry goes upstairs. In a room facing the back, with a view of the garages, a high-end desktop computer with two monitors, sits on a desk. Miller's team takes the computer with them. On the shelf there are a lot of computer- and technology-related books, and an old laptop, which they take too. It seems that Mr Preswick is not the village nobody everybody thinks he is.

"This is a surprise!" Terry says.

"Indeed. Wonder what he was doing with it? It seems a bit unnecessary just to watch porn online?"

"Miles, was Preswick working for Geldenhuis?"

"No, or at least not that we know of. I highly doubt it. Geldenhuis wasn't supposed to have anybody else know about it."

"Did Preswick say anything about Geldenhuis, that he knew what Geldenhuis was doing?"

"Only thing he said was that Geldenhuis had sort of told him that he was running a bit of a side business, a hush-hush porn game thing. That's why Geldenhuis could give Preswick access."

"Such a pity we didn't know about it before. If we had, maybe he'd still be alive," Peter says.

"But Preswick didn't kill him, did he?" Miller says.

"No, we're pretty sure he didn't, but if Preswick found out, maybe someone else did too."

"I see; you have a point. But based on our weekly talks with Geldenhuis he wasn't worried about his own safety. He complained a while ago that someone had driven him off the road, sending him flying into a hedgerow."

"Yes, Geldenhuis told us about it. We now know who it was, Ben Rivers. But, unfortunately, we can't prove it. Too many others used the same paint on their cars."

"Did Rivers kill Geldenhuis?"

"He says no. We have no evidence to tie him to it either. He has a motive, maybe even had the means, but I don't think he did it."

"So, who did?" Miller asks.

"What are you going to charge Preswick with? He killed Marion Rivers and, despite what he says, I don't think it was an accident."

"We're still checking the information he's given us. If it all checks out, he's going to be the star witness. We're now coordinating with the London task force and they're in contact with the teams in other countries. I hope you can keep that local reporter of yours quiet! He called *The Guardian* for fuck's sake! The London chief had to land a ton of bricks on them to keep those bloodhounds quiet until it's all done."

"Right, I promise, we'll make sure he keeps his mouth shut." Peter shoots an angry look at Terry.

"This is one helluva operation, Peter. Including what we've got from Preswick, we're talking about catching at least 150, maybe more pedos, in 9 other countries including Scotland. We can't afford to fuck it up now."

"That is huge, I agree. When is it going down?"

"This weekend."

"This weekend?"

"Yeah, we must get them when they're at home. We have all the proof we need, but the law's the law, ... assumed innocent until proven guilty. And, surprising them at home all at the same time too, makes it harder for those nosy reporters to get a whiff and spread it around, tipping the pedos off."

"Makes sense. Do you need any help from us?"

"No, not one in Faukon Abbey that we know of at least. Your one guy died. And Preswick is not one. At least that's how it looks. Who knows, he may have created an alternate identity, but we don't know yet. Once we turn him upside down and inside out, and get all this stuff checked, then we'll know for sure what he's been up to."

"Okay, we'll leave you to it. Nothing here for us. Just let me know what you're going to do with Preswick, will you?"

"Of course."

Peter and Terry walk away.

"Now, what have you been telling Jimmy Carter?" Peter asks.

"Sir, I haven't told him anything! I swear!"

"Then what does he know and how did he find out?"

"I don't know exactly what he knows. But he found out about the Geldenhuis garage incident. Remember when we went to the garage and Miles Miller showed up?"

"So, it was just a raid on a garage! He saw us going in, that's all. Right?"

"After you left and I was waiting for the locksmith, he came to me and asked me what was going on."

"And?"

"I told him there was nothing going on. And, if he breathed about it to a soul, you'd have him nailed."

"Okay, I most certainly will, and, if I don't, Miles Miller will. So why does Miles know about him? Did Jimmy really call *The Guardian*?"

"I've no idea if he did or didn't. All I told him was that once what we're doing is over and done, I'll give him an interview. I was going to tell you about it, but it slipped my mind. I'm deeply sorry, sir."

"But you didn't tell him what it was all about?"

"No, I swear I didn't. All I said was that it was an investigation concerning the Geldenhuis murder and that was it. Nothing else."

"Hmm, so what does he know? You'd better call him and find out. And when it comes to that interview, we'd better clear that with Mullen. Why the hell didn't you tell me about all this?"

"I'm sorry sir, it slipped my mind. I didn't expect him to do anything much as there really wasn't anything much to know back then, was there?"

"Humph. Right. Let's go and get some lunch."

Wednesday, 11 March

Jimmy Carter, *The Abbey Chronicle*

Jimmy has asked Helen out for dinner. They're to meet in *The Whistle &Tin*.

When Jimmy arrives, Helen is already waiting at their usual table in the corner. He gives her a quick peck on the cheek and goes back to order a full bottle of *Cava* and a small bowl of Spanish meatballs. He takes the bottle and two glasses to the table.

"What's this? What are we celebrating? What's going on Jimmy?"

Jimmy is beaming.

"I did it! I did it," he says, while filling their glasses with the bubbly wine.

"What did you do? Tell me. You've been so secretive lately!"

"Cheers!" says Jimmy and they clink their glasses. The barmaid brings the meatballs and cutlery.

"If you're not going to tell me soon what you did, I'm going to…"

"All right, all right, wait for it!" Jimmy takes out his phone, scrolls a bit and then gives it to Helen. "See that name there, that's me!" he says, pointing to a line where it says '*contributing: James Carter*'.

Helen scrolls back and forth skimming through the article in *The Guardian*, while Jimmy sits grinning widely.

"Woo hoo! You got your foot in there. This is so fantastic. Congratulations, sweetie!" Helen leans over, gives Jimmy a quick kiss and raises her glass. "Cheers! So, this is why you've been totally incommunicado recently?"

"Yeah, sorry about that. I wasn't allowed to talk or say anything until the police here, in Exeter, London, and in nine other countries had arrested all the pedos during the weekend. A total of about 150 or so of them. Couldn't even tell Mike Kings about it."

"Nine other countries too? Wowser! That's huge. How'd they manage to catch them all?"

"Geldenhuis."

"What you mean Geldenhuis? He's dead, isn't he?"

"Yes, he is, he is, but he was instrumental to the entire operation."

"And you found out about that?"

"Well," Jimmy blushes, "yes and no. I sort of found out what he was doing, but I only found out later that it was the police who had set him up."

"What do you mean set him up? Was he a pedo too?"

"Oh no, no, no! Gosh no, he wasn't! He had set up a server in his garage. Those pedos could then connect to it, log on and share their filthy files there. Terry said the little he saw, he wishes no one else would ever see again. Kids abused, you know, and by grown-up men. Just terrible." Jimmy downs the rest of his glass and fills their glasses again.

"Oh my God, that's absolutely awful! So horrible. Poor kids! As far as I'm concerned, those pedos should be castrated and thrown into some deep dark dungeon somewhere so that they could never do anything of the sort again!" Helen bangs her fists on the table. People seated close to them look at her in alarm. Jimmy takes her hands.

"Yes dear, I agree. And I'm ever so glad I didn't have to see any of it. Just listening to Terry and Peter Greene talk about it made me want to puke. Such totally horrid acts!"

They sip their wine and sigh. Jimmy pours the last of the wine into their glasses.

"So how did you get to know about it in the first place?"

"I heard on the police radio that there was something going on around where Marion and Geldenhuis lived. I saw some guys sitting in a car, one of them looked familiar and then I saw Peter Greene getting into that car. He sat there for a good half an hour. I waited. He went back to the garage, then left, and Terry stayed. I walked over and asked what was going on. Terry made me promise I wouldn't tell a soul anything I'd seen. If I did, I'd endanger the Geldenhuis murder investigation, and he'd throw me into jail for a long time."

"Jeez! You think he meant it?"

"Yes, he did. He was dead serious too. Never seen him like that before. Of course I promised. And he promised that once things calmed down, he'd tell me about it. Which he and Peter Greene did on Monday."

"But that was just about the Geldenhuis murder? So why was that a super-secret thing? Where did this pedo stuff come from? You said Geldenhuis wasn't a pedo? Where did *The Guardian* come into this? Were they on it too? Or how did they find out?"

"Hold on hold on, I'll tell you. I told *The Guardian* what was going on over here."

"What, that Geldenhuis was murdered? How was that connected to anything? Did they just take your word for it? They didn't know about this pedo thing already?"

"No, I didn't tell them about the Geldenhuis murder *per se*. You see, instead, I got a tip as to what it was all about. I called *The Guardian* and said they might want to check with the cops over there too."

"What you mean a tip? I thought you only talked to Terry and Greene on Monday?"

"I had another source."

"Oh, and are you going to tell me?"

"We reporters don't reveal our sources," Jimmy says, looking very smug.

"For sure. So come on, who told you what?"

"No, really, I can't tell you who told me and what they told me. I promised. Only it was someone who knew a bit of what was going on. Who had, you could say, a good view of goings on."

"All right, be that way. And you called *The Guardian*?"

"Yes, I called them. There's this one guy I know. I called him, said I had received a hot tip about something going on. Told him briefly what I'd heard. He said he'd check. He did, and a few hours later he called me back. They had also been told to keep it under wraps until today."

"Pretty big deal then."

"Yeah and they wanted me to send them what I had found out here and said they'd put my name on it too!"

"They did."

"They did. On Monday, after I'd interviewed Terry and Greene, I told *The Guardian* that they'd said there was more than just Devon and London, but they didn't know which other countries. That's what *The Guardian* then found out too. They sent their best team to find out and they were also slammed by the cops to keep their mouths shut until the police had finished with all the arrests. The cops all over had to act fast since, with Geldenhuis dead, they could only keep the service running for a short time."

"Hmm, I don't know much about computers, but I thought that if you put something out on the internet it stays there forever?"

"That's true. But in this case, the server Geldenhuis had was a secret one, and it allowed these pedos to do all sort of things. And it sent out postcards."

"Postcards? Who sends postcards these days?"

"Apparently the pedos needed to know when there was new material, so it sent postcards to those who wanted to see it. They couldn't just send emails; those could be traced. But with postcards, they were just sent to the 'Occupant'. No name, just the house number. It was a brilliant and careful set-up to make those pedos feel safe and in control. I mean they know what they are, and they obviously want to keep their horrible and disgusting doings well hidden, although they don't consider those as a crime really. They even say they love kids! Of course, Geldenhuis wasn't planning to die, so how it was all set up died with him, as they'd wanted to keep it all secret, no leaks. After his death the cops didn't want to risk losing the ones they knew about already, so they just about closed the operation and arrested a whole lot of pedos."

"Now why would this Geldenhuis set up a server and work with the cops? I mean it's obviously great that he did, considering the results, but why'd he do something like that?"

"Not sure. Terry and Peter didn't say anything either. It could just be that he wanted to act like a spy, you know? Secret mission and all that."

"Hmm, I guess so. People are strange."

Jimmy drowns the last of his *Cava*.

"Are you hungry or did this spoil your appetite?" Jimmy asks.

"Yes and no, I need to eat something."

Just as they're about to order food, Ingela arrives. She's beaming too.

"Sit, sit, you look happy. We're just about to eat."

Ingela plops down.

"Food, yes please, I could eat a horse! But I think I'll settle for the lamb meatballs."

"I'll go for those too," says Helen.

"Great, I think I'll have them too. So, for the drink? A carafe of the house red?"

Both women nod and Jimmy goes to order and brings back the wine and three glasses.

"You're looking happy," Jimmy says.

"Yes, I am! Thanks to your boss's advice, I could remove myself from being the executor of Marion's will, or, rather, I renounced my executive duties, as they say officially."

"That's good news for sure. Cheers!"

They clink their glasses.

"What happens with her will now?"

"I don't know, and I don't care. I'm free of that horrid Ben. I can't believe that Marion actually thought I'd get together with him! He's a slimy, stinky, creep!" Ingela flicks her arms up in the air. "EEEWW!"

Jimmy and Helen laugh. "Wow, you really don't like him."

"No, I don't. I don't want to have anything to do with him ever again."

Thursday, 19 March

The Abbey Chronicle, Page 1

Shocking Testimony Emerges in Ben Rivers' Trial

Ben Rivers' trial began yesterday in the Crown Court for his role in the death of Ryan Bolan. In his opening statement, Rivers' defence claimed that Bolan's death was an unfortunate accident, as Rivers had honked his horn because Bolan was driving erratically and had failed to move over.

However, during the testimony of Dr Slater, it was revealed that Bolan's death was not caused by the initial impact between Bolan's bike and Rivers' car, but by a stone to the back of Bolan's head. Bolan wasn't wearing a helmet. It was found tied to his pannier. Rivers' attorney suggested that a large boulder had rolled off during the incident and potentially struck Bolan. Slater countered this argument stating that the stone was found with Bolan's blood on it, and that the shape of the stone matched the laceration in Ryan Bolan's head, suggesting it had delivered the fatal blow.

After Dr Slater, Ben Rivers was called to testify. When asked why he had not called emergency services after the alleged accident, Rivers claimed he had been planning to do so, but had been distracted by a phone call from his mother and had subsequently forgotten. The defence's argument was met with incredulity, with the prosecuting counsel questioning how one could forget that one had killed someone. Trial to continue tomorrow.

DI Peter Greene and DC Terry Ford

Mullan has granted both Peter and Terry the following week off. Investigating three murder cases has taken its toll on them both. Terry had spent time in court too, testifying.

Peter and Terry go for a late lunch to *The Whistle &Tin*. They'd worked hard and filed all the reports and paperwork. To celebrate the occasion, they each get a pint of beer and order the meatball special of the day which turns out to be the spicy Moroccan one, with lamb.

"So, Terry, what are you going to do? Take Christine somewhere?"

"Planning to go to Scotland."

"Not to Gretna Green?" Peter chuckles.

"Nah, although it would've been great. This waiting is killing me! Unfortunately, you can't get married there that fast anymore. You need to apply ahead of time and all that. Just like a regular wedding."

"Oh, too bad. I didn't know that. Can't you hurry it all along? You could still go to a registrar's office and be done with it. Then have a big do in the summer?"

"Her parents wouldn't go for that. They're a bit old-fashioned, quite old-fashioned, actually, and she's their one and only." Terry looks morose.

"Well, cheer up, she'll be yours soon enough. You said she was worth waiting for, no? What are you going to do in Scotland?"

"Maybe go hiking if the weather permits. Don't really know yet. We haven't made any strict plans. What about you?"

"I'm taking Maggie to Paris for a few days. Got tickets for Eurostar tomorrow afternoon."

"Oh, that's nice, I'm sure. Lots of things to do there, museums, and such." Terry grins.

"Right, not sure about museums." Peter chuckles too. "It's different! Food is different and no need for a car, we can walk all over."

"Yeah, didn't Jimmy praise those pork trotters to be the most fantastic food or something?"

"Who knows, we may try those too, you never know. What about you? Planning to test haggis?"

"Right, sure! No! We'll drive. Taking the slow route, though, avoiding the bigger roads. Christine has a cousin in Sheffield, so we'll drive there first, stay with her and then head north."

"Sounds like an enjoyable trip. You'll get to see plenty of the countryside too. Hopefully the weather stays nice."

Their food arrives.

"Man, these are spicy!" Peter says. "Tasty, but spicy."

"Yeah, these are good, lemon and pepper. Those salty lemons have a kick."

"I'll get a second round."

DI Peter Greene

After lunch Peter drives to Asda to do some last-minute shopping and then drives home. Maggie should arrive around 5 p.m. He lays out nosh for them: fried halloumi, chorizo, cheese, and olives, with a nice bottle of Spanish red wine. The bottle of scotch is on the side table.

He's fidgeting, puttering about, feeling happy and nervous, and he can't really understand why. They've spoken on the phone a few times since their reconciliation, or getting back together, or whatever you'd call it. But he's been so busy with work. *Yes, he likes her, likes her a lot, but that was a big fight. And then there's the issue of money. It's not about class, or is it? He's just a grammar school copper, she's from old money.* He walks around, fluffing up the pillows, checking for the umpteenth time that the loo is clean and the towels newly washed. Polishes the glasses again. Walks about like an uneasy ghost. His phone rings.

"Hi Dad, is it okay if we come around tonight instead of tomorrow?" Andrew asks.

"Is everything okay? Has something happened?"

"Yes, yes everything's fine. We just got a chance to leave today. Is it okay if we come tonight?"

"Sure, Maggie will be here too, just so that you know."

"Oh, but that's so cool. She's a keeper in case you haven't noticed. We'll be there in another hour or so."

Now what? His quiet evening with Maggie has been scuppered. The funny thing is, Peter feels somewhat relieved. Good thing he had loaded the fridge and freezer with food. Andrew and his girlfriend are going to stay for a week while Peter and Maggie are in Paris. If they still are, remains to be seen. Peter checks the roast, there's enough for two more people for sure. He'll just have to throw in a few more potatoes.

The doorbell rings.

"Hi Maggie! There you are, let me take your coat and..."

And then they just stand there looking at each other.

"No kiss?" Maggie smiles.

He takes a step forward, kisses her, and they stand still, hugging. "Gosh, I've missed you. Let's get your bag here. Andrew and his girlfriend, I hope it's still Gina, don't know for sure, are coming tonight. They were supposed to come tomorrow to stay here while we're gone."

"It's fine. It's fine. Relax Peter. Where's the wine, or maybe you need something stronger?"

They walk to the kitchen and Peter pours them both a glass of wine.

"Cheers," they say and clink their glasses.

"So, you're jittery because I'm here and Andrew is coming too?" Maggie asks.

"It's a bit new for all of us, no?"

"Really? You think so? We've all met before, eaten your grilled chickens and drunk wine, so why is it different now?"

"I don't know, I'm sorry. It's been a tough couple of weeks and I've missed you."

"I've missed you too." He hugs her again.

"Let's take these *tapas* and the wine to the living room and sit there. I guess we'll wait with dinner until Andrew and Gina show up?" Maggie says.

"Yes, is that okay with you?"

"Of course, it is. Come now, come here and relax."

They sit quietly for a moment and then...

"Did you accept ..." "How did your cases ..." Both talk at the same time.

"You first," Peter says. "Elm House?"

"Yes, I took the job after Robert's final offer. As I told you on the phone, it was tough to negotiate, I've never done anything of the sort before, but I thought I could do it, so I did," Maggie says, and smiles.

"Yes, well done! Cheers! And you'll move to Faukon Abbey?"

"Well, first I'll have to figure out what to do about my B & B in Penzance and all that. If I can sell it, that would obviously be great. But the market there isn't that good right now. We'll see. Robert Hughes has been surprisingly helpful."

"What about Lizzie?"

"Her life's mostly in London. And Faukon Abbey is closer for her to visit if and when she decides to come."

"Has she said anything?"

"She thought it was absolutely hilarious that I'd move to Estelle's old house."

"Are you going to move in there?"

"I don't know yet."

The doorbell chimes. Andrew and Gina are at the door with two big bags.

"Hi Dad, hi Maggie." Andrew gives a quick shoulder hug to Peter and waves to Maggie. He grabs the bags and makes a beeline for his old room.

"Hi Peter, hi Maggie!" Gina waves too.

"Hi Gina and Andrew, how are you?" Maggie calls.

Gina stands waiting in the hall, holding the door. Andrew comes running back.

"Bye Dad, bye Maggie. Later, don't wait up."

The door closes and they're gone. Peter is standing by the door, a stunned look on his face. "What the heck was that all about?" He goes out and sees Andrew's car speeding off. "What the hell?" Peter comes back in and closes the door, shaking his head.

"They said nothing?" Maggie asks.

"Nope, they just left."

Peter's phone pings, a text message:

Hi Dad, sorry about that. We're heading to a lecture and will come back later. Don't wait up. I still have my keys.

Peter reads the message out loud to Maggie.

"I guess it's just going to be us for dinner then?" Maggie says.

"Looks like it. Let's have some more wine."

Thanks to the wine, Peter's finally starting to relax and, by the time they've finished it and get to dinner, he's feeling good.

"Yum! This roast is delicious. You put quite a lot of garlic in it."

"Well, you know, going to France, I thought we'd better be prepared." Peter grins.

"Indeed. And it'll keep the vampires away too for sure. Speaking of vampires, you've found all your killers now? The deaths were all murders, right?"

Peter tells a condensed version of Ryan Bolan's and part of Marion Rivers' cases to Maggie.

"So, the son didn't kill his mother after all?"

"No, he didn't."

"And the one who killed her was her neighbour?"

"Yes. Let me show you one thing about it." Peter grabs a print-out from *The Guardian* article and brings it to the table. "You may or may not want to read this while I clear the table. It's a very unpleasant story I must add."

Maggie goes for her handbag and pulls out a pair of reading glasses.

"Oh my God, how terrible! So fantastic that you caught them. How awful! Those poor, poor kids. That's truly the worst kind of crime there is. I sincerely hope those guys rot in hell! That they're never ever let out of prison!"

"I hope so too."

Peter has finished clearing the table and stacking the dishwasher.

"I've got a chocolate cake; would you like some? And a cup of coffee too?"

"Yes please, cake and coffee sound lovely. Did you bake it?"

"No! My culinary skills don't extend to baking. Here, can you take the cake and I'll bring the coffee?"

"Yum, this cake is sublime. Where'd you get it?"

"From *Mocha,* the little coffee shop on Castle Road."

"Tasty." Maggie licks her spoon.

Peter pours them both two fingers of whisky.

"Now, what about that guy in Gwedrow, the one Terry came to pick you up for?"

"Geldenhuis."

"He was a big shot at Gwedrow. What happened to him? Was he murdered too?"

"It's a bit complicated that one. And related to that article too."

"What? Was he a paedophile too?"

"Oh no, he was the one who set up the sting operation together with the Met. He set up a server in his garage. Then all those who have been arrested now, used it to upload, share and view their filth."

"I see. So, who killed him? Was he found out? The same neighbour who killed the librarian?"

"No, he was killed at work by a guy who worked for him."

"So, it was an accident?"

"Yes and no."

"If you don't tell me, I'm going to pelt you with this pillow!"

Peter smiles and pours them some more whisky.

"All right, all right. Yes, the coroner concluded it was an accident. I got a call earlier today."

Maggie raises a pillow. "Spill!"

"As I said it's a sad story. You see, Geldenhuis had set up the server to catch the pedos. He also had two mobiles. One was his private and work phone, and the other was to deal with those pedo-server related things as it was all very hush-hush. That neighbour who killed Marion Rivers used to take care of deliveries for Geldenhuis. You know how you can set up photos for everybody who is on your list, so that you see who's calling you?"

Maggie nods.

"Geldenhuis had the picture of three colourful cartoon rats jumping up and down as a picture on his secret pedo-server phone. What we've been able to establish, and this will never leave this room, promise?"

Maggie nods. "Of course!"

"Geldenhuis was good at his job, but he was also very exacting as a boss. As in everything had to be just so, not just nearly, but exactly so. You should've seen him when he was still alive. I mean he looked like a walking advertisement for starch and iron. Everything so well creased you could cut yourself on his shirt sleeve!"

"Really? Wow. I've met a few people like that. They tend to be real pains to deal with, nothing is never good enough no matter how well you try to do it!"

"Yup, that's just about what the people who worked for him said. He knew his stuff, but he was a pain to work for. That Friday he died..."

"But it was Tuesday, no? That's when Terry came?"

"Yes, he was found on the Tuesday morning."

"Good God! Dead for a few days and nobody missed him? That's harsh, even for someone like him. Poor guy."

"If you live alone, that can happen, as we know. But in this case, he didn't die at home, he died at work. They..." Peter raises his hand, "... they were setting up things in their server room. Only he and three other people had access to it and, due to all those servers and computers, it was kept rather cool."

"No smell then?"

"Exactly. We found out that he died late on Friday afternoon, was last seen and heard from around 4 p.m. He was supposed to meet his ex-wife at 7 p.m. but didn't show up. The Gwedrow offices are closed on the weekend, and then on Monday he didn't show up. But, as he was a manager, everybody thought he was in meetings in Exeter all day, or something. They started missing him, called him, but received no answer. He was found on Tuesday morning by one of his team who went to the data centre and heard his phone ringing there."

"So, nobody went there on Monday?"

"No. And they were worried about another employee, named Mark, who also hadn't shown up. They found him in a terrible state at home when one of his co-workers came to us and requested a wellness check. Mark was in such an awful state he had to be sedated and taken to the hospital. Then Gwedrow IT team was down to one." Peter takes a sip. "Then, early Tuesday morning, Geldenhuis was found."

"Who killed him, then? His wife?"

"We investigated and investigated, interviewed and questioned many people, including his ex-wife. But nobody, including the ex, seemed to have any actual motive for killing him, yet he was killed, according to Slater, he didn't do it himself. The neighbour, who, as it then turned out, had killed Mrs Rivers, was on our list of suspects, but he had an alibi. Ben Rivers, whom we suspected of killing his mother, was also on our list of suspects. Ben wasn't going to inherit the house he grew up in, instead, his mother had decided to leave it to Geldenhuis."

"What? To Geldenhuis? That makes little sense. Were they a couple or something? Why'd she leave her house to a neighbour?"

"That was odd, for sure. Apparently, Mrs Rivers, who was 66 when she died, had developed very warm feelings towards Geldenhuis, who was only 50. We interviewed him after her death, and he was adamant that there was no mutual affection and no plans to get married. To him, she was just a neighbour."

"Was she, as Lizzy is often keen to point out to me, 'losing it'?"

"Could be, we don't know. But if her son found out about the inheritance, he had a motive to kill Geldenhuis. But he didn't. Neither did the wife."

"So finally, who did it?"

"It was Mark."

"Mark, the guy who worked for him and was taken to hospital?"

"Yes. We had no reason to suspect him or anybody else at Gwedrow of killing Geldenhuis. Well, we suspected one foreman there, but he, too, had an alibi. Geldenhuis may have been a demanding boss, but he'd only been there for about a year, so nobody really knew him or enough about him."

"Except this Mark?"

"Actually, he didn't really know him either. It was an accident."

"Hold on, you just said he was killed."

"Yes, but it was an accidental killing."

"You know that's not a legal term, even I know that."

"Very true. But here's what Mark told us once we could finally talk to him last week. On that Friday, Geldenhuis had been a total pain, Mark's words. They'd had a big delivery of equipment for the data centre and all the cabling needed to be labelled properly, fastened and so on. Geldenhuis had come every five seconds it seemed, to jump on Mark for not doing a good enough job. Mark studied history in Exeter uni. Had no formal education in IT. He'd learned and done a lot of computer programming on his own, but knew less about servers and networks. But he'd been working in IT in Gwedrow all these years and learned on the job. But for Geldenhuis, he wasn't fast or careful enough."

"Even so, that's hardly a reason to kill someone? Surely not?"

"No, it wasn't. What was, was Geldenhuis's phone, or rather, a phone call Geldenhuis received. While Geldenhuis was at the data centre ranting on about some missing cabling, his phone rang, the one related to his 'own' server and the picture for it was those jumping rats." Peter takes a sip again, but the glass is empty. Maggie pours them both some more. "Mark said he recognised those jumping rats for what they were: a front for paedophiles! He'd been abused when he was a kid by a rich relative for five years before he ran away."

"Oh God, poor guy! How terrible!"

"As a grown-up, he'd been trying to trace these pedos and he'd been collecting information on the internet, the dark web, everywhere he could get to, about them. When he saw the rats, he just snapped, since he thought Geldenhuis was another pedo, abusing him again."

"Oh my God, that's terrible!" They both take a sip.

"He saw the picture and just grabbed the nearest thing within reach, an old hole-puncher and threw it at Geldenhuis. He didn't mean to kill him, of course; he was just at the end of his tether, all the pain over the years had caused him to snap. The hole-puncher hit Geldenhuis's forehead. That wouldn't been bad had Geldenhuis not lost his balance and fallen backward. The back of his head, you know that small triangle in the back, hit the sharp corner of an old metal computer case. It severed his spinal cord and killed him just about instantly. Mark wasn't aware of his death, just saw that Geldenhuis had fallen. He said he went and shook him a bit. He wasn't dead, or at least Mark didn't think so, so he dragged Geldenhuis behind a rack, placed him half-sitting and put his phone near his hand, thinking that Geldenhuis could call for help. Then he just grabbed the hole-puncher and his bag and fled. Mark was in shock for two reasons: for injuring Geldenhuis which would probably cause him to lose the only job he had ever had, and secondly, because all the issues caused by the years of abuse had flooded his mind. The recent stress caused by Geldenhuis at work had added to this. When he was found the following Monday, he was in a catatonic state and obviously couldn't be questioned. But then we had no reason to question him, anyway. There didn't seem to be any motive. Until there was."

"What a miserable and sad story all around. All those kids."

They sit quietly for a while.

"Do you know why Geldenhuis was doing what he did? Seems a bit, I don't know, strange to go to such lengths."

"According to Miles Miller of the Exeter team, it was Geldenhuis's own idea. You see, the company Geldenhuis worked for in Exeter was doing some security-related business for them and somehow, they got talking. One thing led to another and then Geldenhuis was building this whole server with a game type of thing. Obviously, Miles wanted to make sure that Geldenhuis wasn't doing it for his own benefit, so to speak. As it turned out, he'd been a victim of abuse himself, and wanted to help. He had this rather pronounced limp which was caused by poorly-healed bones. He'd been a late comer, both his siblings had already moved out when he was born, and his father didn't believe he was his. So, every chance he had, he abused the poor kid. Miller's team of course checked it out. They had to, considering. And it was true."

"So, in a way, Geldenhuis and this Mark were on the same side?"

"Indeed. That's what's makes it so sad."

"Does Mark know? What's going to happen to him?"

"As it is, nothing. And no, we didn't tell Mark. The coroner called. His verdict in the Geldenhuis case is accidental death, as Mark was deemed to have been under diminished capacity when it happened. So, for our part, the case is going to be closed. The only public information announced will be Accidental Death."

"Poor Mark. What a terrible, sad thing. Is he getting his job back?"

"That's highly likely. There's also a co-worker who cares about him, so I think, I hope, he'll be okay."

"Good, glad to hear it! At least something positive in a miserable case. I'm going to…" Maggie waves her hand.

"Go ahead."

While Maggie wanders off, the front door is pushed open.

"Oh, hello Dad, you're still up. I thought you'd have gone to bed by now."

"Just about to. What was the hurry?"

"It was supposed to be a lecture and a film about octopi in the Pacific near the coastal waters of Oregon. We thought we were going to be late, but the event didn't happen as scheduled. The organisers had some issues with it so we only saw a few pictures and then chatted to the others. Went to *The Whistle & Tin* and had great Indian meatballs without meat."

"Okay, I was just about to ask you if I should heat up the roast for you, but I guess not."

"Nope, we're good. We'll head to bed now. What time are you leaving tomorrow?"

"I'll have to go to work first in the morning, but I'll come back and collect Maggie about noon. Then we'll drive to Exeter for the train."

"Okay, good night."

"Good night."

Friday, 20 March

DI Peter Greene

Peter drives to work on Friday morning to check whether there's anything urgent. There is only one item in his inbox, the coroner's official verdict concerning the death of Jon Geldenhuis.

Peter calls Ruth Johannsson to inform her of the coroner's verdict. She doesn't answer so he leaves her a brief message.

Just as he's about to leave he gets an email from Jacob Smithers. It is very short, stating that his mother had investigated and could confirm that Jon Geldenhuis wasn't a war criminal. While Geldenhuis had served in the SA military, he'd been stationed in a hospital, for those wounded during the war, as a data clerk.

Peter takes the coroner's verdict to Mullan who tells him to close the case, get the heck out of there and enjoy himself.

Saturday, 21 March

The Abbey Chronicle, Page 1

Ben Rivers - found guilty

In the trial at the Crown Court, Ben Rivers was found guilty of manslaughter yesterday in the case involving a tragic incident. After two hours of intense deliberation, the jury reached their verdict.

During the trial, witnesses from both Penzance and Faukon Abbey, which included police officers, provided testimony. As previously reported, Dr Slater, who had performed the post-mortem, testified that Ryan Bolan didn't die due to being struck by a car. Instead, he died of blunt force trauma to the back of his head. A rock with blood on it, which was a match for Mr Bolan's blood, was found near the body.

The prosecution presented traffic camera footage from Penzance which shows a car colliding with the bicycle of Lucas Hart, propelling him headfirst into the shrubbery by the Eastern Road. Mr Hart was quickly discovered and taken to the hospital. Thankfully, he was not permanently injured. Traces of paint residue matching Mr Rivers' car were found on both Mr Bolan's and Mr Hart's bicycles. Mr Rivers' defence argued that the paint was commonly available. The Prosecuting council noted that Mr Rivers had recently, in early January, purchased the paint which was found at his workplace. According to his co-workers, Rivers had painted the lower part of his car after the purchase, and again in early February, using the same paint.

The prosecution also claimed that Mr Rivers' ability to focus and his driving speed were impaired due to alcohol. Witnesses from *The Scowl and Lint* Pub in Penzance testified that Mr Rivers had purchased and consumed more than just a pint of beer. Mr Rivers had consumed two pints of scrumpy, the high-alcohol cider, in addition to a pint of beer, thus contradicting his defence's claims.

The prosecution presented photographs of the road, covering a 100m stretch in both directions where Ryan Bolan's body was discovered, highlighting the absence of skid marks that would typically indicate sudden braking. The defence countered by stating that Mr Rivers had applied his brakes, but the traces had been erased by a week of inclement weather.

Although Mr Rivers' defence admitted that he was responsible for causing Ryan Bolan's bicycle to veer off the road, they maintained that it was an unintended accident. They argued that Rivers' lack of attention due to his focus on a call from his mother had been exaggerated by poor visibility caused by darkness and rain. The defence also pointed out Bolan's erratic movements on the road.

After only two hours of deliberation the jury reached their verdict. Ben Rivers was found guilty of manslaughter.

The Abbey Chronicle, Page 3

Jon Geldenhuis case closed

The Faukon Abbey police has now closed the case investigating the death of Mr Jon Geldenhuis. The coroner's verdict is accidental death. After interviewing Mark Woods and others who worked for Mr Geldenhuis, the coroner determined that the cause of death was due to an accident which took place in the small, enclosed space in the data centre in Gwedrow.

Sunday, 22 March

Jimmy Carter, *The Abbey Chronicle*

Helen and Jimmy are enjoying a late, lazy brunch.

"What happens to those houses now?" Helen asks.

"Umm, which houses?" Jimmy asks. "Are you really sure you have to open the shop today? It's cold and raining. It's nice and warm here..."

"Didn't Ingela say Geldenhuis was going to inherit Marion Rivers' house? And Geldenhuis's wife, as his next of kin, inherits everything from him? Ergo, the ex-wife gets two houses?"

"I don't know. Maybe. I think we should just stay inside, watch some old movies or something, or go back to bed?"

"She seems to be the one who benefits greatly. You sure she didn't do it?"

"The case was closed, my dear. Case closed."

THE END

Appendix

About The 'Brides in the Bath' Murders

The 'Brides in the Bath' were real criminal cases which took place in England in 1912 - 1915.

In 1915, one George Smith was found guilty of the murders of Bessie Williams (nee Mundy) who was found dead in a bath in July 1912, Alice Burnham who died in a bath at Blackpool in December 1913, and Margaret Elizabeth Lofty who was found dead in a bath in Highgate in December 1914.

<u>The Victims</u>

Five days before her death in July 1912, *Beatrice Bessie Williams, nee Mundy*, had made a will in favour of her husband, Henry Williams (alias George Smith). The husband was questioned but Dr Frank French thought the cause of death was death asphyxia brought about by drowning. When Dr French was asked if the death could have been due to something else, the doctor said no. The inquest jury returned the verdict, 'Death by misadventure'.

Alice Smith, nee *Burnham,* wife of George Smith, had taken a bath, on 12 December 1913. The inquest held later in December returned the verdict that Alice had accidentally drowned because of a heart failure while in the bath. It transpired that Alice had insured herself for £500, a considerable sum at the time.

Margaret Lloyd, nee Lofty, and John Lloyd (alias George Smith) had taken rooms in a boarding house in Highgate, London. On the afternoon of 18 December 1914, Margaret Lloyd had taken out a life insurance policy for £700 with her husband as the sole beneficiary. Later that evening, John Lloyd went out to buy some tomatoes while his wife took a bath. When he returned, he called out, and, not receiving an answer, entered the bathroom and found his wife dead in the bath. In the inquest on 1 January 1915 the verdict was 'Accidental Death'.

<u>Suspicions</u>

On 3 January 1915, Joseph Crossley, who owned the house where Alice Smith had died, wrote to the Metropolitan Police, and enclosed the newspaper clipping reporting Lloyd's death, remarking how similar the death of Margaret Lloyd was to Alice Smith's.

The Metropolitan Police started an investigation and details about George Smith began to emerge. George Smith, who had multiple aliases (Oliver George Love, Charles Oliver James, Henry Williams, and John Lloyd) had re-married while his previous wife was still alive. He had been married to Caroline Beatrice Thornhill in 1898, then to Edith Peglar, under the name Oliver Love, and then to Bessy Mundy while Edith was still alive. He was initially charged with making a false entry in a marriage register but then things became darker. The similarities of the deaths of his three wives were just too close to be coincidental.

<u>Catching the killer</u>

On 23 March 1915, George Smith was charged with the murders of Bessie Williams, Alice Smith and Margaret Lloyd. But how was he caught?

Enter Home Office Pathologist Bernard Spilsbury. He requested the exhumation of Margaret Lloyd's body. The evidence suggested that her death was almost instantaneous. Spilsbury wasn't convinced. The evidence from the other two deaths was also re-investigated. For weeks Spilsbury pondered over the deaths, the bathtubs, and the victims' measurements. If the victim had experienced violent spasms of the limbs, with the limbs flung outward, the body couldn't go underwater, the bathtub was too small. And then he hit upon a possible solution. When Bessie Williams had been found, her legs were stretched out, protruding out of the water. Now what if Smith, playfully teasing his wife, had seized her feet and pulled them towards him, pulling her body under the water. She would have got water in her nose and mouth which might have caused a shock and a sudden loss of consciousness.

Spilsbury and the investigating Metropolitan Police Detective, Inspector Arthur Neil, decided to hire several experienced women divers about the same size and build as the victims. They initially tried to push them underwater by force, but that resulted in signs of a struggle. Finally, DI Neil did what Spilsbury suggested; he pulled unexpectantly at the feet of one of the divers and her head went underwater before she knew what had happened. DI Neil became alarmed when he noticed the woman was no longer moving. They pulled her out of the bathtub and managed to revive her. When she came to, she told them that the only thing she remembered was the rush of water before she lost consciousness. This, even though she was expecting an attack and was an experienced diver. Spilsbury's theory was confirmed.

<u>The Trial</u>

George Smith went on trial at the Old Bailey on 22 June 1915. He could only be tried for the murder of Bessie Williams in accordance with English Law, but the prosecution used the other deaths to establish a pattern of Smith's crimes. On 1 July it took the jury only twenty minutes to find him guilty and he was sentenced to death. Smith protested his innocence to the end.

Sources: Multiple newspaper and other sources online.

Acknowledgements

F aukon Abbey is entirely fictional, though, hunting with falcons, falconry, has been practised since medieval times and is practised even today. While it is/was mostly practised by men, there were and are women master falconers.

Most of the other places mentioned in this book are real and exist; however, all the events and all the characters described in this book are entirely figments of my imagination.

Special thanks to my editor, Cathy Eberle, and cover designer Biti. The ME's office in Seattle provided valuable information as did a lot of other people both in UK and elsewhere. I am truly thankful for everybody who has patiently answered to my often-esoteric questions. I have followed their advice as far as it suits the plot, and any mistakes are all mine.

A.K. Lakelett

July 2023

PS. I hope you liked my book. The easiest way of making an author happy is to leave a review. And thank you!

More from the author

You can find out more about Faukon Abbey on my website www.aklakelett.com

You can there also sign up to be a member of my readers group and get the Faukon Abbey Companion for free!
You will also be first to find out about the next book in the Faukon Abbey Mystery series.
While all my books are individual stories, to get more details into the background of the characters you may want to read the first book, Remember Me? first.